KU-264-886

BEYOND
REASONABLE
DOUBT

GARY BELL QC
AND
SCOTT KERSHAW

WORN OUT
FROM STOCK

RAVEN BOOKS
LONDON · OXFORD · NEW YORK · NEW DELHI · SYDNEY

RAVEN BOOKS
Bloomsbury Publishing Plc
50 Bedford Square, London, WC1B 3DP, UK

BLOOMSBURY, RAVEN BOOKS and the Raven Books logo are trademarks of
Bloomsbury Publishing Plc

First published in Great Britain 2019

Copyright © Gary Bell 2019

Gary Bell has asserted his right under the Copyright, Designs and Patents Act, 1988,
to be identified as Author of this work

All rights reserved. No part of this publication may be reproduced or transmitted
in any form or by any means, electronic or mechanical, including photocopying,
recording, or any information storage or retrieval system, without prior
permission in writing from the publishers

A catalogue record for this book is available from the British Library

ISBN: HB: 978-1-5266-0612-9; TPB: 978-1-5266-0613-6; eBook: 978-1-5266-0614-3

2 4 6 8 10 9 7 5 3 1

Typeset by Integra Software Services Pvt. Ltd.
Printed and bound in Great Britain by CPI Group (UK) Ltd, Croydon CR0 4YY

MIX
Paper from
responsible sources
FSC® C020471

To find out more about our authors and books visit www.bloomsbury.com
and sign up for our newsletters

The facts of the case were these, though they were few and far between.

The Girl was approximately sixteen years old on the night she died.

Of Middle Eastern origin, with no fixed address, identification, or records to be found.

No name anyone knew.

What little could be traced of her final movements existed in a smattering of CCTV snippets, bookended by two eyewitnesses for the prosecution.

The first, Mrs Donna Turner, saw The Girl wander into the mouth of the storm shortly before midnight on Good Friday, 14 April, in the rural village of Cotgrave, Nottinghamshire.

The second, an elderly man named Harold Kennard, happened across her more than seven hours later, after she'd been spat out onto a disused railway in the countryside.

At some point in the horror of those hours in between, somebody had put her there.

Seven fingernails were torn from her hands. Of the two front teeth lost in the struggle, one was found inside her collapsed left lung. The breakages in both legs had been inflicted posthumously, and there was evidence of fifty-seven blunt impacts upon her naked body.

A national appeal brought nobody to the morgue to claim her; it was as if she'd been a ghost even before the life was strangled out of her.

These were the facts, and they were, by definition, indisputable.

Anything else was nothing more than speculation.

At first.

PART ONE

THE PUPIL

1

She'd been dead for more than five months when I found myself reluctantly involved in The Girl's brutal murder, and it all happened shortly after meeting Zara Barnes.

'You look exhausted, Rook,' Percy told me. 'You need to appoint a junior.'

I'd had my eyes closed for a couple of minutes while he spoke, and now I grudgingly dragged myself back into the room. Around us, early finishers were pouring into the Knights Templar like tanks to the filling station, beasts to the waterhole.

I drew a heavy mouthful of wine and shook my head. 'Not this again.'

'Yes, this again. You've got the legal aid certificate for another pair of hands, so why not use it? What's the matter? Too proud to share the glory?'

I turned to the wilting flower boxes beyond the window, September's amber light splintering upon them, and shook my head. 'It's a fraud case, Percy. I can't see there being much glory to go around. Besides, I'm doing just fine on my own.'

This was Friday afternoon and, true to my word, the weekend lay before me like an unfilled crater. All I had to fill those empty hours was work, and plenty of it.

'You're not still taking evidence home, are you?' he asked. 'Jennifer must be going spare with all that paper-work around the house!'

Ignoring him, I gestured to his own glass. 'You plan on drinking that this afternoon?'

'Oh, please!' he scoffed. 'The *house red*? I'm a man of quality, not quantity, my learned friend.'

I had to smile. If ever there was a perfect phrase for the space between us, I thought, it would be just that.

Percy, the rakish blond mannequin of Savile Row *quality*, with zirconia veneers and a tight, almost adolescent face beneath that middle-aged hairline, opposite me, the sheer *quantity* of us two, a couple of years beyond fifty, a few more beyond trim and handsome.

Even here, in a casual Wetherspoon's on Chancery Lane, he was dressed sharp as a box-fresh razor, and he bristled at my overcoat and hat, the relic of faded black wool tossed onto the table, which was all I could wield against my floppy hair after so many years under the wig. To put it bluntly – as he so often did – Percy found my appearance increasingly shabby.

I had little concern to spare. The fraud case I was working on involved almost thirty solicitors who had allegedly come together to rob millions from the legal aid fund over decades, by systematically billing for clients to whom they hadn't given advice. The prosecution's case went so far as to suggest that the majority of those clients simply didn't exist and, acting for the first defendant, it was my job to painstakingly read through thousands upon thousands of letters, bills and bank statements before the trial began, with the daunting task of confirming the legitimacy of every claim.

The paperwork had been weighed in at seventeen tonnes, and after three months I'd barely made a dent.

Percy had finally introduced glass to mouth when his attention was caught by something at the bar, and he nodded to the newcomer settling there.

'Ted Bowen,' he muttered. 'He's just lost an attempted murder for the CPS.'

Like football fans, barristers and clerks often refer to their clients' indictments as their own.

'Who was he up against?'

'Rigby from Fleet Street, defending. Bowen was sure Rigby would've tried to bargain down to a Section 18, GBH with intent, and serve five to six inside, but the man walked out of there with self-defence.'

'Credit to Rigby. Lose, and it would've been life. He's a lucky man.'

'*Sure*,' he groused, 'you can tell that to the victim, if he ever hears again.'

An uncharacteristic moment of indignation from our senior clerk. It was no secret that he'd wanted the case, and if the defendant had been instructing one of our own, Percy would've been first to celebrate, victim be damned. As it had transpired, the only contender from our set of chambers had been Bowen, and it was a relatively big loss for the set.

'Barristers are like golfers,' I said, shrugging it off. 'The only shot that matters is the next, and there's no point dwelling on the last.'

'You hear he's applied for silk?'

'Who, Bowen?'

'It *would* be great to get another QC in chambers. You think he's got a good chance?'

I looked back over my shoulder and watched Bowen sink neat whiskey without breath. Like most of my fellow lawyers, he was everything I wasn't: spiny, almost barbed at the edges, with thinning grey hair sprouting from the nape of a long, crooked neck. Even after two decades on the scene, I remained the clear outsider of our legal kettle, with legs bred for lifting, fists designed for labour and casual violence.

'Who can say?' I sniffed.

Percy must've caught Bowen's eye, because he sent a mirthless smile across the pub before returning to our conversation.

'Pains me to admit it,' he said, 'but you might end up being the final silk in the set, the way these pupillage interviews are going.'

'Really? That bad?'

A mournful nod. 'Twenty-four interviews this week, and not a whiff of Oxbridge.'

'Is that such a terrible thing?'

The look he threw back was as if I'd just cracked a joke about bedding his mother.

'This is Miller and Stubbs Chambers, Rook, not Fagin's School for Crime. We have certain standards to maintain.'

I had to laugh; if I didn't, I might've floored him years ago.

'You should try the Copper at the Door conundrum,' I suggested, a puzzle of my own design. 'Get them thinking on their feet.'

He reached for his phone – always face up on the table – and started sifting through emails. 'There's a good reason you're not invited onto the panel any more.'

'Because nobody has ever solved it?'

'No.' He began hammering a reply with both thumbs. 'Because we hire by name, grades and calibre, not games, riddles and tricks. Honestly, you should have seen the applicant I had before leaving this afternoon. *Zara something or other*. A sort of, you know …' He hesitated, searching for the proper term, and still fell a mile short. '*Half-caste* girl?'

'Mixed race, Percy, for Christ's sake!' I glanced around, relieved to find us alone at our table by the windows. 'Tell me that's not why you turned her away.'

'Of course not!' he chided, without apology. 'She should have been interviewed at one o'clock but didn't arrive until ten past. Said her train had been delayed.'

'Had it?'

He paused, bewildered by the query, and then laughed. 'What am I, the Fat Controller? I told her she should have got an earlier one. You know what she said?'

'Surprise me.'

'Said she couldn't afford it. Had to wait until the fares reduced at nine thirty. I told her that wasn't my problem, the opportunity had passed.'

'Tough luck. Where had she come from?'

'I don't know. Nottingham, or thereabouts.'

A prickle snaked up between my shoulders. 'Nottingham? You don't say.'

'Frankly, I'm not surprised she couldn't afford an earlier ticket. You should have seen the outfit she chose for the interview; all man-made fibres, not a thread of actual cotton. Or better yet, heard her accent! She sounded like Angela Rayner, a real northern monkey.'

'Nottingham's in the Midlands, Percy, and the East Midlands at that.'

'Far as I'm concerned, if it's further than Watford, it's in the bloody North.'

I sighed. Percy was one of the few people I could tolerate in chambers, but even he had a knack for becoming quite intolerable after a relatively short amount of time. Half an hour usually did it.

'Our country is a-changing,' I told him. 'We'd better start swimming, or we'll sink like a stone.'

He huffed, taking a long, measured sip.

'You realise that they can't all come from Eton, don't you, Percy?'

'Well, they ought to, damn it!' He winked. 'Do they not realise, that's why *we're* the best?'

I tried a grin, nodded stiffly, and emptied my glass.

Non-disclosure of evidence in the courtroom is a serious offence. Perjury is worse.

In the everyday working world, a lie, even by omission, can be classed as fraud.

If somebody makes an assumption, on the other hand – if the prosecution submits a supposition that actually weakens its own case, for example – then there's no legal obligation for the defence to correct it.

I hadn't specifically *told* anybody I went to Eton – not for a long, long time at least – but the lies of foolish youth had proven hard to leave behind.

'I should get back to chambers,' I muttered, reaching for the hat, pulling it down over my hair. 'Are you joining?'

'No. I have three meetings to get through in –' he checked his Rolex – 'a touch over four hours, and then my weekend begins. I'd say I have time for one more. You're certain you won't stay for another?'

'Can't. Those billing receipts aren't going to read themselves.'

'Worried that Jennifer might smell it on your breath when you get home tonight?'

'No.' I got to my feet and fished the cigarettes out of my coat pocket. Turned one out into my hand. 'I can't say I'm worried about that at all.'

I left him to his emails, lighting up as soon as I got outside. I couldn't have afforded an afternoon on the booze even if I had wanted one, but Percy didn't know that.

Divorce isn't cheap, even for a skilled professional barrister, and I was the closest I'd been to skint since my own violent years of sleeping rough on the cold city pavement.

2

Chancery Lane is a 500-metre road that runs one way north-wards from the Gothic halls of Queen Victoria's Royal Courts of Justice.

A hotchpotch of buildings old and new, it remains the backbone of law-land for the Inns of Court, though its renowned legal bookshops and courtroom tailors have been spread thin since the influx of chain restaurants, its barristers pushed out by the unstoppable march of baristas.

It is the sort of narrow bottleneck often favoured by charity campaigners and for half a moment I thought that's what she was; one maverick fundraiser braving the hopeless territory of rapacious lawyers.

I was ambling back from the pub towards Took's Court, and the young woman had the entrance masterfully covered. I'd only half turned in the right direction when she gave chase, at first tentative and then agitated and indignant, and by the time I'd reached the heavy red front door of chambers she'd managed to squeeze her way into my peripheral vision, waving skinny arms like a marionette strung to a ceiling fan.

'Excuse me! Hey!'

I paused, flicking what remained of the fag into the gutter, and looked back. 'Yes?'

I guessed who she was straight away; as obviously out of place as Dr Livingstone must have seemed to Stanley, I almost tipped my hat and greeted her with *Zara, I presume*.

Her suit wasn't quite as pitiable as Percy had made out, but the off-black jacket and matching skirt did look painfully similar to the clothes I used to buy from Nottingham's Victoria Centre Market. Ill-fitting, without labels, and averse to direct sunlight due to the 100 per cent polyester count. The look was finished by a flimsy white blouse, laddered tights, and an incongruous pair of black Doc Martens. Occasionally, when a client turns up for court in a suit, it's immediately obvious that they have never worn one before, nor should they ever wear one again. She wasn't quite there, but she was treading perilously near.

'I don't suppose you know if Mr Percy Peck is still in chambers, do you?' she asked, bobbing on the spot, hands wringing anxiously behind her back. 'I was supposed to have a pupillage interview earlier and I need to talk to him about rearranging, but I don't reckon he's gonna let me.'

'What makes you think he won't rearrange it?' I asked, entirely aware that he wouldn't.

She shrugged and blinked, dense black hair tamed up into a tight knot, wide eyes the colour of roasted coffee behind thick Ginsberg glasses. 'I've been waiting here all afternoon and he won't speak to me. I don't think he knows how far I've come.'

'I'm sure he does,' I said. 'I'm just not sure he really cares.'

A low blow. I watched her features melt in the honey-coloured light that managed to break the surrounding rooftops, and she half-heartedly fingered the names on the small brass plaque beside the front door. There were forty-five junior barristers listed there, headed by four Queen's

Counsel at the top. I was second on the list. Above that was another simple plaque, the deeper red-brown of weathered bronze, unchanged since long before I started: Miller & Stubbs Criminal Barristers.

'You a barrister here then?'

I nodded. 'Elliot Rook.'

'QC?' She lowered her head in a hushed combination of excitement and regret, twisting on her toes. 'I know who you are! Sorry to take up your time. If you bump into Mr Peck at all – I mean, I know you're busy, obviously – but if you could just let him know that, well, it really wasn't my fault I was late, and I am sorry.' She sighed. 'My name is Zara Barnes, and I could really use a break.'

It was her accent that grabbed me. No matter how many years go by, or how much one might've changed in the interim, there are always comforts to be found in the tones of home.

I looked up and saw clouds scudding from the west, just in time for the weekend, and was about to apologise and leave her standing there when I thought of Percy, his derogatory comments, and the Copper at the Door.

'Listen closely,' I told her, 'because I'm only going to ask this once.'

She blinked, suddenly wary, and pulled at a loose thread on her faded sleeve. 'All right.'

'A uniformed police officer wishes to question a suspicious passer-by about a burglary in the area, but the passer-by disappears through the door of a busy nightclub before the officer catches up with him. The copper attempts to follow, but the doorman – who is soon to be your client, by the way, so pay attention – refuses entry.'

'My – wait – *what?*'

14

'What happens next is caught entirely on the club's camera, *with* audio. The officer tells the doorman, your client, that he is there to question a suspicious character. Still the doorman refuses entry. The officer barges forward, exercising his right to enter, and your client throws a head-butt, breaking the officer's nose. Your client is subsequently charged with assaulting a police constable in execution of his duty. Headbutting is considered a weapon equivalent, and our doorman is looking at six months' imprisonment. Only, you're going to get him acquitted. How?'

Part of me knew it was a cruel trick to play. The young woman was a rabbit in headlights, waiting for the tyres.

'W-well.' She cleared her throat. 'I don't know anything about the client! Does he have a record?'

'It doesn't matter. The pieces of the puzzle are all there, and on camera no less. It's simply a matter of perspective.'

She licked her lips, adjusted her glasses, and I could see her hands were trembling. 'Then I'd have no choice but to get him to plead guilty, and have his sentence reduced before the trial ever began.'

'OK. That's fine.' If I didn't sigh on the outside, I must've kept it to myself. 'Thank you, Miss – *Barnes*, was it? I really do wish you the best of luck in finding pupillage.'

I pushed the great red door of the old terraced town house and left her standing on the cobbles there, jumbling the pieces, trying to figure out what the hell had just happened. I was most of the way across reception when I decided that Percy was right, there was a good reason I was no longer invited onto the interview panel.

The last thing I expected to hear was the quiet bump of a boot catching the closing door behind me, and the young woman's voice shout a single word into the old building.

'Galbraith!'

I stopped. When I turned back, I must've looked as if I'd been punched squarely in the face. 'I beg your pardon?'

She was grinning, all the way from the boots up, and it suited her entirely.

'There's no case to answer!' she blurted. 'In the case of Galbraith, the Court of Appeal said that if there's no evidence that the defendant committed the offence, then the court should throw the case out, right? The doorman is charged with assaulting a constable in execution of his duty, but the officer *wasn't* acting in the execution of his duty. He didn't have a warrant, and he wasn't on the premises to stop a breach of the peace. He exercised his right to enter the premises for the purpose of arrest, under Section 17 1B of the Police and Criminal Evidence Act, but he clearly said, on camera, that he was only there to *question* the man. Therefore, he had no right to enter, he *wasn't* acting in execution of his duty, and so I submit that there's no case to answer!'

A long silence followed, in which I gave up trying to count all the people who had failed that puzzle over the years; the Oxbridge elite, seasoned barristers and respected judges alike. It required much more than a textbook knowledge of the law. It took lateral thinking, a wholly different approach, something that wasn't taught in any school, no matter how illustrious.

'All right,' I said, deciding that perhaps I ought to take my senior clerk's advice on appointing a junior after all. 'You want to come inside and discuss your application?'

And she did, grinning still, with no premonition of the danger she was getting herself into.

3

As soon as we reached my room on the third floor, I started snatching as much of the scattered paperwork up from the desk as I could manage, before resigning myself to the fact that there were too many sheets for it ever to be presentable, particularly alongside two empty cartons of cigarettes, the container of a takeaway I couldn't remember eating, a half-completed Rubik's cube with most of the stickers already peeled away, and four mouldy teacups.

I cleared my throat, clenching my shame between my teeth, and told her it had been a busy week.

'Wasn't expecting company.'

She waved it off politely, not quite masking her mien of mild horror, and gazed over the unsteady stacks of cardboard boxes, the unorganised, overcrowded bookshelves, and the battered upright wig box, known as a biscuit tin to barristers.

'Nice fedora,' she remarked as I chucked my hat onto the clutter. 'Very *Chinatown*.'

'Thanks,' I mumbled, feeling a lot less *Chinatown* and much more *Ironweed*. 'A little before your time?'

She shrugged and straightened her jacket, which was a couple of centimetres too large on the shoulders.

As I took a chair, two realisations came upon me at once: first, I was accustomed to a very different kind of interview, the sort involving solicitors and alleged crooks, and didn't know what to say or where to start; second, I was embarrassed by the state of my room, like a Cabinet minister caught with pornography. I sat a little straighter, smoothing the bulge of the gut inside my tucked shirt. There are those in the legal profession – any profession, in fact – who prey on the hope of prospective young interns. I know, because I've defended such predators in my career, and I was hideously conscious of that before we began.

'So,' I said, twiddling my thumbs, 'what do you –'

'Holy shit!'

She literally tried to catch the words before they reached me, slamming a palm over her mouth. A silence followed in which we both must've looked as startled as the other.

'I'm sorry! I'm proper sorry, but, is that real?'

I traced her gaze up to one book turned face out from the highest shelf, the illustration of the bough on the cover almost faded to nothing beneath the title. Of all the clients I'd had in the room, few had noticed it there, and I couldn't recall a single one who'd recognised its worth.

She reached up – 'Do you mind?' – and took the book down from the shelf.

She stroked a couple of fingertips over the spine, over Truman Capote's portrait of Harper Lee on the back, just as I'd done when I'd first removed the wrapping paper on the morning I passed the Bar, before replacing it carefully on the shelf.

'You know they only ever printed, like, five thousand of these first editions?'

'I heard.'

She whistled. 'Must've been a serious effort to get hold of!'

A pang rattled my ribs. I felt my left thumb betray me as always, instinctively twisting the band of useless gold around its third neighbour. 'What do you know about Miller and Stubbs, Miss Barnes?'

She sat slowly in the opposite chair, steeling herself, and gave her carefully rehearsed response.

'It's the pre-eminent criminal set in London. Four Queen's Counsel – including yourself – and more than forty juniors. Clients all over the country. It's about as good as it gets.'

'You aimed high.'

'Is there any point in aiming lower?'

She wasn't rude, just sharp, and so I felt comfortable giving it back just as straight.

'Well, for starters, it'd be easier to get your foot in almost any other set in the country. Cheaper overheads if you ended up with a tenancy. You join a set in the heart of the Inns like this, and you'll be saying farewell to half your income on rent and overheads alone.'

She nodded attentively, cheeks aglow in the slanting light of the window.

'I can only presume that you wish to become a trial advocate?'

Another nod. 'I want to defend those who are powerless to defend themselves.'

'As did I, but as I'm sure you know, barristers follow what we call the *cab-rank principle*. Like taxi drivers, we take the next case that comes our way, whatever the charge, and rarely get to pick and choose. This inevitably involves both defending *and* prosecuting. Briefs, or cases, are sent by solicitors through our clerks. Occasionally, a particular barrister is requested by a client, but mostly the solicitor will leave it to the clerks to make the decision. You can only turn down a case if you have a previous commitment, or if you consider it either too complex or not serious enough for a barrister of your call.' I held out an open hand. 'CV?'

I half expected the paper to be crumpled, it took her so long to fish it out from the clutter in her canvas shoulder bag, and was surprised to find it flattened in a hardback folder.

I leaned back and scanned the orderly typeface. 'Law degree from Hull?'

'Yeah.'

'And you're originally from?'

'Nottingham.'

'Whereabouts?'

'St Ann's,' she muttered, a flash burning her cheeks. 'It's a suburb close to the centre. Gun capital of England apparently!' A thin, watery laugh did nothing to flush the heat out from her face.

'Along with the Meadows estate down the road, isn't it?'

She cocked her head. 'Um, yeah, exactly. Most people haven't even heard of it …'

'I'm not most people,' I said, reading on.

It hadn't always been the gun capital. Not when I was born there, and it had been a sprawling slum without hot running water.

'Pretty average degree, but I see you have a good debating record. I didn't even know they had a debating society at Hull.'

'HUDS,' she said proudly. 'I won the Middle Temple Inter-varsity, too.'

'So did I,' I boasted, before noticing, with a sobering wrench, her written age of twenty-four; I won that before she was born. 'This would be your second six, correct?'

'Um,' she pinched at the laddered nylon around her knees, 'not exactly …'

'Oh?'

Between passing Bar exams and calling oneself a junior barrister, there is a minimum requirement of a year's pupillage divided into two six-month periods, at the end of which successful pupils are typically offered a tenancy in chambers.

'This would, technically, be my third. For my first six I shadowed Roger Walsh at King Edward's, and in my second, still with Walsh, I learned how to conduct my own hearings in the magistrates' court, do basic bail applications and pleas-in-mitigation, and I defended and prosecuted in six summary trials.'

'And you weren't offered a tenancy?'

She shook her head. 'The place went to another pupil from my year.'

'Any idea why?'

She managed a wry smile. 'I wasn't *clubbable*, whereas he was. That was the word they used. I suppose it didn't hurt that he was Judge Sudworth's son, Monty.'

I nodded, rapping my fingertips on the paperwork on the desk; I wished I had a secretary to call for coffee on my non-existent intercom. 'A levels in law, English, film studies, psychology and drama?'

'Oh, yeah.' She cleared her throat. 'I know you're gonna be looking for something more academic …'

'Not at all,' I said, knowing full well that Percy would've been revolted by such subjects. 'I'd say they're entirely relevant.'

Her bright eyes narrowed a touch. 'How's that?'

'Well, some advocates get by on doctrine and formal procedure alone. They know Blackstone's from cover to cover, case laws to fit every argument, but becoming a truly great barrister requires something more. The best advocates are, in essence, *showmen*. I'm not suggesting vaudeville, but enough of a performer to keep the jury hanging on every word can be crucial. Defending at the Criminal Bar might not be the walk-and-talk glamour of American television, we've still retained a great many of our traditions, but drama is, most certainly, relevant. Most trials are won and lost by the closing speech alone.'

'Huh …'

I was glad to notice her sink more comfortably into the chair.

'I'm currently taking instructions from major solicitors in cases involving the embezzlement of millions, which require exhaustive research and come with hundreds of thousands of pages of evidence.' With one hand, I indicated the untidiness around us. 'It is challenging work, but it can also be unbearably dull. I'd need somebody around who isn't afraid of long hours and filing paperwork. That said, I also need somebody who is prepared to help defend some of the most abhorrent criminals and killers one might imagine.'

'Don't you mean *alleged* killers?'

'No, I mean killers. Let's not be naive about this. The fact of killing is often admitted, but *murder*, as a legal concept, is denied on grounds such as self-defence, provocation or diminished responsibility. Only a jury can determine whether or not a self-confessed killer who pleads not guilty is a murderer, but more often than not, it is killers with whom we conduct our business.'

I could hear my tone slipping, burrowing, nestling into the familiar accusatory rhythm of cross-examination. I wondered how long it had been since I'd had an ordinary discussion with a stranger, beyond the formal colloquies of the job. How long since I'd been alone with a young woman. It was more than a year since I'd had a drink or dinner with anybody outside of the legal circle. Somewhere inside, I worried about what social skills I'd retained since Jenny had left.

'The unpleasant reality,' I went on, 'is that most of the clients I defend really *have* committed some of the most depraved acts imaginable. In order to construct a fair defence, emotional detachment is critical.' I saw her eyes narrow and continued before she had chance to interject. 'I took silk after defending a man accused of murdering two young women. One was seventeen years old, the other twenty-one.'

'That's terrible,' she said quietly, 'but everybody is entitled to a fair –'

'He *ate* them.'

I watched the spark fall from her face.

'He ate their flesh in various recipes, which he recorded and rated in a journal. I had the murder charges dropped on the grounds of diminished responsibility; the same defence I used for a young mother who boiled her infant alive inside the dishwasher.

'These are the sorts of people you'll be charged with defending, and to this day I'm positive that both were entirely compos mentis in their actions. Fortunately, it's not for me to pass judgement. We barristers have to trust in the system to provide justice, but reconciling the verdicts with your own private opinion is something you must find a way to deal with, as well as the animosity that can come from all sides.'

She chewed her thumbnail in silence for a moment; cobalt varnish chipped away against white teeth.

'What animosity?'

I picked up the Rubik's cube and juggled it in my empty right hand.

'Defence barristers may well be among the most reviled professionals in the working world, third only to traffic wardens and tax collectors. As far as the papers are concerned, we're the ones who come along after the case is solved, once the Mystery Machine has driven off into the credits, to set the ghoul loose inside the theme park again. I'm sorry to tell you this, but you are aspiring to join what is largely regarded as the bottom-feeding scum of the justice system.'

She dried her palms on her tights and blew out a mouthful of air. 'Jinkies.'

I laughed out loud; it was entirely inappropriate, but warm and natural, right from the belly up, and something I hadn't done in chambers for as long as I could remember. She laughed back, and in the sound, as in her accent, I was reminded of a life almost forgotten. Easy as that, I was sold.

'They didn't mention any of that over at King Edward's,' she said. 'You got any advice on dealing with it?'

'Only this …' I stopped juggling, rolled the puzzle away over the desk. 'When you prosecute, always remember that you're acting as a minister of justice, and it's your duty to see that justice is done. When you defend, do so fearlessly, but honestly. Try and win your cases, but don't ever cheat.

Be *friendly* to defendants, but never, ever forget one crucial point. They are *not* your friends. Don't ever stick your neck out for them, no matter what you do.'

'All right,' she said slowly, straightening her glasses, 'I can do that.'

I smiled again. 'Then I think you'll fit in well here.'

The final point of this conversation was one that would come back to me again and again, in moments of great regret and shame, when my neck was well and truly on the line for the client that was about to change everything.

4

One room filled the top floor of our building.

It belonged to Rupert Stubbs QC, who sat four storeys above the sign over the front door that bore his name. Aston Miller QC, his former partner, had been dead for seven years, leaving Rupert the sole head of chambers at seventy-one, but Miller's name remained.

After meeting Zara, memories of my own first days in the building had resurfaced, and, despite the decades passed, Rupert remained ever the pragmatist and almost indistinguishable from the man who had first invited me into chambers. It was as if he'd acquired the physicality of a gentleman well beyond his years early on, to get the ageing process swiftly out of the way. He'd been grey and crisp in appearance as long as I'd known him, yet the physical bulk of my stature was slight compared to the magnitude of his character and intellect. He could've been a genius in any profession, but as an officer of the court he was both fierce and fair, one of the finest lawyers I'd seen beneath the wig, and the privilege of being his personal pupil had been mine alone.

I still remember his inaugural words when I, floppy-haired envy of every failed Etonian applicant among the Inner Temple, had taken a seat in that illustrious room on the highest floor.

'Never sit with your jacket fastened, boy. It ruins the cut of the cloth.'

I'd laughed about that afterwards, my pinstripe blazer having been so oversized and absurd, purchased for less than two pounds from the Oxfam on Drury Lane. My clothes hadn't seemed to bother him in the slightest.

His room remained a physical paean to *old-world silk*; where my shelves were cluttered and punctuated by the likes of Kafka, Dostoevsky and Dickens, his were organised and imposing, with rows of academic leather-bound spines etched in the green glow of an original Emeralite banker's lamp, even when sunlight illuminated the rooftop cityscape beyond the spotless windows. For many years he had smoked a pipe up in that room, and the woody smell of its tobacco still permeated the leather of the wingback chairs, the walnut of his grand desk.

He was pacing back and forth in front of the windows when I walked in a week after Zara's impromptu interview, moving with the precision of a grey pendulum between the standard barrister's horsehair wig on its plinth in one corner – the same he'd had when we first met – and the full-bottomed ceremonial wig on the opposite side, which he'd had since turning to judging.

'You wanted to see me, Rupert?'

He beckoned me into one of the wingbacks without a smile and shut the door behind me.

'Hat,' he scolded, and off it came. 'It has come to my attention that you've appointed Mr Charles Stein as junior on this fraud case of yours, on the condition that he takes on a pupil who will effectively be working for you.'

'That's right,' I said, slumping back into the smoky stretched hide. I could've picked Stein's name from a hat, for all the thought I'd given it; rules dictated that I couldn't mentor Zara myself – silks aren't given pupils – so I chose the first junior barrister in chambers I could think of and convinced him to take her on by offering him a slice of the gargantuan fraud case.

'You know it's not conventional for silks to have pupils working under them, even if you are using Stein's involvement as a loophole.'

'Have I ever claimed to be conventional?'

Still no smile. 'You *are* aware that it is customary for chambers to vote on pupillage?'

I must've groaned, judging by the look he gave me. Recollections of being a schoolboy waiting for the cane rushed to me unbidden. I had to remind myself that the cane had been outlawed long ago, and I was at least four times Rupert's size; from experience, the latter didn't lend me much comfort. 'Do I get points for guessing who carped?'

'Only the majority of our senior juniors this time, most of whom are still waiting for their own pupils.'

'Yes,' I said. 'That's what I would've guessed.'

'I'd appreciate it if you could refrain from undermining our clerk's authority in future.' He continued circling to the point where I felt dizzy. 'I hear this'll be her third six? Does that mean she'd be happy to take cases of her own?'

'More than happy, I'm sure. You'll like her, Rupert. She seems smart. Eager. Sharp.'

'So were you,' he said, running one hand over the driver in the set of clubs he kept by his desk, 'and yet you've never had a pupil make it to the end of term without leaving chambers or requesting a new Pupil Supervisor. In fact, I believe one of your former pupils turned his back on the Bar altogether, did he not?'

I tried hard not to grin. 'We didn't have much in common, the young Master Ainsworth and me. Besides, she's technically Stein's pupil, not mine.'

He shook his head. 'How far you've come from the young man I found on the street outside, and yet you'll still play the fool of a class warrior at every opportunity.'

I was picking at the edges of my nails, I realised, a lifelong habit in his presence.

'Were you ever ashamed of my background, Rupert?'

'I never lied about you once,' he said firmly, perching on the edge of his desk like a much younger man would do, flattening the lapels of his chequered sports jacket. 'How has her first week been?'

'It's been great. Very insightful. Very productive.'

This wasn't strictly true.

I'd been so consumed by the evidence of my ongoing case that we'd barely spoken during her first few days, and it had taken her most of the week to move her things from Nottingham into a shared house in the capital. There had already been several moments when I'd regretted my impulsive decision – having to share my office was a stark reminder of earlier days, and the tension of our silence had become borderline unbearable – but no moment had I regretted more than the previous afternoon.

While analysing his billing records, Zara had stumbled across one particular day when our client, Mr Kessler, had billed for a supposed thirty hours' work – an especially careless move on the part of the suspected fraudster in our corner.

We invited him into chambers to discuss the issue, and instead of passing it off as a slip of the pen, as one might've expected him to do – as *I* had expected him to do – the client brought with him a home-made cardboard mask contraption, which he proceeded to slide over his head and secure with elastic bands.

The minute he slipped it out of his briefcase, this cereal box wonder, I knew it could only mean trouble. Zara must've thought it was all some sort of introductory prank.

It wasn't.

The front of the mask had a long piece of card separating the client's eyes, and it was this, he insisted, that gave him the power to simultaneously read two documents at once. He proudly announced that he had done fifteen hours' reading with each eye, hence the thirty hours billed, and that was the moment, after months of exhaustive preparation, that I realised my case might be fucked.

'Great,' I repeated. 'It's all going really great.'

'Good. It's nice to see you playing well with others.' Rupert paused, eyebrows knitting together, and sighed. 'God knows you may need all the help you can get if you take this on ...' Until he picked it up, I hadn't paid much attention to the fat courier envelope lying on his otherwise spotless desk, which he now brought up to his chest, refraining from handing it over just yet. 'You have been briefed on a new case.'

'And?' There was nothing unusual about this. A legal aid order is first given for junior counsel and solicitor only but, in cases deemed serious enough, an application can be made for a silk and a junior. Once a legal aid order has been so amended, a silk is instructed. 'Why isn't this coming from Percy?'

Another sigh, deepening the folds already set around the cornflower of his eyes; the recent years of moderate luxury hadn't been enough to iron the creases of his dogged youth, and every line was worthy of respect; here was a man who had truly earned his status. 'Elliot, our fellowship demands I lend you some advice here, and it's a suggestion I've rarely made in my career. Something I've never asked you to do before, in fact …'

He was still gripping the envelope close to his chest.

'What is it?'

A flash in the eyes, dipping his chin. 'Do not take this case.'

I thought I'd misheard him. 'I beg your pardon? Why not?'

'You know that we are never impartial advocates in the eyes of the public or the media. I'm not sure that having your name attached to this case would be a wise move so soon after taking silk, especially considering your connection to the area.'

'My connection?' I could feel my curiosity mounting. 'What's the brief, Rupert?'

'It's murder at the Old Bailey, fixed to start in two weeks.'

'Two weeks?'

He nodded. 'Did you hear about the body of the young woman found on a disused railway in Nottinghamshire several months ago?'

It sounded like the start of a bad joke. 'I vaguely remember it, yes.'

Of course I did. It had happened within spitting distance of my childhood home, the secret I'd kept buried to everyone in law-land except for my mentor.

'I'm up to my neck preparing for this fraud case anyway,' I said. 'Why would I be interested in taking that on?'

'It's the defendant.'

'What about the defendant?'

He finally leaned forward to place the envelope into my waiting hand, and I was surprised to find it even heavier than it looked.

'He says he knows you.'

I ripped back the card and slid the papers out into one hand while Rupert continued, his voice dropping to little more than a whisper.

'The instructing solicitor has already organised a letter of introduction for a conference with the defendant at Belmarsh on Monday morning, if you decide to take the case. The way I've heard it, the client has fired his existing counsel in favour of you.'

'Two weeks before the trial? Who the hell *is* this?'

I was looking down, through the white tape that held the brief together, and for one blissful moment I didn't recognise the name on the paper. Somehow, I hadn't registered it in the news at the time of his arrest.

I'd never known him as William, after all.

Then it all made sense.

To me, and all who'd known him, fought alongside him, and been utterly terrorised by him, he'd only ever been Billy, and now he'd hit the big time.

Murder at the Old Bailey. You silly son of a bitch.

5

Chancery Lane might well have been deserted.

It could've been filled with the charred remnants of a nuclear blast for all the attention I paid my surroundings upon rushing out of Took's Court after leaving Rupert's office. The pavement unravelled like film from a cassette tape, footsteps unsteady and briefcase hanging like a noose from my fist, the name inside as destructive as any weapon.

The secrets I'd kept, the lies I'd told, the things I'd done.

Here, in my hand, was the spark that would blow them to pieces.

I paused opposite the Mexican restaurant at the north end of the road, fished my phone out from my pocket, and turned it off.

I wasn't feeling well. My guts were rocking, ready to tip, unsound as a raft of refugees in the middle of a pitch-black ocean.

Checking back over one shoulder, pulling my hat down lower than usual, I collided with a man coming the opposite way along the path, inadvertently knocking him into the wall beside us.

'Steady on, Rook!'

It was Ted Bowen, scrambling back to his feet, wrapped in the thin smoke of what was now a broken Embassy Number 1. I didn't know he smoked; fewer people seemed to every year.

It was exactly one week since he'd lost his attempted murder, and the defeat that had stooped his shoulders in the pub now riddled his whole frame. I might've paid more attention to the sickly grey in his cheeks, had I not been feeling so ashen myself.

I mumbled an apology as I made to pass, eager to put some distance between chambers and myself, but he sidestepped directly into my route. His eyes, which were spread just a little too far apart under the brow, had a red quality to them as if he'd been crying, or drinking, or both.

There was a strained silence first, in which his thin mouth flapped open and closed a couple of times before he spoke. 'My application was rejected today. Silk. I'm sure you heard. No interview offered. Thirty-one years since I passed the Bar. *Thirty-one years.*'

'Shit.' I hardly knew what else to say about it. 'That's shit, Ted.'

He'd certainly worked hard, much harder than some in more fortunate positions, and made no secret of his expectations. I knew he wanted to take silk, but beyond that I didn't know much about him. Was he married? Was he happy? Was he kind? I couldn't say. I barely cared. My own days – or rather long nights – of networking had mostly passed, my years of *playing the game* had all but settled, and perhaps that was where my mistakes began. I had no allegiances. All I had was my past.

I clutched the briefcase tighter at my hip.

'Two grand it cost me just to apply,' he went on. 'That's without those bullshit courses to help prepare my application. What a waste.'

'Tough luck, old boy,' I managed. 'I'm sorry, but I really need to be off.'

I practically stepped over him in my haste and to my surprise he came along with me, staggering at my shoulder, too close, occasionally bumping into me.

'But *you* did it last year, didn't you?' he said. 'First time no less, after only twenty-two, twenty-three years? And that got me thinking: what makes Elliot Rook so damn special? What's your secret, huh? You've had *how many* consecutive wins now?'

I'd stopped listening. It's a vulgar move for a barrister to discuss winning streaks, and I'd come down with the strangest sensation, as if the briefcase was slipping open in my grasp, just a notch, and a great darkness was trickling out, seeping over my knuckles and up to my chest.

The shadow of Billy Barber, and all I'd left behind, was drawing ever nearer.

I was already turning the corner onto High Holborn when I felt a more substantial presence wrap itself around my right elbow, and looked down to find Bowen gripping it with both hands. 'I'm talking to you!'

I stopped dead. Irritated pedestrians had to walk around us, chattering into earpieces or drinking coffee as they hurried for the Underground.

'What?' I snapped.

He laughed a petty laugh, a laugh I didn't like at all, and I could smell the spirits on his breath. I needed a drink, but first I had to get far away from there.

'How long's it going to be before your name's above the door?' he sneered. 'If I were Stubbs, I'd start checking over my shoulder on the staircase.'

While his tone suggested a joke, there was no humour in his flat eyes, and he was still holding on to my arm, even tighter now.

'There's something about you, Rook. Something I can't quite put my finger on.' He released his grip, but only to wag one skinny finger in my face, before resting it knowingly against his chin. 'Remind me, what house were you in at Eton?'

I swallowed hard, the smirk on his lips, the briefcase in my hand.

He knew nothing. He couldn't. Could he?

'I reckon you should sleep it off, chum,' I told him. 'Start fresh on Monday. There's always next year.'

Now it was he who was barely listening. 'You've just forced Charles Stein to take on a pupil, ostensibly for you, haven't you?'

'The fraud case I'm working on requires three counsel,' I explained irritably. 'Stein is first junior, and his pupil, Miss Barnes, is now second.'

'Never heard of a *silk* needing a pupil before, and *what* a pupil you've chosen! I'd heard the rumours about your marriage, but I didn't realise you had such a thing for the rough stuff!'

What happened must have occurred at incredible speed, because the next thing I saw was Bowen's face twisted up, eyes bulging, as I caught him by the collar and slammed his back into the wall of the building behind him.

'Rough stuff, Ted? *Rough stuff?* You have *no fucking idea!*'

I let him slump to the floor, gasping for air, and barged through the staring pedestrians, storming in the direction of Soho and its bars, briefcase swinging a little lighter from my hand.

PART TWO

THE DEFENDANT

6

Sinatra said that when he was seventeen it was a very good year for small-town girls and soft summer nights. I've always liked that. It sounds so pleasant.

I turned seventeen in 1982, and for me, it was a very violent year.

I was unemployed, homeless for the first time, and a feared fighter in the tight-knit rankings of Cotgrave, my Nottinghamshire home.

Feared, but far from a champion. Such illustrious titles went to an entirely different breed of delinquent, and the Barber brothers cleaned up in every weight division.

The youngest, or featherweight, of the clan was Declan. Three years my junior, his own reputation was cemented one lunch break in primary school after being unceremoniously floored by Al Pickard, the school bully. Declan retaliated by breaking Pickard's leg in the middle of the playground with the groundsman's unguarded shovel. He was eleven years old at the time.

The second youngest, Caine, earned the lightweight title over years of scattered spontaneous violence, culminating in the arson of his ex-girlfriend's Ford Sierra, while she was in the back seat with her new man.

The pair made it out alive at least.

Middleweight was Aidan Barber, the brightest of the family and one of my closest allies throughout secondary school. His screws were fixed somewhat tighter, but he was always ready to flatten anybody who came looking for trouble, as they so often did.

And the eldest of the four brothers – the undisputed heavyweight, ultraviolent embodiment of irrationality – was Billy.

My rare attempts to rationalise small-town, working-class mentality have been accepted with varying degrees of success by the occasional jury panel, and absolute refutation from our therapist in relationship counselling; the esteemed Dr Travers couldn't quite get his PhD around the concept.

In the late seventies and early eighties, people didn't have the money to go on holiday as they might do now. I knew four people who had ventured beyond the borders of the county, and all four went to Torremolinos with Pontinental. Ours was a community of coal – of dark winding shafts and the breaking of rock – and like an ecosystem preserved in a jar, Sea-Monkeys in a tank or bacteria in a spoiled carcass, we were all but sequestered from the bigger picture. Our world view started and ended with the rival teams in the football leagues, and, crucially, scrapping with their supporters.

I knew Billy by reputation, and as my best friend's elder brother, but didn't meet him properly until 6 October 1982. I remember the date for its two pivotal moments: first, Nottingham Forest put six goals past West Bromwich Albion, and a large group – more of a *pack*, including the Barber brethren and myself – had gone out looking for celebratory trouble around the City Ground; and, second, because trouble found us in very little time at all, Billy fractured a rival hooligan's skull, and I spent my first night in prison.

I can even recall the shirt I was wearing through those endless, sobering hours, huddled alone in the unforgiving light of that cell; marking the recent release of The Clash's 'Know Your Rights', it had an illustration of an open book on the front of it, the words *The Future is Unwritten* on one page, and a handgun printed on the other. I was perhaps too young to appreciate the irony at the time.

Watching Billy break another man's head open was only the first of several incidents I'd go on to witness, and it wasn't nearly the most aggressive.

He was the sort of trouble that even the local trouble avoided, a man whose unwanted company kept cropping up over the years, difficult to avoid in the pubs of such a small community.

He might not have been Jesse James, but I can guarantee that everybody who lived in Cotgrave through the seventies and eighties would still have a story about Billy Barber, and it certainly wouldn't help in his defence.

My more immediate concern, however, was not the lasting legacy of the outlaw, but rather what the outlaw might have remembered about me.

It was coming up to midnight when I turned my phone back on and rang Percy. Any testiness he had about the untimely disruption to his weekend was exacerbated tenfold when I told him I was taking Billy Barber's trial.

'Are you drunk?' he snapped, guessing rightly by the hour and the slur of a few beers in my voice. 'You want to risk being ready for the most bankable fraud of the year for a murder on legal aid? What am I supposed to tell the client? That you're taking a two-week sabbatical? Just tell the new solicitor that you have prior arrangements and pass it on to somebody else!'

'I've already done the legwork for the fraud, and I've got piles of comprehensive notes for Stein to be working on. Wasn't that the whole point of being shanghaied into taking a junior? All he has to do is find the missing clients. Besides, this murder case will be long past before the fraud trial ever starts.'

'You'll need a junior for this, too.'

He was right, but after years of carefully fabricating my past, there wasn't a barrister in chambers I could introduce to Billy. 'Barnes, the new girl. Brief her on the murder.'

'The pupil? You want to take a pupil into a murder at the Old Bailey?'

The line was quiet, nothing but rattling breath from the other end, and I could tell he was pissed off. We hadn't really spoken since I'd invited Zara into the building.

'Rook, is there something I should know about this case?'

'Just do your job and make it happen, Percy,' I barked, and then hung up on what might well have been my only remaining ally in the city.

After that I stayed out on the town for most of the weekend, doing my utmost to avoid the gathering tempest I could sense on the horizon. It was the first weekend in maybe a dozen that I didn't spend hunting for my alleged fraudster's supposed clients, now that I'd surrendered the majority of the letters, bank statements and billing receipts to Stein and Zara, but I longed for the distraction. I hardly slept for going over Billy's case, convinced that hour by hour, minute by minute, his unpredictability was drawing him ever closer to ending my career with whatever he might remember about my past, assuming that Ted Bowen and the Bar Standards Board didn't get to me first.

It never occurred to me to simply apologise to Ted. I've always struggled saying sorry. Jenny used to say she could almost see the word clotting at the back of my throat, stubborn as phlegm or a fur ball, and I'd sooner choke than spit it out to draw breath. She might have had a point.

By Monday morning I was exhausted and edgy. October had come without my noticing, and I had to go into chambers to collect my letter of introduction for the prison conference.

That's where I found Zara waiting, looking remarkably more refreshed than I felt in her usual suit, two coffee cups in her hands. In absolute honesty, I'd almost forgotten about her.

'Morning, Mr Rook,' she beamed as soon as I'd put one foot inside the room; she thrust one of the coffees into my grasp and offered her newly emptied hand. 'Here's to our first case together! Well, our first case from scratch, I mean. Percy emailed me the instructions through yesterday. He said you might need some help on this.'

I looked down at her outstretched hand and shook my head. 'Barristers don't shake hands with one another. Men originally shook hands to show they were unarmed, and it was considered a slight on the other barrister's integrity. Don't do it.'

'Oh ...' The arm dropped like stone to her side.

I was being short and I knew it. Every word felt withered and tasted bitter on my lips. When I looked around, I noticed that the mouldy cups and litter had disappeared from my desk, the paperwork there had been arranged into a plastic in-tray I'd never seen before, and there was considerably more floor to be seen than usual.

'This is only a quick stop for me,' I grunted. 'I have to collect the letter of introduction and visit the client at Belmarsh before noon. You keep working through the bank statements you were looking at last week, try to find those clients, and –' I paused. 'Something wrong?'

Her face was almost parallel to the floor, loose hair hanging over the shoulders of her off-black jacket. 'No, I just … I thought I might get to come along with you. It's Belmarsh, and for a murder that was committed almost on my doorstep! Percy said he'd ask the solicitor to add me to the conference and … I thought it could be, well, exciting.'

'That's one word for it.'

'Well, educational then …' She trailed off into disenchanted mumbles, something along the lines of, 'It isn't fraud, anyway …' and then went quiet.

I hesitated, the warmth of the coffee cup softening autumn's bite in my bare palm; it smelled like caramel and almonds, all the right sugars to subdue my growing headache, and I heard myself sigh.

I wasn't sure what was going to happen when I came face-to-face with Billy after so many years, but I was certain that I didn't want Zara anywhere near the man.

So how she ended up in the passenger seat on the drive south-east to Belmarsh, I really couldn't say.

7

'Your letter of introduction, sir?'

The warder at the visitors' reception was superficially polite, but his body language reeked of Monday morning, not unlike my own, and when I handed the letter over he smoothed it out onto the desk with both hands and a grumble, leaning close to read it.

'Stand on the blue cross and look into the camera, please.'

In turn, Zara and I had our photographs taken, printed, and clipped into plastic holders attached to badges, before the forefingers of both hands were scanned into the system through an infrared screen.

'Wear these badges at all times on the premises,' he told us as he passed them over, 'and you can only take loose case papers, plain paper for writing, and two pens in with you. Everything else, including watches, piercings and the contents of your pockets, will have to be left in the lockers here.'

I dropped a pound coin into the largest locker they had, slipped my dulled wedding ring, wallet, watch and phone into my coat pockets along with my car keys, and hung the coat inside with my hat.

'Two more weeks!' the warder called from his spot behind the desk, and I turned back, frowning.

'Pardon?'

'Those pound coins,' he said, resting his chin lazily on one fist. 'Two weeks from now they cease to be legal tender, but you won't be able to use the new ones in the lockers. They're not being converted. We're going to be keeping some of the old coins, though, and you'll be able to buy them for two quid whenever you need to use them.'

'Right,' I said, 'that's very thoughtful of Her Majesty's Prison Service, thanks.'

Fifteen gated doors and another fingerprint scanner safeguard the rest of the labyrinth into Belmarsh. The doors operate in such a way that no two can ever be unlocked or opened at the same time, like a series of consecutive airlocks leading into the abyss.

A stern, silent jailer led us through the maze, our footsteps echoing in unison against the clatter of shunting locks, tarnished hinges and rattling keys, then it was out and across a dull, caged yard under a darkening sky.

The High Security Unit is a separate, even more fortified jail within the heart of the larger prison, a concrete building opposite the inmates' five-a-side football pitch. In a cramped inner reception area we were made to take off our belts and shoes – Zara nervously fumbling with the knots of her clunky Doc Martens – which were bundled together through an X-ray machine, while we were searched with a torch from the insides of our mouths down to the fabric of our socks.

The taste of the inspector's latex glove was bitter when she lifted my tongue; my eyes drifted to the grey plastic chair with BOSS III stamped across its backboard, the Body Orifice Security Scanner, and I was relieved to be spared the further embarrassment.

She indicated the papers in Zara's hands. 'Could you place your papers and pens inside the tray as well?'

'They're confidential,' Zara replied sheepishly.

'I'm not going to read them,' the inspector bit. 'I just need to make sure there's nothing concealed inside.'

We spent five more minutes staring into the dead eyes of cameras lined above a forbidding gate of red iron, while a distant control room used facial recognition technology to confirm our identities. Zara was unnervingly silent and statuesque, occasionally flexing her jaw to bite her lower lip, and I asked if she was all right. All I got in return was an edgy nod.

When the gate eventually opened, it did so with the groan of a burial crypt left long undisturbed. Two men came briskly towards us from the opposite end of the corridor.

One was another warder, a tall black man dressed in a crisp white shirt and immaculate shiny shoes, who was presaged by the jangling of a hundred or more keys hanging from his waistband. The other was a small-eyed, freckled, mousy kid of about Zara's age, dressed in a navy suit with his own visitor's pass hanging from the lapel.

'I'm Senior Officer Wilkins,' the warder said first, steamrolling the other's timid attempt at an introduction, then he turned on one polished heel and beckoned us all to follow him towards the visitors' hall.

The kid squeezed in neatly between us, clutching loose papers to his chest, and bounced along in scuffed Clarks. 'I'm Fraser Hayes from Lennox, Ross and Chapman Solicitors. I appreciate you coming down at such short notice.'

'Our client is here on remand,' I said, struggling to keep up with the senior officer. 'Why is he being held in the High Security Unit?'

'Have you *seen* your client?' Wilkins replied without looking back, still some way ahead. 'Special provisional conditions. This is where we hold the *terrorists*.'

'But he isn't on remand for terror offences.'

'Not this time.' Another corner, and he came to a halt outside a small conference room with floor-to-ceiling glass windows separating it from the visitors' hall. 'We've had more than a dozen racially aggravated attacks on the prison grounds in the last three months, and we don't need men like *your client* spreading his backward ideology to the rest of the inmates. It's for his own safety as much as for theirs, and was all discussed and arranged, at length, with his solicitor.'

'He is quite a character,' the solicitor agreed breathlessly; stationary at last, I could see just how young he was, how inexperienced, and suspected he'd been sold the dud that no one else in the firm wanted to touch. 'The client was moved here after an altercation during his first week in general population. Now, he was very explicit about meeting you – and specifically *you*, Mr Rook – alone ...' His eyes drifted cautiously to Zara. 'I'll be waiting out here, and then we can go through the case in more detail, if that suits you?'

'My junior will be joining me for the conference, Mr Hayes,' I told him flatly, and saw a reassured swell in Zara's chest. 'Let's get this over with, shall we?'

Officer Wilkins rapped on the door, and a final, much larger jailer opened it from the other side, stepping out to allow us to enter.

As we crossed the threshold, Wilkins leaned close to Zara with a wholly unfriendly, stony grin. 'I suppose it would be somewhat redundant to warn you that your client isn't a very pleasant man,' he said, and then closed the door behind us, sealing the room.

Silence.

Off-white walls and off-white lights. A single video camera recording visuals.

A Formica table with chairs.

And Billy.

I wished he'd changed over the years. Grown up and softened in appearance, perhaps. He was approaching sixty, after all. If anything, he'd only hardened in the interim.

Baldness had finally finished the job where I recalled a younger man's skinhead, and his expanse of faded tattoos started with a Celtic cross underneath his right eye, and went on to cover every centimetre of his throat and fists. I couldn't take them all in without staring, but the general theme was clear enough from the red Templar cross that fanned out behind his left ear, to the letters stamped across his chestnut-sized knuckles, crooked from so many breakages over the years: PURE LAND.

What bare skin still remained between ink was hardly more appealing, and it clung to his muscles as if professionally upholstered by a specialist dealing in Scarred Oak, Weathered Leather or Killer's Pelt; his burgundy jogging pants, and what must've been the largest grey T-shirt available, stretched thin over his massive limbs.

He was first to speak, as Zara and I took chairs on the opposite side of the table, which didn't seem nearly distant enough.

'Who's the Jude?'

I didn't deign to answer, but he took it upon himself to continue.

'You know where they're keeping me, don't you?'

When he spoke, he did so without breath, words broken only by a recurring tic that jerked his head back over his left shoulder. It was the sort I'd encountered in many addicts before, skull kicking off to the side like a wounded mule.

'They've only gone and stuck me in the same cell that Abu fucking Hook-Hands stayed in. I swear you can still smell him on the walls in there. Fucking stinks. *Reeks*. Treating me like I'm fucking ISIS or summat.'

Every one of his blinks came down hard, slamming over bottomless gloom with the conviction of a guillotine. His focus narrowed back in on Zara.

'What you meant to be, anyhow? A solicitor? A barrister? You're fucking joking.'

She didn't respond. Billy's head rolled again, lips back, jaw jutting defectively from one side to the other.

'Mr Barber,' I began, but he was on her again.

'Can you even speak English, or did you just get off the boat this morning?'

Silence again. Tic, tic, tic went his massive, dented skull.

I desperately wanted to speak, but words were hard to find. All the murderers, molesters and rapists I'd come face-to-face with throughout the years, and here was something I hadn't experienced in my profession. Here was a man who frightened me.

I couldn't even bring myself to look at Zara when I asked her to step outside.

I was trying for a tone that might've suggested I was doing it for her sake, but the truth was I simply couldn't stand the embarrassment of it any longer. She closed the door behind her, making barely a sound, and then we were alone.

Billy leaned forward across the table with a playful wink, as if it was all some sort of game. 'You fucking her or what?'

His features seemed oddly misaligned, no doubt the result of frequent collisions, with one eye fixed slightly lower than the other, mouth hanging off to one side, like the pieces of an original Potato Head kit all pushed into an old vegetable by a heavy-handed toddler.

'Course you're not,' he quickly decided. 'Look at you, fat fuck. Not that you were ever skinny like, but fuck me. Bet you couldn't see your cock now, even if you were King Dong.'

More of those unsettling skeletal spasms; he was practically convulsing in the chair. His hands landed like concrete on the Formica. 'Last time I saw you would've been our Aidan's funeral, wouldn't it?'

'Nice service,' I managed in a dry voice. 'Good lad, your brother.'

He leaned back, puffing the chest of a bear, and nodded pensively.

'Like brothers, you and him were. Thick as thieves, Mam used to say. Thick as pig shit, sometimes, but family the same. What does that make *us* then?'

'We're not family, Mr Barber.'

'Brother of my brother.' He grinned, a rictus slash through granite, and kept on nodding to himself. 'You're gonna get me out of here.'

I shuffled my papers in front of me, steadying my hands. 'If I *was* going to represent you, Billy –'

'You are.'

'Then we're going to have to go through some of the basics. We're going to need a defence we can run with.

You've already had a psychiatric report, and the CPS is going to reject diminished responsibility, so there's that. I can't work with vague, whimsical allusions to intimidation. We need a defence.'

He considered it for a moment and cocked his skull. 'That's a new voice. Where'd you get it?'

I glanced up at the camera, reminded myself that, by law, it wasn't listening, and told him straight.

'Practice.'

It was true, my accent was no accident.

It had taken many months to break the habits of home, and that was all relatively easy compared to switching cutlery to the correct hands at mealtimes after twenty-odd years, studying my shoplifted copy of *Debrett's Handbook* in a sleeping bag under the shelter of a multi-storey car park, and all the endless research into Eton.

'You're charged with murder, Billy. If you're convicted, the sentence will be *life*. We can aim for a reduction on the minimum term to be served before you're eligible to apply for parole, *if* you plead guilty. Do that before the trial starts, and you're looking at a third off. On the first day of trial, it's going to drop to ten per cent, and the window of opportunity will shrink by the day thereon.'

He shook his head, jerked it to the left. 'I'll tell you the same as I told the last wigged-up ponce the solicitor sent me. I'm not pleading to fuck all. I didn't kill no one.'

'You've got kids now, haven't you?' I asked, taking a stab in the dark. 'Think about them.'

'What do you reckon I'm thinking about?'

I flicked through the case papers as if I was reading them, keeping the pens safely in my grasp, and scratched my head.

'Do you even remember the night of the murder? Witnesses say you were blackout drunk.'

'Rat-arsed.'

'So, what *do* you remember?'

His face held tight. 'I remember I didn't kill no one.'

'Right. It's the evening of Good Friday, and you disappear, drunk. The next morning, an unknown girl is found dead within walking distance of your home. Your phone's GPS places you close to the scene of the crime, right up until you switched it to airplane mode. You have no explanation for that void of five hours, before you were seen burning bloody clothes in your back garden. You didn't answer a single question in your police interview to explain your whereabouts or your side of the story.'

'My right to stay quiet,' he grunted.

'It is, but what are we going to run with? You don't want to plead guilty, but you have no answer as to why you *aren't* guilty.'

'Well, that's not my job, is it? Burden of proof is on them, last time I checked.'

He was smarter than I'd given him credit for. I guess he'd picked up a lot in these situations over the years.

'That's why you're here, anyway,' he said. 'You're gonna make a case. You're gonna find witnesses. You're gonna get your fat arse home and bang on fucking doors if you have to, and you're getting me out of this shit.'

'"Bang on doors"?' Tiredness was starting to outweigh my apprehension; I was feeling irritable with the whole pantomime. 'The investigation is over, Billy. I'm not a detective. I present the facts to the jury, and the fact remains that without an alibi or an explanation, the cops have got you bang to rights.'

He only shrugged. In that moment, he hardly seemed to care. 'You're meant to be the clever cunt, aren't you? I've read about you, your cases. Follow some leads! The lass who died was a Paki. Wouldn't surprise me if it was one of them *shame killings* you hear about. Probably sucked too many cocks and got offed by her brothers or summat.'

I was already on my feet before he'd finished.

'We're not doing this, Billy. *I'm* not doing this.' I swept the papers up into a bundle, but wouldn't meet his eye. 'Good luck with the trial.'

I had one hand curled and pressed to the door, ready to knock for the warder to open it from the other side, when he spoke again.

'Those two lads, what were their names?'

I paused, so near to getting out.

'What lads?' I swallowed.

I suspected I knew.

'Two big fuckers,' he drawled. 'Did you and our kid over in, what, '82? Fucked Aidan's leg up for the rest of his life.'

'I don't remember.'

I did. Their names were Robbie Senior and Jonno Morse.

Aidan and I were relatively big fish in our little pond by then, but these two thugs were considerably bigger and already approaching thirty when they jumped us after a night out. Aidan ended up sharing my ward in the hospital.

Bigger fish they were, but they didn't know about the shark in the Barber lineage.

'Pulled a blade on you, didn't they?' Billy went on. 'Slashed your chest up, sent the two of you to A&E, and who did you run off to once you were out? Not the coppers. Nah …'

I turned back from the door; he was staring off into the deep dark past, head jerking all the while, light shining off his scalp or else swallowed by tattoos.

'The bigger one ... Johnny something? His teeth got stuck in my new Docs. Fucked those soles up good and proper. Ha!'

The noise of his laugh was like breaking glass. More than thirty years had passed, but I could still see him standing there in the night, younger but every bit as enormous, slick with blood, as he stamped and stamped on our attackers at our request, and how justified it had all felt. How thoroughly deserved. How fucking good.

I blinked the image away, dissolving it in spots behind my eyes, and came back to the present.

He had me. He had me, and he knew it.

'That's what I thought,' he snarled, catching my gaze and reading my mind, 'so sit the fuck back down.'

He held his stare like a dog on a leash, humourless and ready to pounce, and even there, under the watchful eye of the camera, his unpredictability left me too wary to turn my back again. Slowly, cautiously, I returned to the chair.

'I'm just saying,' he went on, as if there had never been an interruption, 'it's worth looking into, isn't it? Old Bill's too scared to rattle a few mosque doors these days. Cowards. You know they send girls like her into marketplaces, don't you? Nail bombs strapped to them. They dress them up first. You don't know *what* they're capable of.'

I realised from the intensity of his glower that he believed it entirely, and that belief gave him a sense of power.

As a violent, irrational youth he had been dangerous.

As an empowered, righteous adult, he was downright deadly.

'This attitude isn't going to help in your defence,' I told him. 'If you're going to stand a chance, you'll have to knock it on the head. Furthermore, my junior out there, Miss Barnes, she's going to be representing you alongside me, *if* you're lucky. You need to treat her with respect, because she's part of the package. You don't get me without her, and you don't get her without respect.'

He blinked, another spasm. 'I reckon you're misunderstanding the situation here. Almost sounds like you're in charge.'

'I'm not the one on trial. I can walk out of that door and forget you ever existed.'

'Well, I won't forget about you. About the things you got up to.'

I almost laughed, so surreal was the turn of events. 'You're adding extortion to the list as well?'

'Extortion?' He tapped his feet under the table. 'Wasn't that what you almost got sent down for? Or was it just fraud?'

Whatever colour that remained must've drained out of my face.

'Huh,' he said. 'Turns out my memory's not so bad after all ...' He slid his elbows closer across the table. 'You're going to sort this, Rook. You'll do what you have to do, or we'll see which side of the court you end up standing on.'

I felt a nod betray me. With nothing more to say, I stood, careful not to turn my back on him again.

'One more thing, before you go,' he added. 'Good thinking, bringing one of *them* over to our side. That'll play nicely with the jury.'

And then the door swung open and I stepped out backwards, just about as quickly as I could manage.

8

I was twenty-two years old when I decided to become a barrister. Not the most conventional resolution for a young, homeless fraudster to make, perhaps.

I remember the precise instant as if it came upon me like a beam parting the sky, one of those life-changing, light-bulb moments; in actuality, the idea rolled right up to my feet in a mass of steel, walnut and leather heaving to the kerb alongside me.

I'd only just returned from Europe, which is where I'd headed after pleading guilty to conspiracy to defraud in Nottingham Crown Court. My age had, fortunately, seen my six-month prison sentence suspended for two years, and I didn't take any further chances. I acquired a one-year passport, hitchhiked my way to Dover, and spent what little I had on a ticket across the Channel.

Though my journey didn't help me *find myself* in any grandiose, spiritual sense, I did see as much of the Continent as the mid-eighties had to offer to a young man with a patched-up tent and no money, and I followed the warmth wherever it took me, from sleeping under the stars in the Jardin du Luxembourg, to cleaning out bilges along the Mediterranean for petty cash. Eventually, however, it had to come to an end.

I couldn't face returning home, there was little for me there any more, so I stayed south, riding in the back of a lorry to London, and found myself sleeping rough again, this time at the Bullring, just north of Waterloo Station. Commonly referred to as Cardboard City, the Bullring had become the nation's symbol of homelessness, its community of more than two hundred vagrants banding together to doss on the concrete of the huge open-air space, drinking, smoking and shuddering against the nights. For six weeks, I lived there without purpose, using my backpack as a pillow and wrapping my sleeping bag in cardboard and polythene for warmth, quickly finding myself upon the horns of the miserable homeless spiral; I couldn't get a job without an address, and I couldn't get an address without a job.

I was stuck, too poor to eat, too proud to beg. I had no parents to bail me out and couldn't bear to burden my sisters, who were now under the care of our aunt, with any more grief.

And then I saw *the car*.

For it was, of course, a car that put an end to my aimless itinerant lifestyle.

A brand-new Jaguar XJ6, a gorgeous stretched sedan of fine British engineering, growling as loud as its namesake and driven by a lad not many years my senior in a tailored suit with a stunning brunette at his side. For an aimless waif of twenty-two, the sight was seductive enough to stop me dead in my tracks, if ever I'd had tracks to follow.

'Hey, mate!' I shouted as he stepped out of the car into the daylight. I'd been shuffling through the West End with nowhere to go and nothing to do.

The driver turned, bewildered and on guard.

I must've been a real sight, bouncing on my toes, cupping a burning fag down by my side. 'What do you do for a living?'

'I'm a barrister,' he replied flatly, a little smugly, and then the two of them disappeared inside the bustling restaurant on the opposite side of the road.

And that was that. For the first time in my life I had a plan, and it stretched out like a straight tunnel before me, with that pristine Jaguar parked up and waiting at the other end for my arrival.

I got there, eventually.

However, I didn't manage to afford one until well into the nineties, and what was a brand-new release in '87 was now thirty years old when it coughed its way down to Belmarsh after racking up more than 180,000 miles. The cream leather was faded, stained and shrinking, the exterior, once a racy Bordeaux red, was now victim to the relentless death-march of rust, and the engine rattled and moaned at every stationary moment. It was, to put it bluntly, a relic.

But it was *my* relic, the reward for my efforts, and I loved every scratch.

One of the few benefits of such a dated car was the cigarette lighter receptacle, and I clicked it in with my thumb as soon as we came up to a red light outside of Belmarsh, grinding my foot up and down on the stiff, tired clutch to spare it from stalling. It was raining now, raining hard, and the frayed wipers squealed across the windscreen as they threw bucketfuls into the road. On my back seat were my loose golf clubs, untouched since I'd found myself buried by the fraud case, and they rattled across the leather like bones.

'Mind if I smoke?' I asked, unable to stand the discomfiture in the car any longer.

'No.' Zara kept her face firmly to the passenger window, as she had since setting off, and we returned to the deafening silence beneath the sound of water hitting steel.

'You want one?'

'No.'

I sparked up and lowered the window for the smoke, letting the weather soak my shoulder, and longed for the light to change already.

'What happened in there was inexcusable,' I said. 'If you'd rather not assist me in defending him, I can find somebody else to lead in this and we'll set you up with something else.'

She didn't answer straight away. When I glanced across I caught her expression reflected in the wing mirror, smeared by water. She didn't look upset. She looked offended, and that made me feel so much worse.

'There were more than a thousand graduates from my year at Bar school,' she said, 'with a backlog of another three thousand applicants waiting for pupillage, and only four hundred positions available across the country. I thought I'd made it into King Edward's chambers last year because I'd never lost a moot, not a single debate, and that wasn't down to luck. I worked my arse off, Mr Rook. While the other students were out drinking, I was studying. Before that, in Hull, I worked three jobs around my full-time uni hours to earn the twenty grand to get into Bar school. I'm not telling you this to sound like some preachy, working-class hero, it's just …'

'You wanted it that badly?'

'I did,' she nodded, face still turned to the window. 'I didn't have a choice. Average degree, average background.

After all that effort, you know what they said to me at the end of my year at King Edward's?'

'What did they say?'

She took a long, steady breath and removed her glasses. 'They told me I'd been the perfect candidate because they'd been looking for some *diversity* in their pupils that year. It was only afterwards that I heard about the investigation into King Edward's by the Equality and Diversity Committee that was going on at the time. My acceptance had nothing to do with my work. I was the first working-class woman of mixed race they interviewed. They rolled me out like a mascot, took my photograph for their website, and then let me go.'

I sighed, exhaling smoke. 'You're certain that was the case? As you said, tenancies attract a great deal of competition.'

'I know it,' she said. 'I suppose I knew it all along.'

The rain sounded more like hail now; the light stayed red, but there was no traffic crossing the junction.

'Not all chambers are like that,' I said. 'You've had a lousy first experience, and it'd be enough to put some people off the Criminal Bar for life, but you've stuck it out. You've worked hard to get here. You should be proud of yourself.'

'I'm not doing it just for myself,' she said. 'It's for …'

I waited for her to finish. She didn't. The light finally changed.

I tossed the cigarette, sealed the window, and watched the fences of Belmarsh shrink into grey in the spattered mirrors. 'For what?'

She hesitated. 'I lost my cousin a few years back on my mum's side. Hazeem.'

'Oh.'

'It's all right,' she added quickly. 'I mean, he lived with my uncle in Birmingham, and we hadn't seen each other much since we were kids, but still ... that sort of thing really hits a family hard, you know?'

I nodded. 'What happened?'

'A stupid argument. Some lads got into a fight, I guess. Somebody brought out a knife, and somebody died. Hazeem wasn't there. He barely knew the people involved. Still, his name was somehow thrown out by a witness, another Asian to add to the list, and he was charged with conspiracy. His defence counsel took one look and talked him into pleading guilty for a reduced sentence. He was so scared he did what he was told. He ended up in Wormwood Scrubs, started on the drugs there, and killed himself five months later. He was nineteen years old. Never been in trouble before. He wanted to be a surgeon.'

'Damn.' I didn't know what else to say.

'If he'd had the right defence, somebody willing to look past legal aid and do their job properly, then maybe things would've turned out different. Maybe not. All I know is that if I have to face a thousand killers, one way or the other, at least I'll be able to say I worked to the best of my ability. So, if taking me off this murder case is down to your professional opinion, and you think my presence might incite a response from the client that will impede any progress, then that's fair enough. But if you're saying this for *my* sake, then I should let you know that I've never let anything hold me back before, and I've no intention of being bullied out now. I will be a barrister, Mr Rook, and a good one at that.' She replaced her glasses, folded her arms, and lowered her voice. 'As for

William Barber, well … I should've told him to go fuck himself.'

I smiled. It seemed almost silly, finding myself encouraged by the words of a twenty-four-year-old pupil I'd brought in to help with the paperwork, but I couldn't help it. There was something about her that reminded me of somebody I hadn't seen in a very long time. She had all the fire and naivety of a young barrister by the name of Elliot Rook, who had once been ready to take on the world.

9

The case papers for *Regina* v. *William Barber* read like the exposition of a pulp thriller novel.

My eyes moved sluggishly, pages turning deeper ivory as the afternoon grew late beyond the cluttered windowsill of my office, rain exacerbating the gloom.

Zara was sitting in the opposite corner by the old bureau I'd emptied out for her to use, the small stereo it had previously housed now balanced on top of the nearest stack of cardboard boxes, her boots kicked off and feet tucked up and underneath her on the chair.

She was using her forefinger to swipe across the screen of her iPad, Percy having already forwarded her a digital copy of the brief, and her progress seemed to be matching my own wearisome pace.

Despite my attempts after the interview, I couldn't ignore the palpable tension in the room, and wished I was alone.

I was halfway through the evidence section when I had to turn on the lamp. Receiving copies of the forensic photographs was rare and unfortunate, particularly for Zara's first case; these days, case files are ordinarily filled with simple diagrams of the injuries.

Here was The Girl purchasing coffee at a service station in the village. The image from the security camera had added a slight fuzz to her face, but her physical beauty was undeniable. She was remarkably tall, at least six feet, and even at sixteen she could've been a model.

A turn of the page, and here she was again, only much clearer now, her face blue, swollen and cold. The posthumous breakages in her long legs had caused them to splay unnaturally from her hips, eternally caught in their sad, widened vulgarity, and the softer skin on her back had split like over-ripened fruit.

From across the room, I could hear the pace of Zara's breathing quicken in fits and starts, and when I looked over I caught the same images reflected in the lenses of her glasses. The sudden realisation that the victim had not been entirely dissimilar from the girl sitting across from me sent a wretched turn through my chest.

'You all right?' I asked.

'Yeah. Disassociation, isn't it?'

I nodded dolefully – correct – and yet something about this attack being perpetrated so close to home, most likely by a man I knew, with fists that had once injured on my behalf, made it more physical than any case I'd ever worked on. I couldn't silence the swelling of my conscience, the whispering voice that asked how things might've been if I'd acted otherwise in years long past.

It made my palms sweat, dampening the papers at the edges, and I found myself impulsively opening the small compartment underneath my desk, in which I kept a couple of bottles concealed.

Zara must've heard the clinking of glass, and spoke without looking up from her screen.

'Don't suppose any of that is going spare?'

'Course …' I shook the dust from two heavy glasses and poured a couple of whiskeys out, while Zara started to read aloud.

'Counsel's opinion,' she said, '"Client is unwilling to correspond with counsel on even a fundamental level. His unwavering hostility undermines any redeeming qualities in his character – of which I've discovered none thus far – and jeopardises any decent prospect of him standing before a jury. He appears to lack not only remorse for the victim, but any basic sense of empathy as a human and, in my opinion, continues to present a physical risk to anybody in his pres-ence …" And that's from his former counsel! No wonder he let him go. Oh, thanks.' She took the glass, thinking hard. 'I take it he doesn't want to enter a plea?'

'No,' I said. 'The client has instructed us to take this all the way, so that's what we'll have to do. Anyway, defending before a jury isn't playing poker. It isn't about holding the highest hand. It's about casting doubt. The burden of proof should always belong to the accuser, but the prosecution naturally starts with the upper hand. It's their charge, built on enough police work to take it to the courtroom, so the defender usually comes out fighting on the back foot. That's normal, and it doesn't necessarily mean an instant loss. It's our job to challenge the evidence and find a hole in the prosecution's case. Not to prove that he definitely *didn't* do it, but to prove that he *may not* have done it. We need to give the jury reasonable doubt.'

'OK,' she said, 'so what do we know so far?'

I flicked back through my most recent pages of notes, tracing over my own cluttered, meandering scrawl with one finger while running the other hand through waves of my hair. 'The victim was found halfway along a disused stretch of railway, the old pit line, which runs between the country park in Cotgrave, six miles outside Nottingham city centre, and the River Trent to the north. She was discovered by a dog walker at seven thirty on the morning of Saturday the fifteenth of April. Post-mortem interval determined her time of death to have been between two and four o'clock in the morning. Blood analysis came back clean of drugs and alcohol. The contents of her stomach were partially digested, her legs were broken posthumously, and there was no, um, vaginal bruising to indicate forceful penetration ...' I said the last part very quickly, hesitated, and then drained my drink.

'It's always dog walkers who find them, isn't it?' Zara muttered quietly. 'Puts me off ever having a dog. Must be the nose, I guess ...'

'Hmm. Apart from some CCTV footage and a couple of correlating statements from around Cotgrave, there's not much to explain who the victim was, where she'd come from, or how she spent her last day. The police didn't manage to find any evidence of her presence before then, or even determine her name. There's footage of her purchasing coffee with cash from the service station in the village, but the only thing close to an interaction was when she stopped to use the loo of the Welfare Scheme Social Club at almost midnight on Friday. She spent approximately fifteen minutes in there, before walking north in the direction of the country park and, beyond that, her death.'

'Concurrently,' Zara interposed, 'Barber spends his Friday drinking across Nottingham city centre, kicking off the Easter bank holiday weekend as soon as the pubs start serving. His ex-wife Carol waits all morning for him to pick up their son Michael for the weekend, but he never shows. There's a list of CCTV recordings and witness statements from various bar staff to corroborate his movements between the pubs from ten o'clock in the morning until mid-afternoon.'

'We'll submit those statements as *agreed facts*,' I explained. 'There's no need to call every witness to the stand over indisputable evidence like that, so their statements will be summarised and presented to the jury as agreed material. What we're looking for is any witness whose statement *can* be disputed.'

'All right,' she said, 'so, he's what? An unemployed estranged father to different households, rattling around pubs all day on his own. Why? Is he gearing himself up for something, I wonder? What's he planning?'

'I don't think there's anything to be inferred from a man drinking in his own company,' I countered.

Back to her notes. 'Barber gets into his first scrape of trouble late afternoon, after leaving the Roebuck Inn and heading on to Maid Marian Way, where he has a brief altercation with a man using the cash machine there. "Twenty-five-year-old Ali Abdul Nazir",' she read, adding sarcastically, 'I wonder what *that* could've been about. Nazir says Barber was belligerent and verbally provocative, attacking him without cause. The twist comes when Nazir, who turns out to be a semi-pro boxer, floors Barber in retaliation and bolts, leaving him dazed and semiconscious in the road.'

I nodded. 'There might be camera footage from the cash machine. I'd say that gives us grounds to contest Nazir's statement, get to the bottom of what really happened between them.'

'*Really?*' She caught my eye and quickly bit her tongue, opting for another long pull on her glass instead. 'Fair enough,' she conceded, swallowing hard, wincing as the alcohol hit. 'So, one could argue that Barber is angry, probably humiliated, when he gets on the bus back to Cotgrave. By now he's been putting drinks away for more than seven hours, so it'd be fair to assume he's steaming drunk. He doesn't show up again until he walks into the same Welfare Scheme Social Club at around eight o'clock in the evening. He keeps to himself mostly, propping up the bar and telling anybody who'll listen about getting jumped that afternoon. He's still there when our victim shows up to use the toilet, hours later, and he leaves only five minutes after her, staggering off in the direction of the country park and, beyond that, the railway.'

I ruffled through my untidy scattering of papers. 'Who saw him heading that way again?'

'"A Mrs Donna Turner",' she read. 'Same woman who identified the victim leaving. Barber was next to her having a fag out the front when The Girl came out. It was Donna Turner he spoke to, when he said –' She straightened up, gritting her teeth. '"What the fuck's that Paki doing in Cotgrave? She'll be lucky to make it through the night." Then he wanders in the same direction, away from his own home, which his phone's GPS corroborates.'

'Right, right,' I sighed, 'so that's almost midnight, and it's the last anybody sees of him until just before six o'clock in the morning, when his neighbour in the upstairs flat is woken up by smoke coming in through her bedroom window, and uploads *this* to Facebook ...'

I turned to the printout of her public post included in the evidence, a screenshot captured before the post was deleted once the gravity of the situation had started to become clear. I reread the caption:

MY KIDS WAKING UP TO SEE THIS DISGRACE OUT OF THEIR WINDOW! CHARMING! HAPPY EASTER TO US!

On the same page was a separate enlarged copy of the attached photograph, taken on her phone from the second-floor window. There was Billy, quite clear in the pale light of the April dawn, slumped back against a splintered gate, eyes closed and completely naked apart from one remaining white sock, the rest of his clothes burning fiercely in the open maw of a chimenea. Above a bloated drinker's stomach tattoos covered his broad chest, and his flaccid penis looked particularly sad in its nest of thick, wiry hair.

Zara finished up the sorry tale.

'The same neighbour then rings the police only ten minutes after posting that, as soon as she hears Barber throwing his weight around downstairs, arguing with his wife. By the time the officers get there, a further twenty minutes later, Mrs Barber has a black eye, the kid is hysterical, and our dear client is passed out in the shower with the water running cold, one sock still on his right foot.'

'And the blood is gone and the clothes are ash, and the body is found within the hour,' I added gloomily.

We were quiet for a couple of minutes after that, both mentally digesting the story.

'It's scary, isn't it?' Zara murmured.

'The case?'

'To be found like that, with nobody to claim you. It's so sad. It's awful.'

My mind flashed briefly back to my mother's funeral, the community all packed in around me for the service, my hand-me-down suit a little short on my limbs after a sudden pre-pubescent growth spurt, her sisters all standing in a line like varying reprints of the original magnificent work, and I agreed with Zara. It was very sad.

'He did it though,' she added quietly, 'didn't he?'

Probably, I thought.

'It's not our place to decide. There's only one person who knows with any certainty what really happened on that night, and the dismaying fact is there's a good chance we'll never know the truth.'

'But statistically this kind of crime is more likely to be committed by a man than a woman,' she said, 'and *subjectively*, I think that *this* particular crime is more likely to have been committed by *this* man than almost any other. Granted, I haven't met any killers before now, not to my knowledge, but if *I* were on this jury, it'd take a hell of a lot to convince me to acquit him.'

'It'll all come down to the evidence, and without those clothes, without DNA, without the missing tooth or fingernails, a lot of this evidence is still only circumstantial at best.'

She nodded, and I saw her jot down the words *circumstantial at best* in her elegant handwriting at the bottom of her little spiral-bound jotter. Grim surroundings aside, it afforded me a pleasant warmth, having somebody there to take my words on board, and I briefly wondered what sort of teacher I might've made if I'd never seen that Jaguar at the roadside, and my life had followed a different direction instead. An argumentative one, I supposed.

Zara popped the end of the pen into her mouth and resumed her study on the iPad, so that when she next spoke, it was around a mouthful of plastic.

'It says here that the prosecution plans to make an application for bad character and have the defendant's "form" submitted as evidence before the jury. What exactly does it mean by *form* again?'

'His record,' I groaned, flicking through to the same page in my papers. 'They'll use his previous convictions to demonstrate a propensity to commit certain offences, and then use that pattern to adduce a motive for murder.'

'Oh,' she murmured. 'Shit. That's not good.'

'No, it isn't.'

Since I'd left town, Billy had been busy. Zara read the highlights out loud.

'"Twice convicted of displaying written material likely to incite hatred or cause fear. Convicted of posting material online that was threatening, abusive or insulting. Convicted on three counts of distributing a terrorist publication to a proscribed far-right organisation, contrary to the Terrorism Act. *Eight* convictions of actual bodily harm; served three years in Nottingham for a Section 20 unlawful wounding. Burglary, battery, assaulting a constable in the execution of his duty ..." Looks like he's been inside almost as often as he's been out, and I'd bet those are just from the victims who actually dared report him.'

The sinking sensation of guilt came back harder for dragging her into this, but it was chased away by the sound of Billy's voice vaulting straight at me like a fist from her iPad.

'*Out!*' it yelled. '*We've got to get out!*'

Zara uncurled and dragged her chair over, turning the screen so we could both watch Billy standing there, dressed in a scruffy cap and sweatshirt under an overcast sky in Nottingham city centre, cigarette burning in one hand, skull jerking from side to side.

'What's this?' I asked. 'Where'd you find it?'

'The *Nottingham Post*, via Google. He's all over the paper's site. I guess this is one of those vox-pop pieces from the run-up to the referendum last June.'

'Great.'

He looked positively wired, gritting his teeth and pointing a stubby finger into the camera lens and, by proxy, into the faces of millions.

'*It's time we took our country back, by any means necessary! We want sovereignty! We want our jobs! The public has been betrayed for too long, our Christian land has been flooded, and it's time we stood up once and for all and said it out loud! You're not wanted here!*'

'He's a charmer,' Zara sighed.

I dropped my head heavily in my hands, covering the heat in my cheeks, afraid that she might see right through the facade to a time when my own beliefs had been nurtured by similar xenophobic mindsets, inspired by not only the people around me, but also the seventies television standards of Bernard Manning, *Love Thy Neighbour*, *It Ain't Half Hot Mum*, and the like.

Thankfully, she wasn't looking my way when I glanced back up.

Instead, she'd closed the video and started to scroll down through the field of search results on the *Post*'s website, each article's headline as damning as the last, almost all accompanied by the same unflattering mugshot of a middle-aged Billy in a striped polo shirt, collar turned up to his ears with a blackened left eye opposite the Celtic cross.

'Local Thug Charged with Battery', 'Ecstasy Ring Busted', 'Nottingham Neo Nazi Back Behind Bars', 'Local Thug Charged with Battery Again'. The list went on and on.

'Huh, there's a piece here from March about the railway itself ...' she muttered, adjusting her glasses and leaning closer towards the screen. '"Both Cotgrave and Radcliffe-on-Trent Parish Councils have backed a proposition for a brand-new multi-user green trail to be set up for the pedestrians, cyclists and equestrians of Nottinghamshire, with the planned resurfacing of the couple of miles of disused railway line that once connected the former colliery in Cotgrave, now the site of the country park, to the main railway network north of the town ..."' She paused. 'What's a colliery?'

'A coal mine!' I replied in disbelief. 'I thought you were from Nottingham?'

'Millennial problems,' she said simply. 'This was published before the killing. I guess they must've added his name to the search criteria after his arrest. Seems a bit premature, considering he's only on remand ...'

She scrolled through the rest of the article, murmuring the quotes from local councillors under her breath, until a picture at the bottom of the screen caught my attention like gold through silt.

'Wait!' I reached out for the screen. 'That picture there!'

'What?' She followed my eye to the image. 'Oh, that's just a link to another feature in the Community section.'

'The caption underneath ...' I squinted over the desk. 'What does it say?'

She zoomed closer. '"Inspector Sean McCarthy celebrates Harvest Festival with pupils from Cotgrave Church of England Primary School." What about it?'

'Huh ...' I ran a hand slowly over my cheek, leaning back into the chair, wheels turning in my skull. Could it really be him? It seemed impossible.

He'd grown into a handsome man, far from the gangly Irish lad I'd known. Now he had a sheet of grey hair and sharp cheekbones, and in uniform he was almost unrecognisable from the teenaged Forest hooligan I'd grown up with.

Almost.

I heard my words fall out with a sigh. 'I'm going to have to go to Nottingham. I need to make some inquiries.'

'OK,' she replied without hesitation. 'When are we going?'

10

At the time of its sinking, Cotgrave Colliery was set to be one of the National Coal Board's *super pits*, a crowning glory of the British mining industry; its purpose-built estate would bring the families of fifteen hundred miners along for the voyage into prosperity, with seams that would, they said, provide for more than fifty years.

My family was late to the party, relocating to Cotgrave in the early seventies after our eviction notice had been served and our first home – a tiny red-brick pre-regulation two-up two-down terrace built for the urban poor in the Industrial Revolution in the centre of Nottingham – was demolished under slum-clearing legislation.

In just a few years the rural population of Cotgrave, on the edge of the picturesque Vale of Belvoir, had grown from a couple of hundred villagers to a colony of more than five thousand workers, with bricklayers, joiners, electricians and clothiers as well as the clerical, medical and canteen staff required to keep the coal coming up to the surface. For my young parents, who had up until that point been raising their firstborn son in a bare brick house without electrical sockets, sharing one outdoor lavatory with seven neighbouring families, the new estate was akin to luxury; for me, a city boy from the slum, the endless meadows and rolling woods that circled the village were boundless grounds for adventure.

But I was only ever a miner's son, and never a miner at heart.

The Barber boys, on the other hand, were born of coal.

Despite their unwieldy proportions, the men of the family – all the uncles, cousins and grandparents alike – were well suited to life down at the deep hard seam, where it was pitch-black and jagged, an unforgiving labyrinth of armour-plated machinery and stone. As rippers, they took on the toughest roles in the pit, tunnelling through the rock face with deafening drills, buried and blinded by the downpour of black dust, hands shuddering under the strain of machinery until they grew like heavy, twisted boughs, tearing coal out of the seam.

The dust covered everything. Not only was it poisonous in the lungs, eyes and ears, it was also highly explosive. After leaving school, my own short-lived career in the pit consisted of lugging back-breaking sacks of stone dust – broken cement – down through the roadways, a mile underground, to spread over the surfaces and neutralise the chance of it igniting. I lasted a few weeks, but the men of the colliery kept on, as only they knew how to do.

Even when the National Union of Mineworkers declared the strikes of '84, the men of Cotgrave marched into the shafts, not for allegiance to the government, but for the humble sake of keeping on, and keeping their families fed. To this day, Nottingham Forest supporters are often berated by opposition fans, particularly from Yorkshire and South Wales, as scabs.

The recompense for their allegiance came less than a decade later, the very same year I sat the Bar finals more than 130 miles to the south, when the mineshafts were capped and filled with concrete, the towers and associated buildings were brought to the ground, and the economy was razed along with them.

Hard times, and, like the coal dust I'd quenched with stone, the bitterness that remained buried under that picturesque countryside was only ever a haphazard spark away from igniting.

By the twenty-first century, all that remained of the colliery was the branch railway that had once served it, running from Nottingham, down over the River Trent, hidden from the rest of the world by undergrowth and foliage that grew tall and fierce and wild on either side, forgotten, until the broken remains of the body were found upon it.

11

I felt a little harsh instructing Zara to hold the fort back in London on her own.

She probably thought I'd done it because of her dreadful introduction to Billy, but the simple truth was that her presence could've endangered my personal stake in the case.

Halfway up the M1 the following day, however, when the rainfall had finally abated, I found myself craving the companionship. It seemed the first in a long time for the loner I'd become.

Meeting on the station grounds seemed a bad idea from the off, considering how many adolescent evenings I'd spent at the enforced hospitality of the Nottinghamshire Police, so I'd arranged to meet McCarthy on the country park in Cotgrave, regrettably close to the site of the killing.

It was surreal, pulling into the car park at the south-east entrance in the early afternoon. The last time I'd seen those fields there had been nothing but a spoil heap there, so enormous I'd suspected it might never be moved, another permanent peak in the mountain belt left by collieries across the United Kingdom.

As I got out of the car and stretched my legs, shaking off the tedious drive, I could almost smell that familiar smoky burn of the coal somewhere deep below, dead money buried underneath the damp foliage and grass. There was only one other vehicle parked there, some way off from mine, and it reflected the crisp light in hi-vis yellow, black, white and blue.

I found him waiting on a bench, gazing into the dense reed bed at the bank of the Grantham Canal. He was dressed in full uniform: a padded stab vest over white shirt and tie.

'Inspector Sean McCarthy?'

He looked over, startled, and rose to his feet, those sharp cheekbones locked in a stern cast, green eyes summing me up from head to toe and hip to hip.

'You must be Elliot Rook QC.'

I nodded seriously, and we held on to our guises a moment longer, before a great grin split his face in two, mirrored in my own. A tight one-armed hug, plenty of weighty patting sounds on the back, and we both laughed hard.

'You old fucker!' he crowed, any trace of the old Irish accent I remembered now erased. 'I thought it was a joke when I got the message from your assistant.'

'My junior, Zara.'

'Your *junior*?' He switched to his best attempt at a haughty, snobbish accent. '*Member of Her Majesty's Counsel Mr Elliot Rook QC, Leading Counsel.* Ha!'

'You can talk,' I laughed. 'Inspector McCarthy of the Nottinghamshire Police. District Commander for Rushcliffe Borough and former football hooligan! How did you swindle that?'

'Same way you did, I imagine. Years of hard work for low pay, and just the slightest omission of, well, only the *majority* of my youth! That isn't the same bloody Al Capone hat you were wearing in the eighties, is it?'

It was. We laughed some more, and then he suggested we take a walk together.

If anything could've added to the peculiarity of traipsing through the old colliery grounds after all those years, it was doing so alongside Sean in a civilised meeting between a barrister and a police officer. How times had changed. We rehashed the years while we wandered through the immense sprawl of trails winding between lakes, juvenile trees and immaculate open fields, far away from the smog of the city.

I'd forgotten just how beautiful the sky could be, clear and cold with orange-pink undertones speckling the horizon, and it was a pity when, inevitably, the conversation had to come around to the cheerless reason for my return.

'You're actually doing it then?' he asked. 'You're really defending Billy fucking Barber?'

'Somebody has to, don't they?'

'Yeah, but it doesn't have to be you. He's not blackmailing you, is he?'

'What?'

'Tried it on with me a couple of times, back when I joined the force, but he had nothing on me. No proof, anyway. As if people would give a shit about a few stupid scraps at the footy more than thirty years ago.'

'No, no,' I lied. 'He hasn't tried anything like that on with me ...' I decided to pull focus away from the subject. 'So, on Saturday the fifteenth of April, the morning the body was found, did you visit the scene?'

'Nah, thank Christ.'

'Personal choice?'

'Not really. I'd taken Tracey and the kids up to Scarborough for Easter weekend. Primrose Valley, that

Haven place. Only got us the bronze package, costs a bomb on bank holiday weekends, but it's all right up there. You've got Filey, Bridlington and Whitby all nearby. The kids go mad for the slots. You married? Kids?'

'Divorced. No kids.' A great swell of sadness came upon me, hearing it out loud like that, but when I stroked my third finger, expecting to feel the cold metal, I found only naked skin there.

Panicked, I rummaged through my left coat pocket and discovered the ring, where it must've remained since Belmarsh, rolling around in the lint like so many more crumpled receipts of things I'd lost.

I swallowed hard and left it in the pocket.

'Shame,' Sean said. 'We tied the knot twenty years back next August, me and Trace. Our second eldest, Annie, she's coming up to sixteen now. That's why I was glad to miss the call to be honest, but I still had to cut the jollies short and come back Sunday. Bit of a fucker really, considering it was all over by then anyway.' He hesitated, pausing on the trail. 'I saw her in the morgue though. Horrendous. Breaks your heart, seeing something like that, especially around here. Nobody to identify her either. What they'd call a *Jane Doe* over in the States.'

'John and Jane Doe actually come from an old English law,' I told him, trying to fill the silence left behind. 'They were the names given to fictitious lessees of a landlord in the action of ejectment.' I wasn't sure why I said it; a well-worn habit of trying to impress peers.

'Huh.' He kicked a loose stone, skimming it across the dusty surface of the packed dirt, and then carried on ahead. 'Something new every day.'

I opened my mouth to go on, but a small, rather fussy-looking elderly lady in a quilted cardigan and mittens came towards us down the track, her Yorkshire terrier yapping and pulling wildly on its chequered harness. She smiled apologetically as we passed. 'Afternoon, Inspector McCarthy!'

Sean raised his eyebrows. 'Keeping out of trouble, Margaret?'

She tittered, pulling at the lead – 'Oh, come on, Ruby!' – and we waited until she'd disappeared through the young trees before carrying on.

I laughed, shaking my head.

'What can I say?' he grinned. 'I'm *still* fighting them off with a stick.'

'Christ, Sean, what is she? Ninety years old? That's somebody's great-grandmother you're talking about.'

He shrugged, glancing back. 'I've had worse.'

'At the rate you used to go through women, yes, I'd believe it.'

'Irish charm, Rook,' he winked. 'Couple that with a uniform, and there isn't a girl alive who could resist. Why else do you think I became a copper?'

'Marriage must've slowed you down?'

'Of course,' he laughed. 'What do you think I mean when I say I've had worse?'

This time my grin came out a little forced.

'There's a John DeWitt listed in the prosecution's evidence,' I said. 'Investigating officer?'

'Our illustrious Detective Chief Superintendent,' he nodded. 'Sheriff of Nottingham. You know him?'

'No, and I can't talk to him, either. All I need now is for them to start accusing me of tampering with witnesses for the prosecution. Anything I ought to know about him?'

'Yeah,' he said, 'don't go inviting him to any of your fancy champers-soirées. It's no secret that he fucking hates defence advocates ... So do I, come to think of it, present company excluded. He's a hard bastard, old DeWitt. Came down to us from Sheffield a few years back. Should provide a fun day in court for you.'

'I look forward to it. What can you tell me about Billy?'

'Billy?' A hollow laugh. 'What about him?'

'Anything, really.'

'Anything? You know what he's like. It was handy having their family onside when we were lads, but he has never grown up. He's pushing sixty, and I still pick him up from time to time, out scrapping at the weekends, or else we have Sarah, his missus, ringing the station whenever he goes AWOL. The man's got four kids now, for Christ's sake. Remember Carol Clay? She's got his first, Michael, and the apple dropped straight down with that one, I'm telling you. Seventeen, and he's already on his third antisocial order.'

'Seventeen? He didn't start having kids until his forties?'

'Hard to get your end away when you're banged up for most of your twenties and thirties. Well, hard to get it into a woman, anyway!' He laughed hard at that. 'Then there are the two girls he had with old Big Tits Becky Fairburn, but I don't think he has anything to do with them – probably for the best – and he's got another one with Sarah. Oliver, I think his name is. Must be, Jesus, eight or nine by now.'

I'd forgotten what it felt like to be in a place where everybody's personal business was common knowledge. I pulled it back a notch. 'What do you mean, whenever he goes AWOL?'

'Barber classic, handed straight down from his old man and his grandad before them, remember? Tells Sarah he's nipping out for a swift one on Thursday afternoon, doesn't show up again until Monday or Tuesday.'

'Where's he going?'

'Wherever he can, with whoever will have him, I reckon.'

'Affairs?' I tried not to sound too hopeful.

'Probably,' he reasoned, 'but I get the impression it's more about staying out for the sake of being out of the house, as opposed to getting his leg over. The lads he knocks about with are little fuckers, half his age. Steroid heads. Big boys. Every time a group grows past him – settles down or gets nicked or whatnot – he moves on to the next generation, like a poor man's Dean Moriarty. It must take a certain age and mindset to still be impressed by Billy's shit.'

'You think The Girl, the victim, could've associated with one of these groups? Even been a mistress, perhaps?'

'No,' he replied flatly. 'Bunch of extremist right-wing wreck-heads, just like Billy. Wastes of oxygen, the lot of 'em. They wouldn't stand for that. Not a Paki.'

'Huh.' The term caught me like a knife, and yet I didn't chastise him for it. I should have, and I was ashamed to brush past it, but I had to remind myself that this was life among my old crowd. There was no venom in his voice. He was casual, entirely passive, and that was the worst thing about it. Some mindsets are never changed. 'Billy wasn't with his friends on the night of the murder,' I went on. 'He was alone. Why?'

'Couldn't tell you that. Maybe they'd had enough of his shit.'

We came to a fork in the trail divided by nettles and, through a clearing ahead, I caught sight of a tall mast; a solid black eye reflected the light at the very top of the pole. 'How many cameras are on the park?' I asked, pointing towards it.

'Six, but the only two that could've helped weren't operational at the time, and there aren't any as far up as the old tracks.'

'Is that normal?' I asked. 'The cameras being down?'

'This is Cotgrave, mate. Before this, a complete history of crime in the park must've amounted to Rod Hudson's three separate warnings for fishing without a licence, a few kids getting pissed on Frosty Jacks one weekend, and the occasional spate of travellers camping in the trees by Heron Lake.'

'Travellers? You mean Gypsies?' I wondered if you could call them Gypsies any more.

'No.' He wavered long enough for me to catch a slight shift in his expression, a sudden tightening of the lips, before he led me to the right. 'We had a brief, a *very brief*, rash of vagrants squatting on the land here about a year back.'

'Vagrants?'

'Immigrants trafficked in from Eastern Europe. Couldn't speak a word of the Queen's. We found them here after they got out of Notts, sharing tents, waiting to get their bearings or else waiting for the benefits to start. They were drinking water right out of the fucking lake, catching fish to eat.'

'Were any of them working girls?'

'Prozzies? Wouldn't surprise me, but we couldn't find much before they moved on.'

'Any connection to the victim?'

'Rattled a few bushes, but nothing of any use came out.'

'What about interviews with other local working girls? You reckon I could get my hands on the transcripts?'

'Might if we had any.'

I glanced across, trying to withhold my frown. 'You didn't interview them?'

He shook his head. 'Truth is, off the record, when we're handed a slam dunk like this, we don't have the resources to take it that far. It's the same story across the country: under-staffed and over budget. It's not like the old days, when a pair of cuffs and a swinging truncheon did all the talking. Now it's down to administration, liaising with the CPS on what we can or can't do, and waiting around for charging decisions. We've got our best uniforms out on the motor-way with hairdryers fishing for tickets. Even if we *could* spare the manpower, those women aren't going to talk to us. Besides, she died a virgin, what are we going to learn from a bunch of prostitutes?'

'She might've been trafficked in to join them, but escaped before it happened? You didn't talk to *any* of them?'

He sighed.

'We're in the age of the Internet now. For every one of *these* –' he tapped a compact box of black plastic clipped near to his left epaulette, which I only now noticed had a glass lens watching from the middle – 'there are a dozen bystanders filming on mobiles, and we've got to keep *them* from pressing charges against *us*. It's a fucking joke, I know, but if we go booting doors down, *we're* the ones who land in the shit for harassment.'

We came out of the narrow trail and up to the edge of a smooth green field, cordoned off by a makeshift fence of portable steel railings. Sean checked around to make sure we were alone, then fumbled in the pocket of his trousers, offered me a cigarette out of a pack, and lit them in turn.

I realised it was a menthol one a little too late, but thanked him all the same.

'I'm sorry to say it,' Sean said, exhaling smoke, 'especially for the poor lass, but the sooner that railway is torn up, the sooner we can all put this behind us. It's not fair on the area.'

'I saw that they're resurfacing the tracks,' I nodded. 'Planning to make a nature trail, aren't they?'

'That's the one. Another of the council's big plans for this place.' He gestured around us. 'They've got new housing estates cropping up all over the derelict pithead site too, and then it'll be the old shopping precinct after that. A hundred million it's going to cost. Ninety acres of brownfield and rubble transformed into affordable housing in the next six years, and then that'll be that. Like the colliery was never here. A hundred million quid investment, twenty-five years too late, if you ask me.'

All of a sudden, the surface of the field ahead of us seemed to ripple and bubble.

It wasn't grass, I realised, but the opaque surface of thick, slimy water, the exact green of fibreboard underlay.

'Toxic algae,' Sean said through a plume of minty smoke, answering the question I hadn't asked. 'A dead zone. Something to do with the pH in the water, killing all the fish and frogs. Poor little fuckers.'

'You reckon I could get much from talking to the council?'

'I don't know, mate,' he said slowly. 'With regards to a murder trial? Seems a bit dodgy.'

'Just trying to get a better grasp of the bigger picture. Feels like I'm at a bit of a dead end already.'

'The bigger picture?'

He walked up to the edge of the nearest barrier, checked in both directions once more, and then spat into the green, splitting the surface like an axe. Uniform and grey hair aside, I could still see the tall, arrogant lad I remembered in there; the lad who'd loved only one thing more than fighting, and that was fucking almost anything that moved. Every month he'd have a different girl or two dangling from an arm, and it was strange to think of him being married.

'This place has gone through a lot since you left, Rook. It all changed after Thatcher, but now ...' He shook his head and drew on his cigarette. 'There's something growing across the country, you know what I mean? You feel it, don't you? Twats like Barber might pull focus by being the rowdiest of the lot, but it goes deeper than those idiots, and it'll always be the outsiders that get the blame.' Another spit, widening the void. 'It all comes down to territory, like it always has. Lines in the sand. Survival of the fittest. The Peace Walls were already up when Dad brought us over from Ireland, but I used to get the shit kicked out of me every day through junior school for being Irish Catholic. See, it used to be us or the West Indies, and now Brexit is just another scapegoat to distract from Tory mistakes. Mark my words, Rook: this is how the Troubles start.'

Of course.

There were things I'd forgotten about Sean over the years, and one was his need to top-trump every situation with anecdotes from growing up in seventies Belfast.

You were running late? Sean was late once, after a loyalist firebomb targeted the morning bus.

Your uncle was reckoned to be hard? Sean's Uncle Pat killed three members of the B-Specials in '68, and then formed his own paramilitary.

You had a cold? Sean had pneumonia, after his family had been forced to hang wet blankets across every window of the house to slow stray bullets and shrapnel from the street outside.

When his father left home in '82, like so many others who were never to return from the Welfare or the book-ies or wherever, there were rumours of him being captured for running out on the IRA seven years earlier; rumours started, I'd always suspected, by Sean.

'All the boys we lost under here …' he went on, tapping one foot sharply on the ground beside the railing, crushing soft leaves underfoot. 'And for what? Two hundred acres of open space for horses and dogs to come and shit on? The seams all flooded, shafts filled with concrete …' He sighed.

'Least you've got somewhere nice to bring the kids,' I said. 'Nicer than headstocks, anyway. Remember the first time your old man brought us here?'

'Nineteen eighty-one. Sixteen years old.' The edges of his mouth turned up into a wan smile, as he gazed over the dying lake. 'Never shit myself as much as I did getting changed and going through that lamp room. Queuing at the deployment centre, all belted up with the self-rescuers on, waiting at the pit bank for our turn to descend …'

'Miss your ride, miss your shift,' I said.

'Yeah, well, you never did make a very good miner.'

'Claustrophobes don't.'

He checked his watch and flicked the butt of his fag into the eerie green water, where it extinguished with the faintest trace of a hiss.

'We'd better wrap this up,' he said. 'I'm on the bloody clock. Come on, car park's this way.'

The return stroll was quieter than before, less jovial, as Sean led us down a different, shorter trail. He seemed to know the place like the back of his hand. When we eventually got to the car park he fished the keys out from his pocket and unlocked his bright patrol car with the click of a button.

'Nice car,' I noted with a whistle. 'What is that? Brand-new Fiesta? I thought you boys were supposed to be on a budget? Looks like they're treating *you* all right.'

He rolled his eyes. 'She isn't *mine*. You should see the squabble in the parade room after every morning briefing; we've got three new keys on the board there, with thirty uniforms scrapping over them.'

'Don't you get to take it home with you? Perks of the job?'

'Yeah, sure. I just park it up on the kerb outside my place every night. That'd be nice and inconspicuous, wouldn't it? My neighbours would probably shit a brick, you know what they're like round here.'

'You're still in Cotgrave?'

'No …' He hesitated, grinning slyly, and couldn't resist a final boast. He never could. 'You remember Ralph Dickinson from the footy? Rich boy. Lazy eye. Used to throw those massive parties whenever his parents were away in the summer?'

I nodded. 'They had that big old farmhouse up in Radcliffe? Beautiful place.'

'Well, not any more they don't. We got it for a fucking steal during the recession.'

'The recession? Which one?' I smiled. 'It's a nice place, Sean. Sounds like you're doing well for yourself. I'm glad.'

'You'd better believe it.' He adjusted his tie, smile fading, car keys swinging from his knuckle. 'We'll have to get a crate in some night.'

'That'll be the next time one of our acquaintances gets arrested for murder, I suppose.'

He clicked his tongue, patted me on the shoulder, and handed me a card with his mobile number on it. 'Save that *junior* of yours a job.'

'Cheers.'

He started to walk away, then stopped, turned back, and gestured towards the nearest bunch of trees. 'A million years from now,' he said, 'all this … all these trees, the plants and the animals. You know what it'll be?'

'Dead?'

'Coal,' he said. 'It'll all just be coal, a mile underground.'

'A morbid thought there, Sean.'

He didn't smile. 'Do us a favour, won't you, Rook? Do yourself a favour.'

'What's that, Sean?'

He fiddled his thumbs under his belt, scrunched his nose, and then looked me dead in the eye.

'Throw the case. Let them bury that cunt. The world's a better place with scumbags like Barber behind bars.'

And then he walked away without another backward glance, the shadow of a hooligan's swagger still pulling at his shoulders, heavy soles clomping across the dull surface of the macadam.

12

I couldn't face the drive back to London this close to rush hour, and I still had so many unanswered questions. I opted instead for the short journey north-west into Nottingham to spend the night.

Out of my three sisters, I knew that Shannon still lived in Cotgrave, and Tina and Sue would never move beyond the borders of the county, but I hadn't been in touch with any of them since Jenny had walked out, and I didn't have the strength to lie to them, nor to embark on what would surely be a long and raw conversation were I to turn up for the evening unannounced. Instead, I rolled into the centre of the city and checked myself into a room at the Ibis.

I'd kept my sisters relatively close over the years, which was to say I hadn't turned my back on them completely. We shared Christmas cards, and I'd done the uncle thing at plenty of birthday parties, though that was mostly down to Jenny's efforts.

My agnate siblings, on the other hand, I barely knew by anything more than their names. I don't know if any attended our estranged father's funeral in '99. All those leftovers of the families he'd started and departed over the years, like a smattering of oil paintings half-finished and abandoned, never a picture completed after ours.

I did hear from Shannon that the wake was held at the Miners' Welfare, the former Welfare Scheme Social Club, and it resulted in a bloody punch-up and an untimely raid by the cops, and I couldn't think of anything more befitting the aggressor they'd laid to the soil. Even in life he'd belonged to the ground, and never did adapt well to the above.

The last time *I* had been home was in 1988, when I made a fleeting return for a different funeral, the burial of twenty-three-year-old Aidan Barber. If anything could've bolstered or justified my recent decision to become a barrister, it was watching the ground swallow that wooden box whole with my childhood friend inside.

Aidan had always wanted more from life, more than the colliery could offer, and certainly more than his brothers, uncles and father had desired between them, but for all his good looks, intelligence and wit, he never could outrun his surname. It attracted trouble and violence wherever he went, like nails to a magnet, and though he longed to break the cycle, especially after seeing me leave, the pull of the pit was strong, as if gravity intensified around the open maw of its bottomless chasm. The longer he stayed, the less of a chance he ever had, and, like almost every other coal miner's son, he ended up following his family into the pit. It was there that he met his fate.

At the end of another gruelling shift, Aidan, a robust six-footer, couldn't face the back-breaking stagger to the lift, which waited almost half a mile away at the opposite end of the low, narrow tunnel. His damaged leg was stiff in the warmth of the sunlight, let alone in the cold, dark damp.

There was, however, a quicker way to get to the lift; it defied every safety regulation on site, but he'd seen his reckless brothers do it time and time again without getting caught, and this day he fancied his chances. A conveyor belt ran through the warren of the mine, carrying tonnes of coal to the shaft to be lifted up to the surface, and a man could save himself the gruelling trek home with a sly joyride along the apparatus.

But the coal cutter was also hidden somewhere along the belt, a colossal piece of machinery that chewed the rock face into manageable chunks, crunching and mangling anything that the belt brought sliding into its jaws.

With a great swell of heartbreak, I couldn't help but wonder, as I helped lower his coffin into the cold dirt of the churchyard, how much of my friend they'd actually managed to salvage from the chained teeth and knuckles of that machine, or how much of the weight I was holding was merely the coal that had been blended into his remains.

Billy didn't cry at the funeral. I remember that. He only stared off into nothingness, statuesque as the headstones that grew crooked and weathered around us, surrounded by his friends of the time, all those brawny young white men.

Seeing Sean McCarthy as the strapping married man he'd become, father and professional success, had rekindled memories I'd long left behind, and these were the things that haunted my steps as I ventured out through the unseasonable frost to the nearest off-licence to withdraw some cash and buy a bottle of Jameson's for company in the room.

I poured a handful of fingers into the water glass provided in the plastic-covered en suite and then sat back to watch the video files on the disk included in the brief.

Several times I played through the CCTV footage of The Girl's final day, the scant seconds yielded from security cameras across the village. The first footage came from the service station on Main Road at half past ten on Friday morning.

In it, she entered the forecourt on foot, polyester down jacket fastened against the April wind that rocked the pumps; it was the same bright, canary-yellow jacket that would end up muddied and tossed over her naked body, long after the rest of her clothes had been taken by the night.

Inside the kiosk, she used the Nescafé machine to purchase a small black coffee with loose change from her pocket – no purse – and left without any interaction, exiting the forecourt the same way she'd come in.

The next camera – fixed outside the Sainsbury's Local on Bingham Road – captured her walking east only minutes later, disposable coffee cup in hand, neither noticeably hurried nor cautious in the pace of her boots on the pavement. So blissfully ignorant to the horrors that were in wait. She didn't show up again until thirteen hours later, when she used the toilet in the Welfare Scheme Social Club, and was followed into the storm by Billy.

Drinking, watching, I found myself longing to know who she really was. I tried to put myself in her position, imagining what it must've been like not only to meet such a terrifying, brutal end, but to do so with total anonymity, with nobody to mourn her. Into the glass, I absently muttered the words of Emily Dickinson.

'I'm Nobody! Who are you? Are you – Nobody – too?'

The whiskey wasn't helping – how naive to hope it might – and I had to force myself to stop replaying the footage and move on to the recording of Billy's interview at the station from the following day.

He looked even more massive than usual, practically swelling against the four walls of the small interrogation room, a black box recording in the centre of the table, two officers facing him from the side nearest the camera's high-angle viewpoint. One of the officers must've been DCS DeWitt, while the boxy little solicitor at Billy's shoulder wasn't trying too hard to disguise her expression of being a woman dragged in over bank holiday weekend to back a losing horse.

Where were you last night? Why were you burning clothes in your garden this morning?

Did you know the victim? Did you kill her?

No comment. No comment. No comment. No comment.

It went on and on that way, and it wasn't until I'd drained more than half the bottle that I finally slumped into a deep, drunken, dreamless sleep.

I woke to rain galloping like mustangs against the windowpane.

In summer, the curtains would've been paling already, but the early hours of autumn were a deep and solid dark.

For a moment, lying in semiconscious delirium, I thought I was home. Not in Nottinghamshire, or even my present London apartment, but really home. Darkness so thick makes it easy to be fooled.

I reached out into the area beside me, fingers outstretched, and found only empty space and a horrible sinking sensation. We'd fought again, I realised. She'd be off in the spare bedroom, or, worse, over at her parents', and I'd been left to sober up and think about my actions.

I couldn't remember what we'd rowed about, but it was almost definitely my fault.

It usually was.

Then I recognised the papery quality of the pillowcase against my cheek, and registered the dense silence behind the fireproof door, and the hotel swam mercilessly into being all around me.

For what it was worth, I still could've been in my own studio flat in London. It was just as impersonal and void of any individuality, like a show house with an unwanted squatter. Not like the home we'd shared, which had glistened and glowed with character and warmth all year round.

Jenny's taste had always been so effortless. While I was off working twelve to sixteen hours a day in chambers and courts across the country, she'd single-handedly fashioned us a home that was as classically beautiful and quirky as she was, bolstered by an endless array of objects and ornaments amassed from Portobello Road, or else handed down through the generations. When it came to family heirlooms, I brought nothing to the table, inheriting only my father's occasional temper.

Jenny had been born into more money than most would earn in a lifetime, and it had afforded her the enviable opportunity to follow every whim she desired, though I didn't know anything about that when we first met at the Whitechapel Gallery. It was an exhibition for celebrated figurative artist Lucian Freud, elusive grandson of Sigmund; I'd gatecrashed for the free canapés and wine, but what I found was a woman who was beautiful, grungy, and outspoken in all the ways I'd never known. A talented illustrator, she was struggling at the time to make an impression on the city's busy art scene, after failing to make an impact with the violin.

Ironically, it was my attendance at Bar school that saw me swiftly snubbed by the mob of sculptors, painters and shabby pseudo bohemians she called her friends, who unanimously scorned me for being a barrister, an elitist slave to the status quo, before scurrying back to their parents' mansions in the west of the capital, far from my bed under the open sky.

But Jenny wasn't like them. She wasn't like anybody else at all.

The Jameson's was sweating out through my pores and into the hotel sheets, taking my mood along with it, dragging my thoughts off to dark places, and my mouth felt as if I'd eaten a bagful of flour. I grudgingly swung my feet onto the thinning carpet and staggered through the darkness for the taps in the en suite.

I hit the light, shielding my eyes against the glare, lapped mouthfuls straight from the cold tap, and then watched myself piss lazily in the hotel's unforgiving full-length mirror.

The man shaking himself off there looked old and overweight. His features were weathered, somewhat squashed, and framed in lines I hardly recognised. He looked stern and unapproachable, everything I'd never wanted to become, and stretch marks patterned his pale stomach in streaks. Two scars marked the groin in a V shape, mementos of symmetrical inguinal hernias, while a more sinister scar swept across the breadth of the chest.

I faced my reflection every day, but it felt like a long time since I'd seen the whole picture spread out so boorishly before me. I couldn't be sure if it was the alcohol vacating my bloodstream, or the effect of returning to my home county that had turned my perception so morose, but seeing myself like that, alone in the double room, made me thoroughly depressed.

Compelled by gloom, desperate to reach out and touch something, I found myself fumbling for my phone on the bedside table after I'd slumped back under the quilt.

The clock onscreen told me it was almost half past four, and I had a message from Charles Stein, my newly appointed junior on the fraud case, which I didn't even bother reading.

Instead, I had another whiskey straight from the neck of the bottle and embarked on the mother of all self-loathing text messages, riddled with lamentations, apologies and pity.

I didn't know what I was doing. I wasn't even sure if she still had the same number.

Last I'd heard, she'd gone back to using *Jennifer*. I wondered if she'd kept the Rook.

She'd known all about my background, eventually, and she said she didn't care.

She said she didn't care, but I never allowed myself to believe it.

Even after she took me in off the streets, into her elegant Kensington apartment; even after I passed the Bar and proposed, desperate to, as they say, lock her down; even after our first, second and fifteenth wedding anniversaries, I was always doubtful, worried that I might've been just another phase of rebellion against the class to which she'd been born, destined to become as short-lived as her ventures into veganism, Buddhism, Hinduism, blue hair, skiing, cycling and sculpting.

She accused me of building walls.

At first, she'd tease. 'Why don't you ever talk to me about your work? I tell you everything!'

Which must be easy to do, I'd think to myself, when your days consist of doodling mischievous bunnies for an unpublished series of children's books ... but, of course, I never said that to her. Not in the early years. That didn't come until much later, long after the cute and playful repartee had descended into absolute ferocity, and we could hardly be in the same room without rowing.

'You really want to know what I did today? You *really* want to know?'

'Yes!' she screamed one night. 'I really want to fucking know!'

I plunged my hand into the recycling, pulled out the morning's copy of the *Guardian*, and launched it across the dining table.

'Front page.'

She looked down at the mugshot of McGrath there, convicted paedophile, recently released after more than twenty-five years and subsequently alleged to have raped another two pre-pubescent boys.

'Him?' She shrugged. 'I read it already. He's disgusting.'

'He is,' I told her, 'and if tomorrow goes well, I'll have him back outside the playgrounds before nightfall, because one of us has to actually *work* for a living.'

And that was the beginning of the end.

Even before the death threats started to find their way into our mail.

Halfway through my mortifying magnum opus of a text message, I had a sudden change of heart, a flush of common sense, and, thankfully, deleted it all.

Idiot.

Instead, I found myself scrolling through my contact list, right down to the very last name, and typed a much shorter message.

Borrow some cash off Percy for a morning train to Nottingham. I could use your help here. Rook. X.

And then, with a second thought, I deleted the X.

I had to preserve *some* professionalism, I told myself, before hitting send at almost five o'clock in the morning.

13

'It looks different to the photographs. It's darker. Lonelier. Even sadder in real life.'

Zara was right.

I must've fallen straight back to sleep after sending the untimely text, so when I was eventually woken up later in the morning, roused by one of the hotel's cleaners unceremoniously opening the door, I found a list of missed calls and texts asking where we were supposed to be meeting.

Shit. I must've cringed all the way through brushing my teeth, before scrambling into yesterday's creased shirt and trousers, and then rushing out to collect her from the station.

It was long past noon by the time we'd found the right bend in the old railway, intermittently referencing our photographs of the crime scene as we traipsed north from the country park, my takeaway tea already lukewarm, miserable and pallid under the surface scum of long-life milk, the compost smell of the recycled paper cup. Disappointed, I forced the last of it down my neck, crunching through the slush of five sugars in the hope of clearing my headache, and then crushed the cup and stuffed it into my coat pocket. I couldn't bring myself to toss it to the ground in that sorry place, despite the mass of faded, weather-bleached litter that had already blown in over the years, clinging to the tracks.

Zara did nothing to alleviate my hangover.

She'd turned up like a rocket, overly enthusiastic and eager to be out of the office, powering several paces ahead of me in her apposite Doc Martens.

It was cold again, overcast. Leaves had begun to fall from the overhanging trees on either side, forming a brittle, tangled carpet of reds, mustards and yellows that had decomposed under the surface layer. The earth below was swampy, and it forced us to balance on the tracks, which had sunk slightly to form a long, twisted fossil of rust, like the spinal cord of some prehistoric beast.

No human being belonged there. It was a dreadful place to die.

Zara checked her own copies of the crime scene photos once more, holding them up to the environment and nodding. Then she pushed into the thick knots of foliage on each side and came back shaking her head.

'More nothingness. Some woodland in the distance to the left, and you can almost see the brook up there to the north, but everything is overgrown and the fields are like bogs. What are we looking for, Mr Rook?'

'I don't know,' I admitted, squatting down on my haunches and taking off my hat, passing it between my hands. 'Just trying to get my head around it all, I suppose.'

From that height, I could smell the dust in the ballast, the blood-scent of the iron.

Zara started moving nimbly up and down the tracks, much too lively for my whiskey eyes to follow. 'I thought we might've seen some deer. That'd be nice.'

'Why's that?'

'Deer need iron in their diets. They gather at old tracks like these and lick the rails for the iron filings.'

'Really? I didn't know that.'

She nodded. 'I've never heard of a barrister coming out to the scene of a crime before.'

'We call it a *locus in quo* visit. Sometimes it's the only way to make sense of a situation. Did I mention that working with me would go beyond ordinary court hours?'

'I'm not complaining, it's cool. Feels like we're detectives, you know? Sleuthing around like Sherlock and Watson. Mulder and Scully ...' A thought, and then: 'Rook and the Rookie!'

A smile tackled my headache like the ghost of a southbound train. 'Hey, that's actually pretty good!'

She grinned back, proud of herself, showing all her neat little teeth in a row, and there was something bitter-sweet in it; not for the first time, I couldn't help but see the reflection of The Girl killed less than a metre from where she was standing.

If she'd been only half as pleasant as Zara, I thought, then what a terrible waste it had been.

'All right then, Rookie,' I said. 'What are you thinking? First thoughts? It's a long walk out here. You think she ran?'

'Hmm ...' Zara paused, looking back and forth. 'I don't know ... It rained heavily that night. You think she'd be able to run all that distance in a storm?'

I closed my eyes, picturing the darkness, the desperation of the night.

'She would if she was being chased. The dogs found broken fingernails at various points where she'd fallen along this track, right from the country park, which would suggest falling at some serious speed or force. We don't know anything about what happened on that day. She could've been hiding out in Cotgrave. Maybe she ends up in the park by accident. Gets lost. I didn't notice any lights there yesterday. It'd be pitch-dark when the storm comes, and there are miles of spiralling trails.' I opened my eyes. 'She could've gone in circles for a long time before she even got here.'

Zara looked up through the space between the overhang. 'Why doesn't she use her phone?'

'Maybe she doesn't have one,' I reasoned. 'Not by the time she gets here, anyway. She doesn't have ID, nobody can find where she came from. I think it'd be fair to say that she probably doesn't have one to begin with.'

'OK …' She hopped off the track, soles landing with a heavy crunch. 'So, she's lost in the park. All she has is that yellow jacket against the rain, and it's coming down harder and harder by the minute. She stumbles across the tracks by chance, and follows it because, well, *surely* a railway has got to lead her to *somewhere*. But we've passed over two roads since the park, and come within metres of the cricket club, the RSPCA sanctuary *and* a holiday campsite! It was bank holiday weekend, so why wouldn't she go there for help, or try one of the roads for a passer-by? Why stay on here?'

'She might've been confused,' I proposed. 'She might not have been able to make them out through the storm. She might've been too afraid to try.'

'Which begs the question of when does she come into contact with the killer? Is it a chance run-in with a random opportunist? Some psychopath lurking in the park? On the railway? Or does Barber follow her here?'

'Could be anybody,' I countered. 'Murder between strangers is very rare. Inspector McCarthy mentioned migrants in the area. Working girls. If she'd been trafficked into the country, it could explain the absence of ID. It'd explain why there were no family members to claim her. Maybe she tries to get out of the city, but only gets as far as Cotgrave without any English, before the pimp trying to recruit her tracks her down.'

'*Pimp?*' Zara, I noticed, was frowning.

'Trafficker,' I revised. 'He chases her through the park and up along here. It could take him hours, hunting her like that, until …'

I looked back down the track; a solitary leaf drifted to the ground, bright as a yellow bird downed, another skeleton on the ballast.

'I don't know.' Zara put her hands on her hips. 'Traffickers? You think so?'

'You ought to check the Home Office findings,' I chided. 'They've been found to be operating in every town and city across the UK.'

'You ever worked with any?'

As it turned out, I had.

'A case in Wolverhampton a couple of years back. They were smuggling workers in from Pakistan for a thousand pounds a head, which the workers would have to repay once they got over here. They were paid a hundred pounds a week, and once they'd repaid the debt, they were free.'

'Oh …' She thought about it for a moment. 'Well, it's not *great*, but at least they let them go once they repaid the money, I guess.'

'They did,' I nodded, 'but that's without the interest on the debt, which was ten per cent every week.'

I could see her doing the maths. 'But … that's the entire hundred they earned! They'd never break the cycle.'

'And isn't that the point?'

'What a bunch of *bastards*!'

'Yes ...'

I decided not to tell her about how I managed to have them found not guilty.

We went back to studying the photographs; hers on the iPad, mine on paper.

'There's something about the scene,' she said. 'It just doesn't add up. Where's all the blood, for a start? The signs of a struggle, not to mention the rest of the finger-nails and teeth?'

'Forensics say the evidence could have been contaminated or lost in the storm. They dug up the ground, searched the surrounding areas, but it had already turned into a swamp by the time the rain subsided, and besides, they had their man by then.'

'A night of rain just *washed away* all traces of finger-prints and DNA?' She shook her head in disbelief. 'Surely a killing like this would take time. Effort. Organisation. It'd take skill and precision and planning.'

'That's good,' I said brightly. 'We can use that to counter the pathologist's analysis.'

'That's not exactly what I meant.'

'Oh?'

She looked over my shoulder, measuring the track with her eye. 'What if she was killed somewhere else, and then her body was moved out here?'

'It's possible ... They haven't been able to say with any certainty whether she was killed elsewhere, led here, or followed and killed *in situ*.' I shook my head, unconvinced. 'But why leave the body out in the open, if you've already 'gone so far as to remove the evidence? Why all the way out here?'

'Maybe it was a statement? Migrant girl, dumped on the last remaining site of the mine, only weeks after a newspaper article publishes plans to have it torn up and resurfaced?'

'You're seriously reaching. You're bending the case to suit a narrative of your own fabrication. Where did you even get the connection between the colliery and a migrant girl? It's nonsense.'

She frowned then and turned away, muttering under her breath. 'No more far-fetched than your *pimp* theory was ...'

I could tell from the abrupt shift in temperature that I'd embarrassed her with my argumentative tone, irritable, hung-over barrister that I was, so I gave her some more room to explore the idea, trying to pull it back to amicable.

'Let's say you're right,' I said softly, my own feeble version of an apology. 'Who would do something like that? What type of killer would we be looking at?'

She turned back, eyes bright again, lighting her face like a candle. 'Somebody who was proud of what they'd done, maybe? Like ... a serial killer?'

I groaned, standing up straight. 'It's *not* a serial killer.'

'I know *that*, but we could be looking at a similar mentality, couldn't we?'

'How's that then?'

'Well, for serial killers there's no satisfaction in committing the perfect, evidence-free murder. Their actions can't be empowering if nobody else ever finds out about what they've done, that's why they look to repeat the buzz, and why most eventually boast and go on to confess, simply because they want to show people what they've done. It's about superiority. For somebody who *enjoys* killing, I suppose it'd be like painting a masterpiece, only to burn it before anybody else ever gets to see it. The actual act of painting is only so much of a reward.' She paused, nodding over her own train of thought, and then met my eye. 'Criminological psychology.'

At once as enthusiastic as a teenager, and yet as clever as any one twice her age.

'Well ...' I said, trying to stay polite, 'it's an entertaining theory ... Anything else stored away from your college days?'

'Not really,' she admitted, 'just a lot of Emile Durkheim. You know him?'

'"There can be no good without evil, no justice without crime"?'

'That's the one. Durkheim said that these acts were a necessary part of society; that people learn right from wrong by them, and a serious act of deviance forces people from all backgrounds to come together to react against it.'

'Like a jury,' I grumbled. 'I don't buy into all that criminology and behavioural science malarkey. They'll never *cure* crime, so what's the point? And if they ever did, then we'd be out of a job.'

She shrugged it off. 'Medicine hasn't cured depression, but it doesn't mean we should stop smiling.'

It was a nice sentiment. The sort they could print on a coffee mug, I thought, but it reminded me of something Jenny would say; ever the left-leaning, picket-wielding, vocal enthusiast of the human rights movement, until it came to the amnesty of the vilest criminals in my diary, and all that liberalism up and vanished post-haste.

'So,' she said, 'what's next on the agenda? This place is starting to freak me out.'

'Lunch.' My stomach, raw from the whiskey, rumbled in appreciation. 'And, after that, I was thinking we could check in with the local mosques. She was Middle Eastern; it might be worth trying to find out if she'd attended any prayers before she died. Maybe we'll get lucky.'

'All right. But you know there are almost thirty mosques inside the city? Which one do we go to?'

I sighed, turning back to face the long, winding way we'd come.

'I suppose we'll have to start with the biggest.'

14

The imam of Nottingham's Central Mosque and Islamic Centre was a short, stout man, with round cheeks and bright grey eyes. When he leaned forward to shake our hands I could smell the surface of his skin; nothing unpleasant, it certainly wasn't unclean, but rather a very human scent, humble, and void of cologne or perfumed soaps.

'*Al-salāmu alaikum*,' he said, and I was both thankful and surprised when Zara responded.

'*Wa-alaikum al-salām*.' She looked down at his outstretched hand and shook her head apologetically. 'I'm so sorry, but barristers don't shake hands.'

'That's only with other barristers,' I muttered, accepting his hand, and she blushed and did the same, apologising profusely.

'I am Dr Musharaff Badour, imam of the *masjid*,' he smiled. 'How can I be of help today?'

We were standing in our socks on the carpet of his modest little office, tucked away behind the great prayer hall, and, with so many more mosques to get through, we wasted little time pulling out copies of the stills from the CCTV footage of the victim.

He leaned close to study the photographs, and answered almost immediately in a slow, raspy voice. 'I've seen this girl before.'

'You *have*?'

'Yes, these exact pictures, I mean. The police issued us copies as part of their witness appeal earlier this year.'

Crestfallen, I cursed myself for assuming it could've been so easy. 'Did you show them to the members of your congregation?'

He nodded, running fingers through the dense grey of his vast beard. 'It was on the noticeboard for several weeks, but when it became apparent that she was unknown to our community, we were forced to file it with the others.'

'I'm sorry,' Zara interposed, 'others?'

The imam shuffled over to a dented filing cabinet in the corner of the office, opened the top drawer, rummaged through a thin folder from within, and handed me a selection of papers. The top sheet had the same image of our victim on it, underneath a Nottinghamshire Police hotline. I held them out at an angle for Zara to follow as I thumbed through at least a dozen more printouts, mostly homemade, featuring photographs of young women, the loose leaves now palimpsests of Arabic annotations.

'We still hand them out from time to time, whenever we see new faces have been added,' he muttered glumly.

'But, some of these are dated eight years ago!' Zara said. 'They're all missing?'

'They were reported to the authorities at the time, but we never had much of a response.'

She stopped me halfway through turning the pages, catching one of the sheets.

'This girl!' she said, straightening it out. '*Parinda Malik*. I think I *recognise* her …'

I moved it to the top of the pile. 'Really?'

Parinda Malik had been twenty-three years old, according to the poster, when she stopped showing up to the mosque more than three years earlier. The only photograph was badly cropped and impossibly grainy; presumably, it had been taken of an entire congregation, with tiers of shoulders and robes surrounding her face, giving her all the standout qualities of a head-scarfed wallflower.

'From around the city?' I asked. 'It's kind of difficult to make her out, isn't it?'

'I'm not sure ...' Zara bobbed on the spot, eyes closed and straining, rummaging through the clutter of her memory. 'I think the poster was up around my area a couple of years back, when I was home one weekend, maybe?'

I took another long look at her blurry features, and then continued through the set, which turned out to be much more of the same. More faces. More dates. Few names.

'With all due respect, Doctor,' I said, when our victim came back around to the top, 'the Islamic community seems to be pretty tight-knit around here, and yet some of these posters don't even have names to their faces.' I held one up, case in point. 'I mean, this one is just a loose description of a teenager suspected to be lost? Doesn't it seem unlikely that these women, the victim in our case especially, could simply appear and disappear without any interaction within the community? Where could she have come from? What was she doing here? Somebody has to know, don't they?'

He perched on the lip of his desk, adopting a pose reminiscent of Rupert, and I couldn't help but notice something familiar in the crocheted skullcap pulled down like a wig, the gown flowing to his ankles like silk, and the tall bookshelves stuffed with daunting, weighty tomes. Our traditions weren't so dissimilar.

'I think you may be surprised by how many Muslims across this city have fallen through the cracks of the asylum process,' he replied matter-of-factly. 'In giving zakat we can only do our best to help, but it's getting harder by the year.'

'Zakat?'

'Almsgiving,' Zara answered for him. 'Charity is the third Pillar of Islam.'

'Precisely.' He wrapped a single curl of his beard around one finger. 'As a registered charity, our centre works closely with the Nottinghamshire Refugee Forum, but their last estimate suggested that there are up to three hundred unregistered migrants currently living in the city and surrounding areas. If an asylum claimant should fail, then more often than not they will find themselves forced onto the streets, into abysmal, desperate lives. We can provide them with tickets for hot meals at our community restaurant, *if* they come to us, and even a clean bed when we are able, but in the wake of recent events, with an increasingly negative portrayal of Islam, sponsors are getting harder to come by ...'

'Desperate lives,' I repeated. 'Have you found any links to human traffickers?'

'We're aware of the practice, but I'm thankful to say that there's no connection to the mosque and its attendees.'

'What about William Barber, the man charged with our victim's murder? Are you aware of him?'

The sudden cloud behind his eyes told me that, yes, he most definitely was. 'I know the sort he belongs to. We've had two mosques in the city attacked with petrol in the last year. Windows smashed, attendees attacked upon leaving.

Just last week, one of our young girls was assaulted after madrasa in this very mosque. A group of grown men tore the hijab from her head and knocked her to the pavement. She is nine years old.'

'Awful,' Zara whispered.

'Yes.' He crinkled his nose and sighed deeply through the nostrils. 'On your way out of the building, look over to your left, directly opposite the entrance. Perhaps you'll have a better understanding of our current climate.'

I nodded. 'Are there any other local mosques that you think might be able to help us with our inquiry?'

'They will all open their doors to you,' he said, getting up to stand before us in his discoloured white socks, 'but the elders meet regularly, and I know that you will only receive the same answers I've given you today. As I said, we maintain a strong community between us.'

'Thank you for your time, Dr Badour. We appreciate it.'

I held the stack of papers back towards him, and he waved them away with one hand. 'Keep them, please. We have plenty of copies to spare, and the further they travel, the more chance we have of finding answers for the families involved.' He opened the door for us then, and bowed his head. '*Ma al-salāmah*.'

'*Fi amān Allāh*,' Zara replied, bowing her head in return.

As instructed, I glanced to the left as we stepped into our shoes and out of the entrance, and saw words painted on the brick wall.

GO HOME.

'Disgraceful,' I sighed, flattening my hair with the hat.

'Damn right,' Zara agreed, following my eye. 'As if I'd want to go back to St Ann's, anyway.'

'Doesn't that bother you?'

'Of course,' she shrugged, 'but I've grown up here. I'm used to it.'

'That doesn't make it right.'

'I'm not saying it does.'

I lit a fag as we walked back to the car, the dome behind us blooming upwards like an emerald mushroom in the middle of the city, rivalling the spires of the church directly opposite; the two edifices were separated by St Ann's Well Road, itself named after a spring once believed to have had magical healing properties for the blind. It was a crossroads of superstition, with none of the three managing to sway me.

'That was impressive,' I said, 'what you did in there. You speak Arabic?'

'Hardly. A few phrases here and there from my mum's side of the family, that's all. She was a strict Muslim when she first came over from Pakistan. Not so much after meeting my dad. I guess that caused some problems when I was little ... She was only seventeen when she had me.'

'And your father?'

She laughed. 'Rotherham, originally. Not quite as exotic, I know. He teaches primary. Kids with learning difficulties, mostly. He's a good man.'

'So, you're not ... That is to say, you've never been ...'

'Practising?' She smiled. 'No. Let's just say my lifestyle doesn't quite meet the criteria.'

'No? In what –' I stepped into the road for the driver's side and was interrupted by the screech of a car coming to a halt behind me, causing me to jump out of my skin.

I spun, startled and irate, papers now scrunched in my fist, and found myself face-to-face with a slick black Mercedes,

117

its fine German engine growling only centimetres from my chest.

From inside, its crew of three young black men were staring straight back at me.

'Watch it!' I bellowed, but they didn't reply.

The nearest passenger, however, was outright glaring, and I felt the slightest niggle of recognition somewhere in the back of my mind.

He lifted his right hand up to the glass, pointed his index finger at my head like the barrel of a gun, and fired; then the tyres spun, and off they went tearing up the road and out of sight.

'Great to be home,' I whispered to myself, ducking into my car, feeling much too old and tired for that sort of shit. I reached across and unlocked the passenger door manually, and Zara climbed inside.

'What was that about? You think they're part of the congregation?'

'I have no idea.'

I stuffed the collection of lost girls into the glovebox, alongside an empty can of de-icer, a fistful of receipts, some McDonald's napkins and two unpaid parking tickets, and put the Mercedes to the back of my cluttered head. That would prove to be a near-fatal error.

We visited only three more mosques, receiving the same response from all, before taking the imam at his word.

15

When he wasn't behind bars, Billy lived in a ground-floor flat in Cotgrave with his second wife Sarah and their young son, only a handful of metres away from our own respective childhood homes.

Like all the neat little buildings in the area, it had originally been constructed for the workers of the colliery, and, despite later being divided into flats, was almost identical to the house I'd grown up in, the one my mum had died in, which I couldn't bring myself to look at as we drove past.

Even after nearly forty years, the memories evoked by those short roads and little brick houses hurt; I don't think it's something a person can ever truly get over; I don't think a person ever should.

It was Zara's idea to go and speak to the wife after we'd given up on the mosques, and I couldn't think of a decent enough excuse not to go, put on the spot as I was. As first impressions go, however, the flat wasn't what I'd been expecting when we pulled up in the cul-de-sac at nearly five o'clock. Missing were the English Defence League banners and St George's crosses of my imagination, and from outside it looked like Sarah Barber maintained a tidy, if humble, little home.

Inside, though, it didn't take long to recognise the signs of a strong man's rage; doors hung slightly crooked in their frames, replacement latches didn't match up to original hinges, and the beige feature wall of the cosy living room was punctuated with cracks and indentations, roughly the size of a large and weighty fist.

The woman also defied my expectations. Nearly twenty years younger than her husband, her voice was as soft as her curves, her mannerisms polite and her movements attentive. I couldn't help but notice, once she'd invited us inside, that the bright, kind eyes she boasted in framed photographs along the hallway seemed wearier in the present. She was a tiny little thing, still dressed in her supermarket uniform of a purple blouse with orange trim, her auburn hair tousled from her day of stacking shelves.

'I hope we're not disrupting you or your son, Mrs Barber,' I said, removing my hat like a wartime officer delivering news of an overseas fatality.

'Not at all, me duck.' She poured us Yorkshire tea from a pot, the proper way, and then hurried in flustered, apologetic circles around our feet, collecting scattered Lego up from the carpet.

In this way she, too, reminded me of my mother. Struggling and stressed, but ever accommodating. The brave face of the working class. I've often wondered how much longer I might've had with my mum, had she not been too proud to see a doctor when the pains first came.

'Olly's having tea at his nana's tonight,' Sarah Barber said. 'She picks him up from school when I'm working.'

'Your mother-in-law?' I asked.

'No,' she said, finally collapsing into a two-seater that ran across the living room at a right angle to our longer sofa. 'No, Billy's mam passed away about, Jesus, must've been eight or nine years ago now.'

'Sorry to hear it.'

I could still picture Jan Barber as I'd known her in my youth: peroxide hair, fag in her mouth, breasts pushing up out of her dressing gown at any time of the day. The lads and I would make an extra special effort to call for Aidan.

It was bizarre to think of her as an old woman, never mind dying.

'How did you meet Mr Barber?' I didn't know Sarah. She must have been a child when I left the area, so I hoped I could hold on to anonymity a little longer.

She thought about it, sipping tea, eyes wide in the lamplight, and then shrugged. 'Everyone round here knows Billy. We started seeing each other about eleven years ago. Got married after I fell pregnant.'

'He has three children from previous relationships, doesn't he?'

'That's right. Mikey still stays over from time to time, but he's seventeen now and, well, you know how boys are at that age …' She trailed off, leaving a big empty space and a look that said it all. 'Then he had the twins, Lottie and Lizzie.'

'Do they have much to do with their dad?'

'No,' she scolded. 'No, their mother wouldn't allow that.'

'Why not?' Zara interjected sharply, pencil poised over a spiral-bound jotter that she seemed to have pulled out of nowhere. 'If you don't mind me asking?'

Sarah buried her nose into the vapour rising from her teacup; I noticed a chip in the bottom of the ceramic. 'We don't get along,' was her flat reply.

'Because of your husband?' Zara was pressing with the subtlety of a shotgun, and it showed in Sarah's writhing shoulders.

'Is this relevant to the trial?'

'Maybe,' I assented. 'We're just trying to get a better sense of context. I hope you'll forgive me for saying it, but your husband hasn't been entirely communicative so far.'

I could feel Zara bristling, dying to interpose, but she kept her opinion private.

'Well,' Sarah sighed, 'if you must know, it's me their mam hates just as much as Billy, if not more. We started seeing each other while the two of them were kind of still together, I s'pose. Billy had moved out by then, but Becky was pregnant with the girls, and the whole thing was ...' she frowned, pondering the word, 'messy. A fitting start for things to come, eh?'

I nodded, the scratch-scratch of Zara's pencil filling the room.

The next part was awkward, but she had teed it up better than I could've hoped for.

'Mrs Barber,' I said, 'I don't like asking you this, but if there's any chance it could help to pin down your husband's whereabouts on the night in question ...'

'You're going to ask me if he was having an affair, aren't you?'

'I understand that it's probably not something you want to discuss, but, honestly, adultery would be an improvement on a murder charge right now.'

I was sorry to see her tired eyes redden.

'He's out a lot of the time,' she muttered. 'I knew that was the case when we got together, he's always been like that ... I think, in a way, all Billy's women came to him with the same arrogance I had back then. We all thought we could change him. That it would be better with us. That *he'd* be better ...'

She needlessly straightened the chequered throw that was folded over the two-seater, then returned her arms to her front, crossed and always guarded.

It amazed me, as it had with countless thugs throughout my career, that this timid, attractive and very ordinary woman could ever have paired up with the wrecking ball that was her husband. I looked at the wedding photo framed on the ledge of the television cabinet, and it really put their sizes into perspective. Her big, beauty queen hairdo only just reaching the shoulder of his suit jacket, her pregnant belly tight in white satin.

Beside that photograph was another, taken years before at what must've been a fancy-dress party during Billy's twenties or thereabouts; an odd juxtaposition it was, seeing him smiling like that, having what appeared to be genuine fun in his camp cowboy costume, dressed in a black hat and fringed buckskin like Jon Voight in *Midnight Cowboy*, surrounded by friends. Thirty years later, and he'd still be playing cowboys and Indians if he could. There were familiar cheering faces in the background, all from the social club, and I even spotted Sean McCarthy storming across the dance floor with a pint in what looked to be a replica of Hugo Boss's all-black SS uniform, a lifetime before he stepped into the get-up of the local constabulary. Classy, I thought. That's how he'd been back then, always keen to shock.

I was still gazing at the photograph over the top of my teacup when my eyes shifted to the frame beside it.

I almost dropped the cup.

There I was, grinning loutishly with almost thirty lads in Forest gear including Sean, Mike Smith, Paul Sinclair and, crucially, every one of the Barber brothers.

Sarah must've registered whatever horror had struck my features, as she followed my eye to the photograph.

'Yeah, that's Billy there on the left, a long time before we were together. Sad, really. It's one of the only photos he has of him with his little brother, Aidan.' She sighed again, ignorant of the hooligan at Aidan's side, the smaller, angrier version of the man sitting across the room. 'Aidan died in the late eighties. Down the pit, same as the rest. I don't think Billy's ever got over that. He's crazy about his brothers.'

I nodded stiffly, shaking the ringing sound around in my ears, the alarm now warning me to get out of there fast, to snatch the photograph and bolt.

I managed to prise my eyes away, trying to remember who the hell had even taken it, but I'd been a few drinks deep by then.

'What was your husband doing for a living, before the arrest?' Zara asked.

'Oh, just all sorts, really …' Sarah mumbled, eyes on the carpet. 'Proper work is hard to come by these days, you know? Gets a bit of labour here and there, but he's struggled ever since they filled the pit.'

Zara looked up from her scribbling. 'And what happened on that morning your husband came home? Your neighbour says she had no choice but to ring the police out of concern for your safety. For the safety of your boy.'

'Who, Denise?' She glared up at the ceiling, and there was a surprisingly fierce strength behind it. 'She's a pathological liar.'

'What makes you say that?' I asked through a dry throat.

'Everybody knows it. She got herself in a mess a couple of years back for making false allegations. Claimed that these two blokes had raped her after a night out. The whole thing was a load of shit, if you'll pardon me saying so.'

'How do you know that?'

'What, you mean apart from hearing it all through the ceiling? Silly cow didn't know that one of them, whichever was behind her I suppose, was filming it all on his phone. He turned up to court with footage of her kneeling on the floor begging, and I mean literally begging, for them both to –' She managed to compose herself before the literal finish line. 'Well, I'm sure you can imagine ... Her kids were in the flat and everything. You should've heard the racket. She ought to check her own bedsheets before getting her nose into someone else's business.'

'That's ... enlightening,' I said. 'Did Mr Barber's last counsel know about this?'

'No idea.'

'But on that morning,' Zara returned, pressing harder, waggling her pencil in the air, 'you're saying your husband *wasn't* aggressive with you?'

Sarah's feet started tapping; cheap, black work pumps bounced off the carpet. 'He's a very loving man, our Billy. You might not believe it to meet him. I'm not saying he's a *soft* man, not by any means, and he's opinionated when it comes to politics, but he can also be the most tender, loving person you could hope for. He has a lot to live up to, I think. His image, and what it means to be *Billy Barber*. Do you understand?'

I understood exactly what she meant, and as I glanced into the small adjacent kitchen I found myself thinking,

125

strangely, about all those bottles of champagne I'd shared with judges, barristers and even politicians over the years. None of them would ever know that, to me, champagne would always be the plastic-corked Pomagne Mam used to break out on Christmas morning in our own identical little home. What strange secrets we keep.

'As for aggression …' Sarah went on, pushing her fore-arms hard against her knees, planting her feet to the floor. 'You might not know this, but marriage is complicated.'

I tried to ignore the pale strip of skin on my left hand.

'He'd only ever hit me once before that morning … He loses his temper a lot, throws his weight around a bit, but that was the only other time he actually *did* it.'

'What happened?' I asked, soft as I could manage.

'It was around a year ago.' Sarah mumbled. 'Halloween time … It wasn't all his fault, though. I lost my temper. He lashed out, sent me into the wall there …' She indicated one of the cracks I'd already noticed in the plasterboard.

'I'm sorry,' I managed, 'but do you remember what caused the argument back then?'

Her feet were full-on drumming now, sending her whole body into a quivering frenzy. I could feel the vibrations from a metre away.

'Cheating,' she quietly relented. 'He'd spent the night with another woman. I'm pretty sure it was a prostitute.'

And just like that, a whopping piece of the puzzle came slamming down into place, and I felt Zara stiffen in response like a wave through the cushion beneath me.

'Did he tell you that?' I asked.

'Eventually …' She fumbled through her pockets for a bobbled scrunch of tissue and wiped her nose clean.

'That's what they do, those lads he hangs out with. Go to the footy at the weekend, take a load of gear, and then go and stick it up some slag. Billy came home at about ten o'clock in the morning one Sunday. I caught him stuffing his clothes into the washing machine. Managed to wrestle his underwear away from him and it was … stained. It was fucking disgusting. So, I started hitting him, and hitting him, and he retaliated, and …'

Zara was bobbing alongside me, still mortified, but clearly unsure whether to cross the room and offer an arm.

My own sympathy was, perhaps, stifled by the excitement of the revelation itself.

'Do you know who it was, and if he had any further contact with her?'

She shook her head, wiping her cheeks carefully as if to preserve the make-up she'd stopped wearing, and slumped forward.

'I'm sorry,' she said into the tissue. 'I'm sorry but I just can't talk about this any more. I don't want all this dragged up in court. In the papers. I don't want to prove to the world that it was right about us after all.'

16

We ended the day in the Welfare Scheme Social Club, three blocks away from the Barbers' flat.

The last place The Girl was seen alive.

It had changed a lot in thirty years, and was almost unrecognisable from the Miners' Welfare as I remembered it, with thick patterned plush and carpets adding a softer, nineties feel throughout. I was fairly confident that the decades would give me enough cover to get into the building without being hassled, but didn't fancy my chances in the sports bar, where I could see moderate crowds gathering around the pool tables and dartboard.

Instead, I took Zara into the quieter lounge; here, I could sit with my back to the room and its white-haired patrons, who were too busy reading newspapers, sipping mild and playing cards to notice.

For all its lack of opportunities, there were things I'd missed about Cotgrave. London might have been the greatest city on the planet, but it didn't have the same sense of *community* that had endured in such small villages across the rest of the country, places proud to keep the *civility* in the civil parish. As a lad, I'd known not only every employee in the corner shop, butcher's, greengrocer's and Miners' Welfare, but their families too, and could send my regards along with them after every brief encounter. Things were different in the city. I didn't even know the names of my upstairs neighbours.

'Thoughts, Miss Barnes?' I asked, after we'd been up to the bar and then collapsed into one of the booths in the back corner of the lounge.

She shrugged, all the morning's excitement beaten out of her, and sipped her Coke. 'Feels like a lot of effort for no real progress, doesn't it?'

'You were hoping for answers after one day?'

Another shrug. 'I just thought things might've been a bit clearer. All we've really learned is that there's not going to be any point in asking his wife to stand up in court, if all she's going to do is give the prosecution a perfect opportunity to ratify Barber's proclivity for violence towards women.'

'Maybe,' I agreed, 'but she can also confirm his use of prostitutes, and *that* could provide us with the answer to where he went and what he got up to on that night.'

'You really think Barber would be willing to lose the past six months, and potentially the rest of his life, for a murder he didn't commit, if he could just get out of it by admitting he'd spent the night with a prostitute? Seems a bit of an extreme alternative ...'.

She wasn't wrong, but it brought another trial to mind.

'You know anything about George Ince and the Barn Murder of '72?'

She undid her knot of hair, rolled it back over her ears, and leaned forward on her elbows. 'I don't think so ...'

'Well,' I said, trying to recall the finer details, 'as I remember it, the Barn was a restaurant in Essex, and the site of a botched armed robbery. A woman was killed, and George

Ince, an acquaintance of the Kray Twins, was charged with the murder.'

'OK ...'

'Thing is, the cops *knew* that Ince had an airtight alibi, but they also knew it was one he'd never use ... He'd been in bed with the wife of Charlie Kray, the twins' older brother, at the time.'

She gasped, slapping her palms down onto the table, looked around the room, and hissed, 'You're saying that the police are *fitting Barber up*?'

'No! No, I'm absolutely not saying that. But I told you that Sean said there'd been migrant girls working around the country park area, didn't I?'

'*Sean?*'

'Inspector McCarthy,' I swiftly revised. 'If that were the case, it could explain why Barber's being so cagey about coming out and admitting it, considering his personal politics. I'm betting he wouldn't want his skinhead mates finding out about him sleeping with migrant girls, would he?'

She frowned, and I wasn't sure if I'd used the most sensitive terminology.

'Surely losing the respect of your peers is a small price to pay for freedom?'

'Maybe he's optimistic,' I suggested. 'He seems arrogant enough to believe that he's going to get off with the indictment anyway. He might just be waiting to have his cake and eat it, too. I once represented a man charged with drug dealing, and part of the evidence included cocaine recovered from his wife's coat pocket. He claimed it was his, for personal use, and told me, off the record, that he was a cross-dresser, but he would never admit to that in court. You'd be surprised what punishments people will seek, if it allows them to hide a truth.'

'Maybe … *But*, what if we submit that theory, that he was with a prostitute or whatever, and the prosecution turns it around on us anyway? What if they argue that the victim *was* the working girl, and that Barber followed her into the park for, you know, *business*, only he lost his temper, and this time he didn't stop at breaking walls?'

I shook my head. 'There's no evidence to suggest that the victim was a prostitute. The autopsy says she died a virgin. No drugs. But if we could only find out where he *did* spend the night, we could find an alibi, and that'd be enough to –'

'*Rook?*'

I froze. The voice hit me from behind like a smack to the back of the head.

I turned round, slowly, and there was old Geordie Yates, dressed in a greasy striped apron, balancing the food we'd ordered on huge oval plates. I couldn't believe he still worked there.

'Said you'd be back,' he gloated. 'They all come back. Now, I've got one steak and kidney with chips, one vegetarian, extra gravy.'

'Vegetarian here …' Zara said, scratching her head.

He placed the pies on the table between us and then walked back behind the bar and out of sight into the kitchen.

I didn't say a word. Just swallowed a mouthful of lager, reached for my cutlery from our shared basket of condiments, and pretended I hadn't noticed a thing.

Zara, on the other hand, was staring after him, trying to work it out.

'Well,' she said eventually, lifting her eyebrows, 'now I know where you came last night ... Thought you might've had a rough one when you picked me up this morning, but I didn't want to say.'

'Oh yeah?' Relieved, I broke through the pastry with my fork, sending a plume of rich, beefy, home-made goodness up into my face. 'What made you think that?'

'Smoking. You've hardly smoked all day.'

'Huh ...' She was right, though I'd barely noticed; cigarettes were a one-way ticket to nausea on a hangover.

'You drink every night?'

'Not every night ...' I lied around a mouthful of steak. 'Now, that upstairs neighbour. If she's a proven liar, we can move to discredit her statement, submit a bad character application like the prosecution is doing for Barber.'

'Hmm ...' She poked at her own food. 'It's not great though, is it? When we know that he really *did* hit his wife. Feels sort of ... underhanded, I guess.'

'You're not having second thoughts about the job, are you?'

'No! Absolutely not! It's just a little more ... *visceral* than I'd expected.'

Another mouthful and I agreed that, yes, sometimes it was.

We ate in silence for a few minutes after that.

I realised, glumly, that sitting there, sharing dinner with a young woman, talking about the brutal death of another, was the closest thing I'd had to a date in years. Sarah Barber wasn't wrong. Marriage was complicated.

'Hey!' Zara suddenly perked up. 'What about that *dead brother* she mentioned? What's up with *that*? Could explain the bitterness Barber might have for the collapse of the mines or whatever. Pains me to say it, but it might even make the jury empathise with him, don't you think?'

'No,' I said, shooting the idea down. 'I don't think that's relevant.'

It was also a story I didn't want to get into.

More silence. The rhythm of bass from the jukebox on the other side of the wall.

'The old Miners' Welfare club,' Zara whistled, eyeing the room. 'I suppose you didn't see anything like this at Eton?"

My knife skidded across ceramic. 'Eton?'

'Yeah. Everyone at my last chambers was always talking about the place like it was the only school that mattered, or else it was *Cambridge* this or *Oxford* that … Did you see that report about Oxbridge universities offering more places to Home Counties applicants than the whole of northern England put together? They reckon the bias is actually getting *worse*.'

I nodded, polishing my plate clean. 'If it makes you feel any better, I went to Bristol University.'

'Really?'

'Uh-huh.'

'I assumed you were an Oxford man.'

'Don't ever assume.'

She leaned back, resting her cutlery neatly across the plate with almost a quarter of her meal uneaten. 'It's weird, isn't it? This was the last place she ever came. I mean, why here?'

I couldn't say.

She gazed from corner to corner, absently wiping her mouth with the edge of her paper napkin, and then a thought caused her pupils to flare behind her glasses.

'I've just realised something!' she whispered, leaning closer across the table. 'If Barber *didn't* do it, and I'm not saying that he didn't, but if that was the case, then that'd mean the killer is still out here, wouldn't it? He might even be in this building!'

I nodded stiffly and seriously, more to flatter the possibility than because I actually believed it, and lowered the brim of my hat before peering back over my shoulders. We were the youngest in the room by twenty to forty years respectively. Everybody else seemed to be wearing the same brand of fleece and stretch-waist trousers, and one table had moved on from cards to dominoes. Killers indeed.

Zara checked her phone and groaned loudly, instantly abandoning her suspicions. 'I should probably start heading back to the centre soon. Train's at half eight. Not that I need to see another track for a long time after today.'

I slipped my arms into the coat on the back of my chair, and patted through the pockets for my cigarettes and car keys; the jangling fobs included a battered Heineken bottle opener, a Tesco Clubcard I'd never redeemed, and a telephone number encased in plastic for O'Malley's, the small, family-run garage I'd got the Jag from, which had been absorbed by a Subaru dealership shortly afterwards.

I sparked up outside the automatic sliding doors, leaned back against the dated, boxy building as I had countless times in my youth, and looked up at the evening sky and the stars beyond, lost in the heady rush of nostalgia. I tried to imagine Billy standing in the same spot, under the same stars, on a night not so different. The Girl coming out from behind, only to disappear into the dark.

Why had he followed, if not for malice?

She'll be lucky to make it through the night.

Was it unfortunate prophecy, or genuine intent?

'Don't your family live in Notts?' I asked, trying to shake the thought and his words from my mind. 'If you can't face the train, I can always take you there tonight, and then drive you back down tomorrow?'

'Really?' She was gazing off in the same direction, following the path of the ghost with her eyes. 'That'd be ace, but I've already bought the return ticket ...'

'Your call,' I shrugged. 'I won't tell Percy if you don't.'

Instead of going home, Zara asked me to drop her off at the Horn in Hand on Goldsmith Street in the city centre, just round the back of Rock City, to meet some friends.

I watched from the kerb to make sure she got into the pub safely. Then I watched for a moment longer to see who she was meeting there. They were all so bloody young.

I was old enough to be their dad, I realised, and that stung as I drove back to the hotel.

It's not that I hadn't wanted children. In fact, the mulish part of me wanted to become the type of father I hadn't had, just to prove how easily it could be done. But there was another part, a quieter part, that worried I might end up becoming precisely the type of father I'd had. I convinced myself over and over again that it wasn't a good time, until there was simply no time left at all.

Jenny wanted to be a mother, and for somebody who spent her life arriving late to every date, meeting and event, she kept a damn close eye on her body clock. I ended up a thief, in her eyes. My career had robbed her of the chance.

As soon as I got back to the Ibis, the receptionist flagged me down; the key card must've sent some sort of room alert to the computer beside her, because she called out to me by name the moment I entered.

'Mr Rook?'

'Yes?'

'There was a call for you this evening.'

'To the reception?'

'Yes, a gentleman telephoned at –' she checked the Post-it attached to the bottom of her monitor – 'six thirty-five and asked if you were on the premises.'

'Did he leave a name? A number?'

She shook her head. 'The number was withheld.'

'All right,' I muttered. 'Very helpful, thank you.'

Back to the bed, back to the bottle, trying to focus on the events of the day, too tired to concentrate, too keyed up to sleep. My eyes were feeling scratchy and raw. The room stretched out like an empty hall around me.

Alone again.

I tried not to dwell on it, which wasn't too difficult with everything else that was already clattering around in my head. I turned the television on for background noise, any sort of presence, but hardly gave it a glance.

It was well after midnight and I was half cut on the whiskey when I decided to go in search of the hotel's smoking area. I left my hat by the bed but took my coat and a handful of the case papers along with me to read. I left my phone in the room. I wasn't going to need it.

After padding back and forth through the corridors on every floor, I realised that the hotel didn't have a designated area for smokers, and I'd have to brave the street outside. It never occurred to me to go back for my phone. I'd only be a minute.

The reception was empty by then – the receptionist having gone home for the night – so I let myself out into the cold, pocketing the key card.

The road was just as empty as my room. Fog had started to roll in, a million fine droplets suspended in the air swallowing what little light there was. I stood close to the outside of the hotel and blew smoke up towards the tram lines that run back and forth above Fletcher Gate. It was too dark to read, so I shuffled a few metres over to the right, nearer to the lamp post, leaned back, and turned to those CCTV stills of The Girl once again.

If it hadn't been for that cup of coffee, I thought, then it would've been as if she'd fallen right out of the sky and onto those tracks.

If she'd only talked to the cashier. To anybody.

That's when I noticed the car mounted askew on the kerb a little way off, directly outside the Lace Market car park where my own Jaguar was sitting.

It was a black Mercedes. Disturbingly familiar.

Then I heard the flurry of movement closing in on me.

Instinct afforded me one good swing at the nearest of the three. My cigarette burst into orange sparks against his head, sending him back into the road, but it wasn't enough to stop the other two, and all of a sudden, fists were raining down like bricks, smacking me onto the pavement in a heap, and scattering my papers into the empty road.

17

I balled myself into a tight coil, shielding myself against the toecaps swinging in from every side, and tried to hold the wind in my lungs. Alcohol could only desensitise me to the impacts for so long.

Wet grit spattered my lips, my teeth, in the hyper-awareness that comes with a good kicking. I managed to roll, snatching a glance up through the frenzy and the hoods and scarves, and still had enough breath to splutter:

'Nelson!'

Everything stopped.

Nobody moved.

I heard a car drive down a neighbouring road, too far away to help, and then there was nothing but the noise of animal-panting in the low light.

Exposed, the tallest of the attackers yanked the scarf down from over his face, revealing a thin jaw, mottled skin, and a panic-stricken gawp at being identified; I'd finally recognised the passenger from the black Mercedes earlier that afternoon.

Though Barber was unique in his use of extortion to acquire my counsel, he was not the first to have crawled out from my past in search of aid. There had been others, rolling back around like bad pennies or venereal disease, and Nelson's father had been one of them. A well-known villain of the West Indian community that had been allocated some of the worst housing on the slum in which I was born, he'd been a friend of my father's, or rather, a financier to my father's addiction to gambling, and had remembered my name when fate saw our paths eventually cross in the courtroom years later.

After three successful trials for him, this pseudo Yardie hired me to defend his youngest son, Nelson, on a charge of armed robbery. Nelson had decided to help himself to the valuables of a student house in Hyson Green, allegedly using a hefty knife to subdue the three young lads living there, while he pocketed their girlfriends' handbags. He was caught only a mile from the scene with the stolen goods, riding a stolen bike, and then identified upon parade. During the trial, however, I managed to prove that the victims had fabricated the knife out of embarrassment about failing to confront the intruder. I'd thought the day was won.

The three pairs of size elevens that had just battered my sides were a stark reminder of why a barrister should never make guarantees of success to a client before the jury's verdict. Oddly, failed defendants never blame the coppers who arrest them, the barrister who prosecutes, the jury who convicts, the judge who sentences, or themselves; it's always the defence barrister's fault.

One of Nelson's cohorts panicked, voice muffled by a scarf that I only now noticed, with a sting of irony adding to my injuries, to be the red-and-white stripes of Nottingham Forest.

'Fuck! Shut him up, man!'

Nelson's hand went into his pocket, and this time the air in my lungs escaped me, as the sliver of a blade in his hand caught the yellow of the nearest street light. The scar on my chest burned with fear.

'Stick him,' one of them hissed. 'Do it, Gangsta!'

They spoke with Notts-interpretations of Jamaican accents, but I would've wagered that none of them had ever stepped foot in Kingston.

I swallowed hard. 'You're going to stick me on camera, are you, Nelson?'

He hesitated; with a careful tip of the head I gestured to the front of the hotel behind me, hoping it was dark enough to prevent them from calling my bluff.

I must've split his lip with my only successful swing because blood was gathering in dark lines between his bared teeth, flecking onto the ground, and a smudge of grey ash had burned across his dark, bony cheek like chalk.

I got painfully to my feet, the sound of blood pounding through my ears, pushing heat up and out of a gash in my hairline, and stepped closer to the edge of the blade. Adrenaline can make even the wisest man a fool. 'You see that on the floor?'

His eyes darted down and then back up to me in a fraction of a second, the tremble in his hand bringing the knife nearer.

The dark spatter he saw on the ground was, I knew, most likely my own blood, but I'd split his lip, and he'd never been the sharpest kid to begin with.

'That's your DNA,' I told him. 'Hard evidence. You do this, leave me here to die in a puddle of *your* blood, on camera, and it won't take Sherlock to look back and figure out a motive. You're still sobbing about a few months? You'll go down for *life*, and it won't be a fucking nursery like the last time. You think you'll make it with the big boys in Category A?'

His tongue quivered fast and snakelike, collecting the blood from his chin, eyes burning from under his hood.

'Let's take him up to the water!' one of his accomplices cried through his scarf. 'Do him there!'

'My partner's inside!' I could hear my words falling faster and faster, betraying my cool, and I showed them my empty palms. 'She knows I came out for a cigarette, and she can ID your car from the mosque. I'm guessing you rang every hotel in the city to find out where I was staying. Clever! You think they won't be able to trace that? You reckon they won't have your car picked up on automatic number-plate recognition?' A pause, an exchange of nervous glances, so I swirled a gobful of metallic spit and propelled it onto the pavement. 'Just making sure there's a decent trail.'

The closest assailant quickly scrubbed at the spit with the sole of his Nikes, as if to wash it away.

'That's it,' I said, 'you just get that DNA all over your person. Good idea!'

I could see they were rattled, each waiting for the other to make a move, and I risked no sudden gestures; if my work has taught me anything, it's that there are few things more lethal than anxious men forced into a corner.

Nelson pressed the blade up against the wool of my coat, undergoing what appeared to be a serious internal struggle, then he pulled it back to his side, and gritted bloodied teeth. 'See you're still the fucking clever cunt.'

'It's a curse,' I shrugged, and reached into my pocket for another cigarette; when I brought it up to my lips, it was vibrating wildly in my grip.

'Fuck him. Let's get the fuck out of here,' Nelson muttered to the others, and they started to storm away, returning to the car. 'Don't come back, Rook. If I see you again, you're a dead man.'

I didn't dare respond with any sort of rejoinder. My head was pounding, dizziness almost throwing me over as I bent to collect my scattered papers from the gutter, and then I looked at the crumpled sheets in my hand and paused.

'Wait!' Even after the attack, the hard-wired barrister inside had sensed an opportunity. 'I want to ask you something!'

They turned, car doors already open, Nelson at the passenger side.

'You what?'

I wiped a thin streak of wet warmth from my forehead, smearing blood onto the back of my smoking hand, and thrust one of the sheets towards them; it had curled almost closed in the damp.

'Any of you ever seen this girl on your scene?'

'Our *scene*?'

'You know,' I said, 'whatever you're into.'

Nelson glowered truculently, clenching his jaw, kneading his right fist. 'We ain't *into* nothing.'

'No? What is that?' I nodded to the car. 'Last year's registration? What are you, the Midlands' three amigos of investment banking? I don't think so.'

They exchanged glances, bemused, and I had to admit to myself that it was a strange turn of events.

That's just how life is sometimes. Every fight has to end somehow.

'Come on,' I said, checking the road in both directions, the emptiness of the fog, 'just look at the fucking picture.'

Nelson scoured the empty windows overhead, leaned forward, cagey.

'Could be anyone,' he muttered. 'What'd you take this on, fucking Nokia 3210?'

'All right,' I growled, rummaging through the damp, creased pages in my hands, 'then how about this one?'

I shoved it up to his face and he reeled back against the car. It was indeed of a much clearer quality, her face now beaten, bloated and broken beyond repair. I shouldn't have done it, but a few fists to the head tend to provoke the worst in me.

'I don't know nothing about that shit!' Nelson cried. 'You ain't pinning that on us!'

'Why?' I jabbed. 'Did you do it? Some of your *homeboys* get a little carried away one night in spring?'

'I ain't never seen her in my life!' Nelson spat, and I switched my glare to his cohorts, who were hastily shaking their heads.

'What about working girls? Prostitutes? You ever heard about that going on down in Cotgrave?'

Nelson shrugged. 'Happens everywhere, doesn't it?'

'This would've been about six months back.'

He nodded slowly, circumspectly, still checking around. 'There was a pop-up down there for a bit, but it ain't there no more.'

'A what?'

'Ain't you meant to be a lawyer?' He rubbed his lip with his free hand; both were swelling by the second, and a youthful part of me was glad to know I could still throw a good punch.

'You mean a pop-up brothel?'

'Yeah. They find a place for rent, send one of their gals round to check it out, dressed up all nice, pay deposit in cash. All happy families, far as the landlord's concerned. Then they move the rest of the gals in and run them until they have to move on.'

'You're talking about, what, a gang?'

'I don't know. Albanians or some shit, straight-up Bad Men, they bring them over here and put them to work.'

'Any idea where they're set up now?' I asked, perhaps a little too eagerly.

One of the others laughed, shaking his head in disbelief, and pulled the scarf down from his face; he was much younger than Nelson, only twenty if he was a day. 'Man wants some pussy, is it? Course we know where it is!'

'Reckon you can take me there?'

I heard myself say it without thinking, and Nelson's jaw actually dropped.

'Now I know you're playing. You think we're gun' get your blood and mess in our car for the courts? You can fuck right off, Rook. Take your games elsewhere.'

'Come on,' I said, folding the case papers and slipping them into my coat pocket, flicking the filter of the cigarette off into the fog. 'I bet you've got a couple of napkins knocking around in that glovebox to clean me up. I'll keep my hands to myself. Just get me to the right place, and it might help me forget about *that assault with a deadly weapon* that just happened on camera …'

He glowered, weighing his options, and now the driver spoke. 'No fucking way. Not in my car!'

'Shut the fuck up, Ross!' Nelson snapped, and then he went rummaging through the glovebox, cursing under his breath, and tossed me a single-sachet, lemon-scented hand wipe, before checking the street one final time, and gesturing into the back seat.

It was only once I was inside, sobering fast with my attackers around me, lemon-scented wipe bloodied and blowing away down Fletcher Gate, that I remembered my mobile phone charging peacefully in the room, and decided that this might've been the worst idea I'd ever had.

Nobody spoke a word as the car rumbled into the belly of St Ann's, built on the rubble of my birthplace.

The slick fog lights grinned over the shadows of Hungerhill, one of the oldest allotments in the world, and I tried to snub the nauseating image of being found bullet-riddled or shanked there, eighteen stone of fertiliser left for the autumn squashes.

Even when we got to the place, and I wasted no time scrambling out of the car, I was half expecting to spring a sudden leak from somewhere between my shoulder blades.

'Here we end, Rook,' Nelson snarled as he let me out, pointing one hand off to the shadow of the house. 'We didn't see each other tonight, and we ain't never going to see each other again, you get me?'

'That's fine by me, Nelson,' I said, backing away. 'Let's forget this ever happened.'

And then the door was slammed and the car rolled off into the dark, leaving only the smell of fumes clinging to the fog in the otherwise empty suburb around me.

Darkness, and little else.

Relief rushed through me like iced water to the parched, but the sensation was just as quick to evaporate by the time I reached the house ahead.

18

That place.

It wasn't a structurally attractive building by any means, but at least it matched its dismal, blockish, pebble-dashed neighbours; it might've even made an inviting little retirement snug in another time that wasn't so distant, a universe not too far.

Unfortunately, as with so many other, similar council estates, the area had turned into a clash of generations; the settled elderly residents had suddenly had the young, urban-poor shoved in atop them, and lovingly tended gardens were now interspersed by overgrown yards strewn with litter, hand-me-down see-saws, broken prams and, in one case, an adjustable weight bench, rusting in the damp.

Only one house out of twelve had its lights on in the dead-end road. My watch said it was coming up to two.

Pink, orange and red glowed faintly at the edges of thick, mismatched curtains, and I could hear the steady bass of music coming from within as I entered the unkempt garden, stepping carefully over the scattered glass of a vodka bottle, the ammonia stink of alcoholic piss.

Reason urged me to turn back, sanity told me to leave, but the door ahead opened before I had the chance, making the fateful decision for me, and I froze.

A man was standing in the doorway.

His classic Eastern European buzz cut was marbled by scarring where the hair no longer grew, his brow was a solid brick above a fat, meaty nose, and his eyes were as dead as any I'd encountered in the dock. He filled the door frame completely in his black tracksuit and trainers, blocking all the surreptitious goings-on, except for the music.

Words wouldn't come straight away, so I just stood there, pain prickling around my head, coat held tight against the penetrating chill of the fog. I'd mopped as much of the blood away as the napkin had allowed, but I suspected it had been a poor attempt.

Incredibly, the stranger said not a word, but gestured me inside with one massive hand. Ignoring my own final plea for sagacity, I followed.

What hit me first was the stench.

Beneath the heady soaking of cheap perfume, it smelled of sweat, ash and the musk of cum-stained fabrics, the chemical smoke of crack cocaine drifting from the dark upstairs, sweet and synthetic as plastic and caramel burning in a rusted tin.

I was led through to the kitchen, or what once had been a kitchen, where a thin red veil was now draped over the only lamp on the worktop, casting crimson light onto the rising damp, which lifted speckled wallpaper up in waves beneath the wood-panelled ceiling. Instead of culinary equipment, the sides were scattered with glass ashtrays, empty cans of weak, supermarket-brand lager, and an assortment of erect dildos, with one especially intimidating model drying off in the sink beside an empty plate.

The music flowed through the whole house from a source unseen, but it couldn't silence the pressing moans behind every wall, which suggested I was standing in one of the only rooms that hadn't been transformed into a makeshift boudoir. Indeed, I caught just a glimpse into the old sitting room down the hall, and saw a mattress laid out there like a camping bed, a webcam pointing at the shadow of long legs stretched out and open over the sheets.

Times had changed since Aidan and I had gone down to Forest Road, Nottingham's red-light district of the early eighties, to watch the girls from afar in the small hours after a miserable defeat at the City Ground. That was still years before the Kerb Crawling Taskforce had driven them away from the corners with cameras and plain-clothed patrols, and it was believed then that as many as three hundred were working in the area; copping a look-see was a renowned pastime for the bolder young lads, and we were feeling brave. It was only when we'd reached around the thirty-metre point that we spotted a man who looked a lot like Sean, bartering with two ladies on the next corner, and we scarpered, humiliated, and didn't speak of the evening again.

Since then, I'd never approached a brothel, and certainly never seen such a rank, surreal locale for one, and yet the women of the house were staggeringly attractive, or else might have been, were they not slightly malnourished, or strung-out on whatever poison abounded there. They moved back and forth through the shadows of the building, every curve punctuated by jutting bone under flimsy trans-lucent slips, with dark hair and naked legs. I even spotted a young man in loose pyjama trousers slinking out of the sitting room and up the staircase; barely into his twenties, he threw me a wink from an eye surrounded by burn scars, drinking a pint of milk straight from the bottle and revealing his bare back, where a tattoo of a torero in traditional *traje de luces* fluttered a great scarlet flag.

The alcohol that had bolstered my actions seemed to be draining through a gaping sinkhole, replacing itself with growing unease.

I had no idea what I was doing there.

The intermediary who had let me into the building kept a watchful eye from his post by the bottom of the staircase as the compering duties were handed over to the madam of the evening, a tall woman with sharp features and piercing black eyes, a prominent collarbone and slightly sallow skin.

She looked at the swelling around my face and lifted the arc of her painted eyebrows.

'Rough night?'

Jagged appearance aside, her voice was every bit as silky as the flowing gown she wore, and textured with the undertones of a faraway land; my snap decision to force a local accent, on the other hand, meant reversing my time-worn disguise for an altogether blunter approach.

'Aye, you could say that.'

She studied my face. 'I don't know you?'

'Doubt it, love.'

She shook her head. 'We arrange our business online. The girls are listed on Red Sheets, and you can book an appointment on here.'

'Ah, come on,' I teased. 'You wouldn't believe the night I've had. I could really use some attention,' and before she had chance to refuse again, I fished out the wallet that I'd thankfully kept in my coat pocket, carefully covering my protruding driving licence with one thumb, and showed her the wad of money inside.

I had the strangest memory then, of getting those precious brown envelopes on Friday afternoons, back when nobody I knew even bothered having a bank account. It was a habit I hadn't grown out of – carrying cash – something of a working-class giveaway, but now it paid off.

'I'm good for it,' I said, 'clean, and I won't be any trouble.'

For a moment, I thought we'd hit a wall. Cajoled by the presence of hard cash, however, she quickly changed her mind, and went on to list the price of every available service in crude detail, as pragmatically as a market butcher peddling value meat from a stall. The rates were so low I'd be ashamed to ever repeat them out loud. I handed over the money and then she offered me my pick of the litter, calling for three of them to come and form a neat line like suspects in an identity parade. Two almost looked like they might be interested in what was happening, while the other seemed lost in a glazed, introspective trance. Coupled with the rising hangover, it all made me feel quite sick.

Ever since Sean had told me about girls working in the area, I had been thinking it might hold the answer we needed. Now I was almost sure of the complete opposite, and I'd got myself trapped in another dead end.

Awkwardly, I picked out the most responsive-looking of the trio, a young woman – a *very* young woman, I suspected – with a dark complexion and strong Slavic features, dressed in a chemise of shiny polyester that dreamed of being red Chinese silk. She managed a smile at least, full scarlet lips spreading through a fall of black corkscrew hair, and then led me off through the kitchen and a tiny passage-cum-utility area, into what turned out to be a bathroom at the very back of the ground floor.

It was even smaller in there, with another strip of cheap red cotton pinned across the ceiling light, darkening the grotty pink porcelain of the amenities, candles burning low on the windowsill alongside stacks of folded towels. The girl shut the door behind us and reached into the cubicle of a tight walk-in shower, releasing the spray.

'Come,' she said simply, eyes wide. 'Shower.'

For all its underhanded baseness, there was something unnervingly beguiling about the gloom, the cocoa smell of massage oils soaked into the towels. I could feel myself slipping, falling, intoxicated by her presence and the leaden weight of exhaustion.

She casually dropped her slip down to the stilettos on her feet, and every muscle under my skin tensed at once, bolting me to the spot, all my weakness and loneliness forcing my eyes to the contours of her flesh, her breasts, and the lace of her underwear.

With a quick, practised flick of her feet and a gentle shove she removed my shoes, making me feel even more naked than she was.

She parted my coat and began to undo the buttons of my shirt, working downwards from my collar, and I was very nearly lost. My eyes closed, and warmth spread down through my body.

Then her fingers caught the deep scar on my chest, and the sheer chill of the contact shocked me to my senses.

I caught her wrists, cold and stiff as a corpse, and shook my head.

'Can we just talk a minute?'

She frowned, snapping her hands away, and cocked her head. 'You want we talk?'

'Yes. You can put your clothes back on. Is that all right?'

She just shrugged, not especially embarrassed or relieved, and pulled her scant clothing up again, covering her thin body.

'Some want to talk. Most don't. You still pay.'

'Course.' I pulled my wallet out again and gathered the remaining notes I had in there, which amounted to no more than forty pounds. It felt dirty, thrusting the crumpled papers out towards her like that, and I was painfully ashamed. 'Here. It's just for you.'

'For what?'

'To talk, that's all. I promise. Nothing else.'

She looked at the money, wet her lips, smudging the red there, and shook her head. 'Matka will find it.' She reached to kill the shower.

'That's all right,' I said, 'leave it running.' Her seductive turn had all but vanished, and she was eyeing me suspiciously as I buttoned my shirt, clouds of water vapour thickening around us, dampening the candlelight. 'Matka? You mean mother?'

'Not really.' She sat on the lid of the toilet seat, indicating the room around us. 'Matka has the house. You understand?'

'I think so … What about that man, the one who let me in?'

Her lips tightened. Nothing. I had to pull it back.

'Where are you from? I mean, originally.'

'Bulgaria.'

I couldn't tell whether she was telling the truth. She had no reason to, I suppose.

Beneath the rumbling hiss and whirr of the electric shower, I could hear floorboards creaking overhead, heels clopping in the kitchen.

'You worked here long? I mean, with Matka?'

She blinked, bewildered, and I could sense my time slipping away, as surely as the suffocating flame of the candle.

'How about in Cotgrave, the village? Earlier this year, maybe? About six months ago?'

Another blink, almost bored.

I decided to go for broke, and reached into my coat pocket for the fold of case papers, still damp from the surface of the road. She watched warily, as I flicked through them, until I came to the grainy photographs of the victim at the service station.

'How about her? Do you recognise this girl? Do you know her name, or how she might've got to England?'

'Who are you?' she asked, pulling her slip tighter. The humidity had almost swallowed the candlelight by now.

'Nobody,' I snapped. 'Her name, that's all I need!'

She shook her head, so I frantically raced for the photograph of Billy, the mugshot taken on the morning of the killing.

'What about him? Has he ever come to you? Was he a regular at one point?'

I knew, from the way her eyes bulged at the mugshot, that it was a bad idea before she'd even opened her mouth.

'*Politsiya!*'

'No, wait!'

But she'd already made it to the door, flinging it open and hurtling out through the house.

'*Politsiya! Police! Police!*'

153

'Fuck!' I tried to follow, stuffing the papers back into my pocket, but the giant who had let me into the house was already barrelling towards the bathroom, so I slammed the door shut and forced the flimsy bolt into the jamb.

Crunch. He must've thrown himself into the wood. I pushed my entire weight back, looking desperately at the window, which was barely half my width.

Another colossal slam, and a crack split the length of one panel. The only saving grace was that the passageway beyond the door was narrow, with little room for momentum, but I knew I had only seconds before the hinges gave way, and we reached his inevitable *Here's Johnny* moment.

There have been several times in my life when I've had to take a beating, and known it in advance, if only by a few moments. The best thing to do is accept it, to take it on the chin, and cast aside such terrifying thoughts as one-punch kills.

In this situation, however, visions of that cold, empty railway seemed to come nearer with every shunt of muscle on wood.

I had no phone, no weapon, and no hope of escaping.

Until, out of nowhere, a memory came sharp and sudden as an electric shock.

A client I'd once defended on alleged arson.

A struggling beautician, she'd had a stroke of luck, one might say, when her failing salon inexplicably burned to the ground one night, and the subsequent insurance payout cleared her massive, mounting debts.

I had the charges dropped, after proving that the client used massage oils on a daily basis, the residue of which had gradually gathered in the fibres of her towels, enduring every wash cycle, until eventually igniting on one of the radiators in the middle of the night.

Oils. Towels.

I moved without considering the consequences, gathering fistfuls of oily, sweet-smelling towels from the windowsill and stuffing them into the sink, along with a half-roll of toilet paper for good measure. As the door burst open the lock pinged off and hit the tiles on the opposite side of the bathroom, and I introduced the dying candle to the pyre, taking cover on the underside of the porcelain sink.

It flashed like napalm, hurling heat into the face of the Goliath as he stormed the room, and the split second of confusion – him grabbing for the showerhead in a panic – was all I needed to barge through, bouncing off screaming, scantily clad women and leaving my shoes behind. The skinny young man with the burns around his eye appeared in the hall, leaping over the banister and into my path, but I steamrolled him with little effort.

I managed to sprint for several blocks of the estate, which was something of a personal best, before the pavement took its toll on my feet, the cold air cut at my lungs, and I was forced to slow to a sorry, breathless stagger.

Thankfully, nobody followed.

It was a half-hour walk back to the hotel, but I wanted to get out of St Ann's as fast as I could, and only hoped that a bare-footed six-foot-plus man with swelling bruises, might just look crazy enough to dissuade any more would-be assailants.

Halfway back, adrenaline subsiding, feet wet and numb from the freezing pavement, I caught sight of myself in the window of a parked van on Carlton Road and heard a manic, nervous laugh nearby.

It came from me, I realised; for now, it really was like being home.

Just then, as I was confident in the belief that things couldn't get any worse – the likelihood of trouble for one night having surely been spent up by now – a car entered the dark road I walked, slowed to a crawl alongside King Edward Park, matching my pace, and halted my movement with a single, silent pulse of its blue light, which was swallowed by the fog.

19

It was an unmarked BMW 5 Series, a dark, matte sedan with thin LED strobes still glowing blue in the grille.

The window was already down when it pulled in to the kerb, but I couldn't see the driver inside, buried in shadow as he was.

'Morning,' came a deep, resonant voice from the heart of the dark. 'Everything all right?'

'Fine,' I replied as cheerily as I could manage; was it morning already? 'Yourself?'

A hand must've reached upwards, because the interior light illuminated the inside of the car, the notebooks and flask on the otherwise empty passenger seat, and the driver opened his door with the engine still purring. At first, when he stepped out and I saw how tall he was, I hoped it might be Sean, but even my old friend was short compared to this solid six-and-a-half-footer. He moved into the light of a lamp post, revealing a barrel chest and combed blond hair, a moustache turning auburn and grey at the bristles, and regarded me in silence for a moment.

I turned my socks inwards, connecting toes as if to hide them, but he was already staring down with steely eyes. I couldn't tell if he was much younger than me; he was certainly much fitter.

'Mind if I ask what you're up to?'

'Not a lot,' I said. 'Just on my way to bed. Had a couple of drinks and decided to stretch my legs. There's no smoking at the hotel.'

'What happened to your shoes?'

'Left them in my room. Didn't expect to walk this far.'

He turned his head pointedly between the black expanse of the park on the far side of the road, the empty, bolted faces of the garage and trade shops on the near, and shrugged. 'Can't see any hotels nearby. Want to tell me your name and what you're doing in the area?'

I stuffed my glowing right fist into my coat pocket and felt the papers inside. 'Are you asking officially?'

'Should I be?'

There was something in his accent that was difficult to place; if it was Notts now, then it hadn't been for long, and I couldn't cool the irritating scratch at the back of my head that told me I recognised his face. Strangely, as if reading my thoughts, he was firing the same look back at me.

'Well,' I said, nodding at his zipped rugged barn coat and jeans, 'since you're not in uniform, I can only assume that you're about to show me your warrant card, Officer …?'

He didn't like that, and straightened up to his full height, which was undeniably massive, before flashing both teeth and his identification. 'That's *Detective* to you.'

It most certainly was, I realised when I looked at the card. Detective Chief Superintendent John DeWitt. If it had been any other night then I might not have believed my misfortune, but they do say that such things arrive in threes, after all.

What was it Sean had called him? The Sheriff of Nottingham? If I hadn't sobered up already, I did so in another heartbeat.

'So,' he said, 'shall we try that again? I want you to put your hands flat on the edge of the car.'

'For what, exactly? If you're planning on searching me, then I'd like to know on what reasonable grounds you intend to do so.'

He cocked his head and arched his brow, distantly amused. 'You don't ask the questions around here, I do, understand?'

Though I couldn't be certain, I was fairly sure he'd just lifted one of Brian Dennehy's lines straight out of *First Blood*, and suddenly I was Rambo, hands on the car, legs back, another drifter on the bonnet.

'It's a little late to be going for a wander,' he said, wrapping both palms around my shoulders and sweeping the lengths of my sleeves. 'You going to tell me your name?'

'Sure,' I growled, his hands slipping into the pockets of my coat, producing a fistful of damp papers. 'Elliot Rook, and that's *Queen's Counsel* to you, Detective.'

There were many regrets I ended up with from that evening, but one had to be facing the opposite direction when he stiffened. I'd bet his expression was priceless.

'So,' I went on, shrugging him off and turning round, 'you can tell me all about those reasonable grounds now, as well as what you expect to find on me, and then produce the record of the search that I'm entitled to.'

He blinked down at the papers in his hand, and then glanced up and down the length of the road; a taxi came belting along it, and then slammed on its brakes, dropping to the speed limit at the sight of us standing by the Beemer.

'Rook ...' He scrunched his nose, lifting the moustache, and rummaged through a couple of the pages. 'You're defending in the railway murder?'

'That's right.' I snatched the papers back, by now little better than tattered scraps, and returned them to my pocket. 'Do you perform many random stop and searches, DCS DeWitt, or am I a special case? It's just that usually I'm partial to at least a little foreplay before the groping starts.'

The last thing I expected him to do was smile, but smile he did, though his eyes remained cold as stones; like the wet smell of air freshener hanging in the toilet, I thought, it was pleasant, but only there to remind you that somebody had just taken a shit.

'Can't be too careful these days, can we? What brings you up to Nottingham, Counsel?'

'Visiting old friends.'

'Is that so? Well, how about I give you a lift back to your hotel, to show there's no hard feelings?'

'No thanks,' I said, looking into the second strange back seat of the evening. 'I came out here to stretch my legs, and that's what I'll do.'

He shrugged, imitating friendly, and tightened the collar of the barn coat against the lingering fog. 'Where is it you're staying?'

'Travelodge on Maid Marian,' I swiftly lied. 'It's only ten minutes from here. Enough time to have another smoke, I should imagine, and then it's Goodnight, Vienna from me.'

I fished a cigarette out from my pocket, and before I had chance to find the lighter, he'd opened a brass Zippo in front of me, which cast a glow of orange over his entire face.

'Not yet it isn't,' he said as I lit up, 'but soon enough, I'm sure.'

The lighter closed with a snap, swallowing the flame, and for another moment we held our stares. Then he dipped his head and got back into the car, and despite it being quickly lost into the fog, I could feel him watching me closely in the rear-view mirror.

Fifteen minutes later I collapsed onto the hotel bed, grateful for the three locked doors that separated me from the city outside.

20

The exact same cleaner from the previous morning burst into my room once more, cleaning trolley at the ready, and woke me with another embarrassed fluster of frustrated apologies as she backed out into the hall again.

This time I couldn't blame her. I was already half an hour late for checkout, and all but dead to the world.

I rolled over to check the time, and spots of pain blossomed all over my body. My fist was stiff, the knuckles split. I was filthy, tired, and ready to get back to London.

When I looked at my phone, however, still charging peacefully at the bedside, and saw the missed calls from Rupert, and an accompanying text message requesting – nay, demanding – that I come into chambers as soon as possible, my desire to go south was quickly snuffed.

The only other message had come from Zara, asking if I'd mind picking her up from the city centre, close by, and that was at least a single shred of good news. Going anywhere near St Ann's was just about the last thing on my agenda.

I showered and scrubbed my teeth with my left hand, the right too stiff to close tightly around the brush, checked out of the hotel in my socks, and found, with no small relief, that my car hadn't been torched by Nelson's gang at any point in the night. Small blessings. The pale morning had washed the fog away, but the air remained wet in my lungs as I dug an old pair of golf shoes out of the boot.

It was half eleven when I found Zara sitting, as promised in her message, outside a coffee shop only a few blocks away. Face in her hands, half asleep, blocking out all the bustling city movement around her.

I pulled the car up onto the pavement, narrowly avoiding the pedestrians there, and blasted the horn, causing her, and everybody else, to jump.

'You all right?' I asked, once she'd flopped, deadweight, into the passenger seat.

She lowered the window and dropped her whole head out of it like a puppy gone limp.

'Don't feel well,' she replied in a quiet undertone and, feeling somewhat tender myself, I almost retched on the smell of pure flammable spirits that surrounded her. She closed her eyes and breathed heavily through her nose, holding her temples between two fingers.

'Millennial problems,' I said, and then bounced the car down from the kerb with a crunch, spun the bonnet round to face the south, and let the engine have it.

Zara was soon asleep. So much for good company. Even when I pulled in to the service station for fuel, she didn't stir.

A lady at the neighbouring pump flashed me a smile, but I couldn't find one to return.

I took the unleaded from its sheath, joggled its nose into the tank, and used my left hand to squeeze; as the fuel poured and the dials whirred, I found my mind sliding back to The Girl's final morning, the swaying pumps and the empty lot.

Was it the wrong place at the wrong time, or something more?

The smell of the fuel hit hard, cutting right through me, and I was flung back to the night before, the fire, and how utterly stupid I had been.

One rash, desperate decision that could've cost lives. If the flames had spread, it would've been manslaughter, at least. My great legacy as Queen's Counsel would've come to its abrupt end on a fellow silk's Crown Court agenda, with God only knew how many bodies choked on smoke around my forgotten shoes ...

The pump handle kicked back against my grip, snapping me out of my self-loathing, and I paid up and got back on the road.

More miles. I cycled between radio stations for news bulletins, dreading what might've happened in that house after I left, but nothing came up. I settled on Radio 2, where Jeremy Vine was discussing the ongoing trial of a young homeless man who had been taken in by a generous family, only to return and fatally stab them a year later.

I was just wondering who had got the case, when Zara interrupted my train of thought.

'Do you think people are bad?'

She'd spoken so quietly that for a moment I thought it was another caller on the radio.

'Do I believe, what, that people are Old Testament evil?' I asked, referring to the topic on the air. 'No, I don't think it's as black and white as that. Not to start with, anyway.'

'I don't mean criminals, or whether criminals are born or made, I just mean *people*, in general. You've been around longer than I have, thought maybe you'd have some perspective on it all. Some wisdom or whatever.'

'Some wisdom?' Thoughts of Billy, the flash of a flame in a houseful of vulnerable women. A fleeting anxiety asked if she was reading my mind, if she knew what I had done.

'My family,' she grumbled. 'My ex. Everybody back home, actually. They can all do one, far as I'm concerned.'

I shifted into the left lane and loosened the pressure on the accelerator to show I was listening and glanced across. 'Bad night?'

She shrugged, lowering her head, indicating yes. 'Let's just say it didn't take me long to remember why I wanted to get away from there in the first place. They're supposed to be my mates, but I swear they're all just waiting for me to fuck up and come crawling back home. Just because their world begins and ends in Notts.' She sighed, exhaling more alcohol into the air. 'Then I wake up to my mum going ballistic because of this trial, as if I need *that* on a hangover.'

'The trial? What about it?'

'Oh, just *everything*. She's been reading up on the case. Can't seem to get her head around me defending a racist. Started throwing up a lot of crap from our past, the things she went through to get here, you know? Says it could've been me out there on the railway, and if I do this, if I get him off, I might as well be killing her myself. Can you believe that?'

I could hear her voice breaking at the edges.

'She says I should be ashamed, *sticking up* for a man like that. I told her that the right to a fair trial is what makes this country great, in case she'd forgotten, and oh, she didn't like that. Not one bit.'

I didn't know what to say; I wasn't sure if she was about to cry.

'I'm sorry,' she went on, 'it's just, yeah. Bad night, that's all. I guess you wouldn't understand … It's not easy where I come from, you know? I feel like I have to fight twice as hard as everybody else just to get anywhere, but all I get is crap for even trying.'

I nodded stiffly.

The tyres rumbled, the radio played on to itself, and all I could see littered on the grey road ahead was fire, those naked breasts, a tattooed lad drinking milk from the bottle, a young girl's body, broken on the tracks, a million dead fish floating limply under toxic algae, and Jenny's smile, lost to the years, all swelling against the walls in my chest, pounding, growing until, before I could stop it from happening, it happened.

'I'm recently divorced. I didn't go to Eton. In fact, I left school without a single qualification. I was born in St Ann's, I grew up in Cotgrave, and I was convicted of conspiracy to defraud in 1983, a few weeks after my eighteenth birthday.'

Catharsis by guilt.

An overwhelming deluge of truth, the whole truth, and nothing but.

Still the tyres rumbled, and the radio played on to itself, and slowly, very slowly, Zara turned to face me.

'You … Wait, *what*?' She adjusted her glasses, clearly only just noticing the scuff marks across my head, the thin darkness growing around my eye. 'I don't get it.'

'It's not a joke.' I kept my eyes on the road, which suddenly seemed a lot clearer; when I switched lanes to overtake a lorry, the car manoeuvred as if it were a great deal lighter. 'I'd appreciate it if you kept that between us, it's not something I'm prone to shouting about, you understand?'

I could feel her blinking up at me, waiting for a punchline that wasn't on the horizon. 'Which … which part?'

'All of it.'

'So, you didn't go to Eton, but everybody seems to think you did?'

'Assumptions, mostly. I suspect there are plenty of Old Etonians who have never been near the school.'

'You were born in *St Ann's*, you grew up in *that* village, and you failed to mention that yesterday, or at any point over the past week?' Her voice was getting stronger now; wilder, almost.

'It's my personal business, and I keep it that way.'

'Hold on!' she blurted. 'You're a *convicted criminal*?'

'Conspiracy to defraud, 1983. Suspended sentence.'

'But you're *silk*! I didn't even think that was possible!' She fell quiet then and stayed that way for a couple of minutes. 'Why are you telling me this?'

I wasn't sure. You'd be surprised what punishments people will seek, I thought, quoting my own words.

'Because you shouldn't be entertaining the idea that your background will affect your future. Only you, and your actions from this moment, can do that. You have to fight hard to get anywhere? Then fight hard! Do whatever you have to do. There's nothing holding you back except for yourself.'

It sounded good before I said it – I thought so anyway – but didn't have quite the impact I was aiming for.

'With all due respect, Mr Rook, you've hardly been open about your background. In fact, it looks like you've mostly made it this far by being dishonest.' She had a point, and it tossed another weighty stone back into my gut. 'Conspiracy to defraud? What the hell did you do?'

It was something I hadn't spoken of for many years, but, as any cross-examiner worth his wig ought to know, once there has been a glimpse of a guilty man's truth, the rest usually follows. A copper in the Met once told me that was why so many thrillers end with the bad guy's self-incriminating monologue; by nature, we are storytellers all.

'I had a lot of shit jobs in the years between losing Mam and becoming a barrister,' I told her, and in my accent, as in my dialogue, I could hear myself slipping into the past. 'One of them was for a company testing fruit machines in the early eighties, making sure every machine was paying out the required eighty per cent. Course, it would've taken forever to do that with coins, so the fronts of the machines were opened up, and I just had to sit there all day, clicking up credits on the meter by pushing a metal wire that lay across the coin chute.

'It was slow work, so I went home and drilled a hole into a ten-pence piece, tied a fishing line to it, dangled it into the slot until it hit the wire, and it clocked up a credit. I lifted it back out, dropped it in again, and sure enough, it worked. So, I told the boss to shove it, and spent the next year travelling the Midlands, emptying machines in every pub I came across.'

In the complete silence that followed I glanced to the left, anxious, and saw that her jaw had gone slack.

'You robbed *fruit machines*?'

'Regrettably, I did, until an undercover officer nicked me in Southwell. Wasn't easy trying to run with a couple of hundred quid's worth of ten-pence coins in my pockets, I can tell you.'

And then she did something I hadn't been expecting; she laughed, and laughed hard, slamming her palms on the dashboard.

'I'm sorry!' she panted, wiping her eyes under her glasses. 'I am, but it's hardly Ronnie Biggs, is it?'

A sting of humiliation, but then I, too, found myself grinning like a fool in spite of myself. 'I didn't say I was proud of it, did I? Besides, I was only eighteen, I didn't have any O levels, what did you expect?'

'I don't bloody know!' she crowed, 'I thought you were about to let me in on some *Ocean's Eleven* sort of heist or something, not *fruit machines*!'

'I made a fair few grand from it, I'll have you know! Problem was, I couldn't keep my mouth shut. I let a few blokes in on the secret, who passed it on to a few more, and by the time I was nicked, there was a whole network I'd never met robbing thousands across the country. Hence, conspiracy to defraud. I had my sentence suspended on account of my age, and the rest were banged up at HMP Nottingham.'

Her laugh faded, but she was still shaking her head in utter disbelief.

'That's mad. Like, actually *mad*. Was that the worst job you've had then, testing fruit machines all day? It doesn't sound so bad.'

'The worst?' I cried. 'God no! Just before that I spent an especially hot summer scrubbing the festering bins out behind restaurants. That has to make the top three.'

'*Bins?*' She waved it off with both hands. 'You should try working a few pubs on the student circuit during freshers' week, then you'd see some real filth.'

'I was a fireman once,' I recalled, mentally thumbing through the back pages of a book I'd left long closed.

'You weren't!'

'I bloody well was,' I said. 'Times were different then. A three-month residential training course was all it took, although I didn't actually see a blaze before, ironically, I was fired.'

'Fish factory in Hull,' she countered. 'Mopping up the guts for fourteen hours a day. I reckon that's got you beat.'

'No chance. Try a coal mine in 1981. Dust in your eyes and your lungs, nearly two miles underground. Read 'em and weep, Rookie.'

'All right,' she sighed. 'You've got me there.'

She turned to face the window once more, but I caught her smiling back to herself in the wing mirror, and then, in the rear-view, I caught myself smiling, too.

I might have looked like I hadn't slept for scrapping but felt like I'd lost fifty pounds of baggage.

In fact, it seemed like the first time I recognised myself in as long as I could remember.

21

I left Zara at the cramped, overcrowded house she shared in Brixton, where kids were sitting outside smoking, dressed in the paisley linen garb of backpackers, despite it being a Thursday afternoon. It reminded me of the homeless crowd at the Bullring in the eighties.

I told her to take tomorrow off, to rest, and then come back fresh on Monday. Still painfully hung-over, she seemed grateful for the offer.

I planned to make the trip into chambers as brief as possible, drawn by the thought of my own bed waiting nearby, so I raced the stairs up to the fourth floor, pretending not to see Percy hailing me from the clerks' room below, and blundered into Rupert's office.

It proved a total waste of energy.

The latch had barely caught behind me when a brusque knock rattled the door, bouncing it back open, and Charles Stein pushed his head in through the gap. From his desperate panting, I could only assume that he'd been at my heel up every flight.

'Something wrong with your phone, Rook?' he wheezed, eyes on my tattered golf shoes.

'At least fifty things I can think of,' I said, collapsing into my usual wingback, and pulled the ridiculously dated flip phone out of my pocket for effect.

Straight faces all round. 'Well, I need a word after you're done here with Mr Stubbs, if it isn't *too much* trouble.'

Rupert was standing by the windows, dressed in a bow tie and polka-dot braces, which he pulled at with both thumbs while watching me down his strong nose. 'Might I ask what it's about?'

'Certainly!' Stein said, clearly hoping he might, and pushed his way into the office, closing the door behind him. 'Perhaps you'll be able to offer some outside opinion on whether or not I'm being unreasonable here.'

'By all means,' Rupert said drily, welcoming him into the room with a sweep of his arm.

In the emerald lamplight, Stein looked almost as rough as I felt, his characteristically slick chestnut hair frayed, tie hanging lower than usual over his enormous gut. 'Did you know already, Rook? Tell me you didn't know before you roped me into this.'

I shrugged, batting back and forth between the two of them. 'Know what?'

'Am I right to assume,' Rupert interjected, beginning to pace in his brogues, 'that this is regarding the fraud case you are working on together?'

'*Together?*' Stein raised his eyebrows. 'The generosity, our newest silk, inviting me onto this train wreck! Twenty-eight solicitors accused of systematic fraud, of robbing the legal aid fund blind, and yet they can't even prove between themselves whether half of their clients exist, let alone account for the hundreds of thousands of hours they've billed them for. The summaries alone come to 150 pages of evidence!'

'Summaries I produced out of seventeen tonnes of paper-work,' I reminded him. 'You're welcome to start over, if it doesn't meet your high standard, of course.'

'Don't be facetious,' Rupert rebuked, and Stein pursed his lips.

'Did you know about the mask?'

I glanced into the corner; Rupert's full-bottomed wig stared back at me, always judging.

'Mask?' Rupert asked. 'What mask?'

Stein was carrying a briefcase of black leather and brass fittings, which he now swung up onto Rupert's spotless desk, opening the latches with a fast double-click, as if he was loading a shotgun pointed at my skull.

'Eight days I've found so far,' he replied, parting the case. 'Eight days on which our client, the first defendant, has billed the legal aid fund for working in excess of twenty-four hours per day!'

Rupert frowned. 'That's prima facie impossible, of course.'

'Oh, you'd think so, wouldn't you?'

Rupert shrugged, catching my eye, as I realised what Stein was reaching for inside his briefcase. Sure enough, out came the cardboard contraption hanging limply from its elastic bands, the same mask I'd already advised the client to destroy and never show to another living person.

Rupert leaned over his desk, palms flat on the walnut, frowning harder still. 'This is a mask?'

'Not just any mask!' Stein cried. 'Oh no, what you behold is a feat of both engineering and sheer physics! With this contraption, our client intends on showing the court that he can split his vision down the middle, and read two sets of documents simultaneously!'

He pushed the mask up to his face, his Hugo Boss suit swinging out madly from underneath it, and if it had been anywhere else, at any other time, I might have burst out laughing. When he pulled it away, however, and tossed it back into the briefcase, I found all eyes turning on me, and not a trace of humour in sight.

'I have already *strongly* advised the client *not* to present that as evidence,' I tried. 'At least you got the bloody thing away from him.'

'Oh, no need to worry about that, Rook! He told me I could *keep* it! Said he'd just make another, and it was really no problem at all!'

'Be fair now! You know that we can only advise our client, and if he wants to go ahead and use that as his defence, then it's his decision!'

'Well, next time you need a junior,' Stein snapped, shutting the briefcase, 'perhaps you ought to let them in on the full extent of the case's failings beforehand! Speaking of which, Barnes *is* supposed to be *my* pupil, is she not? It'd be nice to actually see her one of these days, as I could really use a hand with this mess, while you're off doing ... whatever it is you're doing!'

'Don't worry about that,' I said. 'I have total confidence in your performance. I'd say we have our best man on the job.'

'There's a reason nobody wants to work with you, Rook,' he said, and he was still shaking his head and muttering under his breath when he slammed the door behind him, quaking the books on the nearest shelves.

Once he'd gone – footsteps stomping off towards the clerks' room downstairs, for what would undoubtedly be another round of furious protests – Rupert let out a long, pensive sigh.

'Is there any particular motive for torching every bridge available to you at the moment?'

I shrugged, a cornered schoolboy once more, and he retired into the chair behind his desk, an instant warning; Rupert rarely sat down to talk, except in the gravest of situations.

'You have another, far greater problem than that of Charles Stein, and it has forced me into something of a quandary.'

'Which one?'

'Theodore Bowen.'

Ted. Of course.

In the ever-mounting catalogue of shit I had to handle, I'd inadvertently let that slide to the very bottom.

I groaned and squeezed my eyes between forefinger and thumb. 'Has he gone to Bar Standards?'

'Not yet he hasn't, though I suspect it's a near inevitability ...' He sounded positively furious at my total lack of surprise. 'Did you intend to let me know about this?'

'There's nothing to tell.'

'You assaulted him in broad daylight?'

'Assaulted?' I slammed my fists down against my lap. 'Please! He has no evidence, does he? It's his word against mine, and I'm pretty sure that he'd already been drinking on the morning in question. What's he going to do about it, *really*?'

He didn't answer immediately, and I could feel my years peeling away, stripping me back to a younger man.

'It will do neither you nor chambers any good to have the whole of the Criminal Bar learn about your past,' he said. 'Do you really wish for all and sundry to know about your homeless years? Your criminal record?'

Somewhere deep inside, that hurt. 'It was all declared to my Inn years ago, and, with all due respect, that's a dirty move – you knew the score when you gave me pupillage.'

'Pupillage with a condition,' he said. 'The condition that you leave your past behind, and become the best you could be.'

'And I did. I have.'

'Yet here we are, twenty-three years on … You think I don't know why you took this case? The client knows something, doesn't he? Something you've kept close to your chest …'

I didn't respond, and so he leaned further across the desk, scrutinising my face in the light.

'Is that a black eye forming?'

'Fucking Bowen!' I barked, straightening up. 'Sneaking around like a dirty little snake, going tit for tat. He's a grown man for Christ's sake!'

'As are you! Perhaps you ought to remember that, and start getting your act together, Elliot. I'm sure an apology wouldn't go amiss for starters.'

'An apology? If he really has a problem with me, then he's more than welcome to say it to my face and take me on any time, anywhere.'

'Then this might just be the perfect opportunity,' he replied curtly. 'Your murder at the Bailey. Bowen will be junior on the prosecution.'

'The CPS must really be struggling for advocates if they're hiring him for outside counsel again, considering the mess he made of their last trial! How'd he even manage to get this?'

'A favour from the leading counsel, I'd imagine.'

This piqued my interest. 'Why? Who's leading him?'

'Harlan Garrick, with Merton Pike presiding.'

'Brilliant,' I muttered. 'As if this couldn't get any better ...'

He nodded solemnly, smoothed his shirt with both hands, and spun his chair to the window. The light was falling fast there, smothered by a thick grey cloud that blurred the line between sky and London granite.

'Don't go back up there before the trial,' he said. 'Whatever you've been doing, leave it behind. Go home and spend the next week preparing as you ought to, as I taught you to do, and then win the case. Win it, and leave all this where it belongs. In the past.'

22

Gloucester Place is a lengthy stretch of classic London town houses in Marylebone, NW1, four blocks from Baker Street Station and, beyond that, Madame Tussauds, Regent's Park and London Zoo.

Its close proximity to tourist town meant that the twenty-minute journey to chambers would, more often than not, take me at least an hour whether I faced the crowds on the Underground or the queues on the road. I preferred to drive into work, but my car would often have to spend the night on Chancery Lane while I dried out on the Tube home.

Each Marylebone town house was a perfect reprint of its nondescript neighbour, with six neat windows rising up to the third floor in pairs, separated from the pavement by black, spiked iron fencing, and steps leading down below street level.

That's where I lived, in a rented studio flat basement.

In the year of doing so, I'd made not a single impression on the decor of the bedroom–kitchen–living area, nor the cupboard-sized bathroom at the rear. No frames hung from the walls, no rugs brightened the faded carpet. It stank of recent divorce, from the cardboard toilet-roll tubes and empty cans of shaving foam mounting by the toilet – seat almost always upright – to the muddle of whites and darks in the overflowing clothes basket, and the bare, grotty fridge, containing only a few beers, a half-bottle of imitation ketchup, and a jar of English mustard.

I didn't have a wardrobe, but the free-standing garment rack I'd bought for a tenner from Argos had started to bow under the weight of my extra-large shirts, suits and sweaters; the rest hadn't fitted me since the millennium, but I liked to tell myself that they might. The dozens of boxes of paperwork made my office seem bare by comparison.

This was all I had. I'd gone into my marriage with nothing; it was only proper I'd come out of it the same.

I went straight there after leaving chambers and collapsed like a deadweight onto the futon; ordered a kebab from the Istanbul Grill down the road and stared blankly at the television until its busy light faded into nothing.

That was the first evening I had the dream, which would recur every night until the trial.

In it, I was lost. Stumbling through impossible darkness, using only my hands, my sense of touch, to guide me. I could feel rock on either side, worn smooth by the thin flow of freezing cold water that rolled across its face without direction, and I groped stalactites that hung from above. Somehow, despite the running water on the walls, the floor was always dry, the smell of dust and raw iron inescapable.

A distant feminine scream rebounded from every surface and I tried to hurry towards it, but when I moved my hands down I felt a sack of stone dust tied to my waist, holding me back, impossible to lose.

On and on I staggered blindly, legs like shackles, for what seemed to be hours in that illogical sense of time beyond consciousness, until the scream led me towards a glimpse of white-blue light coming from round a final corner.

Thousands of black motes hung perfectly static there, clouding the beam, as if time had now stopped altogether.

But it was never The Girl I found there.

It was Aidan Barber, his face still young but smudged, warped at the edges by my own failing memory; a lamp glaring into my eyes from the top of his head.

We stood in silence – the utter, damp silence of the deep underground – until a single trickle of blood came rolling down thick as syrup between his eyes, and he asked a question, which was more of a sensation than actual sound.

'Where were you, mate?'

And then I woke, and had to get a cold beer to wash the taste of thirty-year-old soot out from the cracks between my teeth.

I'd ended the meeting with Rupert by reluctantly giving responsibility for Zara back to Stein to help with the fraud preparation, and so I spent almost all of the next week at home away from chambers in something of a mental slough, trying to organise my thoughts, preparing for what was to come, and hiding what had quickly developed into an obvious black eye.

There's a great deal of work involved in a Crown Court trial, especially for the defence.

Prosecutors are often able to work like session musicians, turning up and plugging in, sometimes only receiving the brief on the first morning of the trial. I suspected, however, that Bowen might just find the time to ensure that this would be something of a nail in my coffin, especially with Harlan Garrick QC at the prosecution's helm.

Garrick, and my great defeat of 2012.

He hadn't been silk back then, but it was a big case, and I thought I had it in the bag before it ever started.

I didn't.

I was acting for Stephen Stilwell – yes, *that one* – *Match of the Day*'s golden boy of the time, who had woken up one Sunday morning with a severe hangover, and a charge of grievous bodily harm.

The victim, a retired police officer, was blinded in one eye. He claimed that my client had attacked him with a bottle over an autograph request outside a nightclub in Soho.

My client accepted that, yes, there *had* been a confrontation, but the bottle was dropped by an onlooker in the chaos, and the victim's injuries were sustained after drunkenly falling face first into the glass.

It almost came down to a doomed dispute between the statement of a humble former officer and that of the drunken, overpaid premiership striker, but I had a surprise witness.

Not merely a bystander, but a Baptist reverend from the church across the road, who had seen the entire incident, and whose independent statement corroborated that of my defendant to the absolute letter.

'Oh, heaven must have sent you, honey,' I sang to myself on the way into the courtroom.

I had to give it to Garrick. He did such an expertly ruthless job of dismantling my holy witness – who, it turned out, was a season ticket holder for the defendant's team, and regularly wore their colours beneath his cassock – that the jury took no more than ten minutes to find my man guilty.

I hadn't faced Garrick since, but I did hear it that the client in question had turned to peddling heroin since his release from prison, unable to slot neatly back onto the football pitch.

It was Saturday night when I opened my laptop and punched Detective Chief Superintendent John DeWitt into the search engine.

I had *Songs of Leonard Cohen* growling from the record player, and the gravelly, brooding tone was the perfect mixer for a few otherwise neat drinks. I cooked myself dinner – or rather, poured baked beans onto white, heavily buttered toast, with half a block of Cheddar melted in the mix – and washed it down with warm, potent, corner-shop whiskey.

I'd been thinking about DeWitt a lot, and it wasn't just his heavy-handed tactics that were bugging me. What was an esteemed DCS doing patrolling the streets of the city like an average beat copper in the early hours of a Thursday morning?

There wasn't a great deal to find online about DeWitt, and I knew that Zara would've been better at the task, young, adept and computer-literate as she was.

Citations throughout BBC News placed him in Sheffield until around five years ago. I remembered his biggest case well, as it turned out. The grim cause célèbre of '99, it was the racially motivated murder of a fourteen-year-old stabbed to death by a gang of white youths in broad daylight in the centre of the city. Notorious as the killing itself had been, its investigation was infamously botched from the start, and highlighted massive failings in the South Yorkshire Police's handling of witnesses and suspects, in that grey area of slow change between Stephen Lawrence and the Black Lives Matter movement.

Only one detective had risen above the controversial shit-storm, and spent five years single-handedly hunting every one of the killers down.

Far from the common plod, it was quickly apparent that DeWitt was a fierce, old-school copper, sharp as flint and hard as stone. The Gene Hunt of our time. I could just picture him leathering a few crooks where the bruises wouldn't show, and it came as little surprise to read that he'd been cleared in several unspecified misconduct hearings around that time, right before finding himself relocated to Nottingham. He was younger in the photographs they had online, but still rocked the moustache with its pure kicking-down-doors, seventies-detective vibe.

Sean was probably right, I thought. Ours would almost certainly turn out to be a hell of a day in court.

He had no Twitter, Facebook or social media presence whatsoever, which wasn't unusual for man of his age, particularly one of the law. I hadn't had a Facebook profile since the one I'd been roped into sharing, in true middle-aged style, with Jenny – Elliot and Jennifer Rook – and that had been promptly deleted after the first crazed members of the public read my name in the papers and sought me out there.

HOW CAN YOU SLEEP AT NIGHT DEFENDING THAT PIECE OF SHIT? SCUM!

Deleted.

Once I'd found all I could on DeWitt, which wasn't a great deal, and after the Internet had got me well and truly lost in stories of a South African man with the same name, I held my fingertips stiffly over the keyboard, preparing for my next step.

I was suddenly hesitant. Paranoid about IP trackers, cookies and whatever else might be warehousing my searches in those surreptitious government databases. I relocated a couple of metre or so from the futon to the kitchen worktop, sat beside the sink, opened the window there, lit a fag, poured another drink, and blew the smoke out and up onto the pavement of Gloucester Place, clouding the shoes of occasional passers-by.

When I eventually typed the brothel madam's words into the browser's search engine, clamping the cigarette tightly between my teeth, it took only a millisecond to return its top result.

Red Sheets: adult service provider, directory, webcam, movies and more.

'Here we go,' I muttered to myself.

With one final, furtive glance up to the empty pavement, the moonless sky beyond, I clicked on the only available link. Enter.

Inside, there was a catalogue of women organised by thumbnail photographs. A few actually showed faces, captured from slightly above the head and doused in soft lighting, smoothening the skin and brightening the eyes, but the majority were snapshots of naked breasts in every colour, size and degree of maturity imaginable. Usernames accompanied the images, ranging from the likes of CzechMaria, 25, and JuicyKate, 19, up to the more blush-inducing SluttyGrandma, 67. I narrowed the field down to the Midlands, and began to work through the seventy-odd results.

Each escort was rated by Field Reports, starting with pre-set options – out-call or in-call, time, cost, value for money, accurate representation, etc. – and almost always including *good English* as a positive attribute, highlighting a running theme in the girls.

I trawled through every review, hoping against hope that I'd stumble across one left by Billy, as if it could all have been so simple, but the users were anonymous, the reviewing process vague. I had to google acronyms such as OWO and CIM to understand what the clientele had been paying extra for, and none brought me closer to whatever answers I was looking for.

My initial apprehension soon gave way to a deeply shameful sense of arousal, fuelled by the drink and the dozens upon dozens of vulgar, pornographic images, until I came out the other side, entirely desensitised by the overwhelming amount of bare flesh available to order at the click of a button. I wondered if that was how psychopaths viewed the human form, a menu of meat of varying shades and sizes.

Everything adapts, I reasoned, even the oldest profession on the planet.

Leonard Cohen went from 'So Long, Marianne' to 'Hey, That's No Way to Say Goodbye', and, alongside those bodies, his tales of loneliness and loss took my mind to forfeitures and hurt.

There was a time when I was reasonably good at sex. I'm sure there was. There are memories, distant now, of *moderate* athleticism between the sheets; whole days lost in bed with scrapes on my shoulders, the excitement and intimidation of those exploratory years when there were still *firsts* left to be had.

At some point – perhaps slowly over the years, one night at a time, or maybe in a sudden exodus, but almost certainly behind my back – my prime had been left behind. Like my denial of cigarettes, and how I'd assured myself that I only enjoyed an occasional smoke, it was much too late when I faced facts and admitted that I had in fact been a smoker for years, and my lungs were likely blackened beyond saving.

I continued my research, as I kept calling it in my head, for another half an hour or so, but it was useless. The website operated with total anonymity.

At least, it did to any member of the public, but to the police?

I stumbled to my coat, which had been slumped over the garment rail for almost two whole days, and rummaged through the pockets, ignoring the brief sting of cold metal as the abandoned gold ring brushed across my hand.

The card was still in there. It took almost two minutes for him to answer.

'Hullo?' He sounded half asleep, and I realised I should've checked the time before ringing.

'Sean? It's Elliot.'

'Whu ...? Rook?' A long, tired groan. 'It's nearly half eleven, mate, and the kids –' He held the phone away, covering the mouthpiece with one hand, but I could still hear his snappy, impatient replies. '*No, it's just work ... No. No, I know, I'm ... Yeah, I know they're in bed! ... Will you? ... Yeah, but ... You know what, Trace, will you get off my fucking back?*' He cleared his throat, removed his hand from the mouthpiece. 'Look, I really can't talk now, the kids are in bed and Tracey's up for work in five hours.'

'I just wanted to ask if you'd heard of Red Sheets.'

He sighed, and it crackled through the speaker. 'Just, give me a sec, will you?'

I heard his feet bumping along a landing and down a flight of stairs, a door unlocking, opening, the spark of a lighter close to the phone, a deep inhalation, and another sigh.

'Escort agency. Some seedy website for whores and pervs. Why d'you ask?'

'Did you ever find evidence of Billy using it?'

'Barber?' I pictured him shrugging, standing at the door of Ralph Dickinson's old house, most likely in nothing more than underwear, but quite possibly pyjamas, menthol in his right hand, phone in the left. 'I wouldn't know, but the techs analysed his phone, and if it had been relevant, you'd have heard about it.'

'You reckon you can find out for me? Maybe take another crack at it?'

'What the hell d'you want me to do, Rook?' He was considerably less chirpy near the witching hour. 'I'm not bloody MI5.'

'Come on, just do me a favour. Talk to the analysts, see if they had anything to say.'

I could almost hear his thought pattern through the phone, the buzzing of synapses, lured, as I so often was, by the prospect of a mystery.

'I suppose I could have a word with the Kerb Crawling Taskforce, see if they have a list or something, or if he's ever popped up on their radar.'

'Thanks, Sean, that'd be a big help. I owe you a drink.'

'Yeah, yeah …' he sighed. 'I'd better get off, Tracey's going to go through the fucking roof. I'll let you know if I hear anything.'

'Cheers again, appreciate it, mate.'

'In a bit, Rook.'

And just as he rang off, I heard what must've been Tracey's shrill voice rising from the background, gearing up for what would inevitably be a blazing row. I felt bad, but that's the way it went sometimes.

Marriage was complicated, after all.

23

I didn't see Billy again until the end of the week.

I was back in Belmarsh, beyond the scanners and sliding bars, three days before the trial.

Alone, together, he was eyeing the yellowing ghost of the shadow upon my brow.

'Hear you've been to see my missus,' he said. 'She belt you one or what?'

'No, I'm afraid she didn't have that pleasure.'

'Wouldn't put it past her.'

'Really?' I laid my paper and pens out on the table between us. 'She didn't strike me as the type.'

'Harder than she looks, our Sarah.'

'I suppose she'd have to be, wouldn't she? Living with you.'

The flash across the dark of his eyes told me he didn't like that. I clicked my ballpoint into life.

'Get into many punch-ups with the old lady, do you?'

I actually heard his jaw click from across the room while his skull kicked off to the left. 'You married, Rook?'

I didn't answer, just closed my naked left fist, which must've said it all.

'Didn't think so,' he jeered. 'I'll tell you one thing. It's not all happy families all the time. Marriage is –'

'Complicated? Yeah, I heard. Is that why you spend your nights with prostitutes?'

He leaned back, summing me up through narrowed eyes, and folded his hands into boulders beneath his chin.

I caught myself checking that the light on the overhead camera was still blinking, for reassurance. We'd tried talking and the professional approach had got me nowhere. It was time to prod the bull, time to force his hand.

'Migrant girls, aren't they? Seems a bit hypocritical for a man of your principles. Is that where you went that night, Billy? Frightened your mates might kick you out of the Midlands Fascist Brigade if they find out about it?'

He was glaring now. 'You've been busy,' he growled. 'Who you been speaking to?'

'I've had some time to kill,' I shrugged, 'and since you're not going to enlighten me on what actually happened that night, why don't I tell you a story, and then you can let me know what you think about it?'

He only stared, so I went on.

'It was Good Friday, and you were feeling sorry for yourself after getting dropped by an Asian lad half your age in the city centre. Must've been embarrassing, showing your age like that with nobody there to back you up, so you decided to go and lose some steam at the Welfare, where you sank pints for another six hours or so. Maybe you saw The Girl come in and it got you in the mood, maybe not. She *was* a looker. Maybe you just had some anger to take out on an immigrant, so you staggered to a pop-up brothel in Cotgrave run by Albanians. You hang out with lads half your age, so it only makes sense that they would've introduced you to the place through an online escort directory.

190

'But fourteen hours of drinking didn't do your stamina any favours, did it? I reckon you couldn't perform. Frankly, I think you couldn't get it up.'

He had a strange, bulging look to his scattered features, lost between disbelief and fury, but I was on a roll and wouldn't be stopped. It was my turn to talk.

'By then you must've been feeling totally humiliated. Your plan to relieve some stress had only gone and backfired in the worst possible way, so you started throwing your weight around. Maybe you turned your hand to whichever woman had shown you up, and that got you in a scuffle with the big bastard running the show, and he sent you stumbling home bloody and worse for wear.

'Now you've got two knockouts in one day, *and* a public show of impotence, quite literally *under your belt*. So much for a quiet start to the bank holiday weekend. I'm not surprised you went home and burned your clothes in shame after all that. Must've been a genuine eye-opener for you. One of those pivotal moments when it really hits home, just how *old* and *useless* you've become. How am I doing?'

I found myself tensing against the back of the chair, ready for whatever response he was about to launch at me over the table.

As it turned out, he only smirked.

'I reckon you ought to write for the *Evening Post*, making up stories like that.'

'Yes? You could always be my fact checker. Fill in a few of the blanks?'

'Here's a fact for you to write down, fat prick. I *always* get it up. End of story.'

A few teeth on show, but he wasn't biting yet. 'What did happen then?'

He blinked a level stare. 'Maybe I just went for a wander. You thought about that?'

'In a storm, after fourteen hours of drinking? Pull the other one, Billy. You've got a nice little home, a family waiting for you. Most blokes would be thankful for that.' Present company included, I thought. 'Why the disappearing acts all the time?'

He lifted one shoulder in an evasive half-shrug. 'You're gonna talk to me about disappearing? Surprised you could still find the place after all this fucking time. How was that, going back as the big-time barrister? Not quite paved with gold up there, is it?'

'No,' I said, 'but it was all right. Saw the new country park.'

'Oh yeah,' he snorted, 'that'll put food on the table.'

'Or beer in your stomach?' I countered. 'Fags in your pocket?'

'Another fucking pie in your stomach?'

I actually felt a small smile at one side of my mouth. 'It's good for the area, isn't it? All that new housing they're putting up on the pitheads, tearing up the brownfield sites. You must be able to see progress in that?'

He drew his brows together, nostrils flaring. 'That's right. All that new housing, and who do you reckon is gonna get it handed to them? The ones who don't contribute a penny to our country or its economy, that's who.'

'And what've you been doing for work lately, Billy? Quite the tic you've got these days. You sure you haven't been dipping into your own stock over the years?'

'No idea what you're on about,' he muttered, instinctively scrubbing the heel of one hand up against his nose.

'Must be difficult to keep a roof over your head, even without all those CSA payments, on just a few dribs and drabs of labouring. I'd guess most of your time has been spent dealing, or else sponging off the taxpayer, and yet you've got the nerve to sit there and begrudge genuine refugees? All right, so they closed the pit, but they didn't bomb the village. You had options. You still do.'

'The taxpayer,' he smirked. 'Remind me, how does legal aid work again?' He had a point. Legal aid had been slashed, but I'd still made a decent living from it for a long time. 'At the end of the day, we're not too different, Rook. The taxpayer feeds us, clothes us and puts us both in the courtroom. You're going to sit there, in your fucking suit, and give me a hard time about working for a living? Where the fuck was you in '84?'

France? West Germany? Spain? I wasn't sure.

'It all came down to a choice,' he growled. 'Stick with the union and have some pride, or be a fucking scab, but a scab with food on the table. They spat on me, you know that? This, here –' he turned his head and pressed one finger against the white scar of a long-faded gash above the right ear – 'that was a brick, chucked at me from the line by my own uncle. And how did we get thanked for standing by the government? Which side was rewarded, after families had torn themselves apart? We all ended up in the same fucking place.'

His eyes dimmed.

'They're flooded now,' he said. 'Thousands upon thousands of tonnes of fine, usable coal given back to the ground.

Thousands of hard-working blokes suddenly without work, and that didn't leave many options. So yeah, I moved a bit of gear to make ends meet for a while. That makes *me* the criminal, while Thatcher's got a statue up in Westminster … You've got no fucking idea what it's like to be there, Rook. Without work, a man has to force himself to be something, even if it's the something everyone else expects him to be, or else he's nothing at all.'

He fell quiet, and I realised I was fidgeting; I knew what it took to hold on to an image or risk losing everything. If anything, I argued to myself, I'd have only worsened the problem by sticking around, one more on the register when their world came crumbling down.

'Heard about your mam,' I said, surprising myself. 'Jan was always good to me.'

'You were round ours enough, weren't you? More than I was, most of the time.'

I shrugged. 'All I had at home were three little sisters who were more grown up than I was. It was nice, having somewhere to go and get tea cooked for me after school. Proper tea. Corned beef hash. Fried egg and chips. Liver and onions …' My mouth began to salivate at the thought of food that would undoubtedly have made a man like Percy's stomach turn, had he known it existed. 'Christ, I haven't had a fish-finger sarnie for years. Used to wind your brother up something chronic that you could fit four fish fingers from top to bottom, but always needed a fifth along the edge to fill the bread. He used to say that he –'

'That he was going to write to Birds Eye and tell 'em to make them an inch bloody longer,' he nodded. 'Never did get round to it.'

'Shame. That captain needed knocking down a peg or two.'

He almost grinned. 'You should try the dog shit they serve in here. It'd do that belly of yours better than any Atkins crap. Saying that, you must be used to it, living in London. Surprised you're not shitting through the eye of a needle.'

'Why's that?'

'Well, it's like Little Asia now, isn't it? I hear they've got shop signs in fucking Arabic over in the East End.'

'Did you read that on the Internet?' Of course, I thought, you've never left Nottinghamshire for anything but Her Majesty. 'Does it honestly bother you? Bullshit aside, with nobody here to impress, just you and me. Are you really upset about a few shops 130 miles away from your front door?'

'It's worrying that it *doesn't* bother you. How many terror attacks have we had this year? It isn't just the Middle East no more. The holy war's *here*, Rook. It's us, and it's them, and it'll always be that way. Then a Paki gets killed and people act surprised! They pin it on me because, fuck it, that's the easiest thing to do. They tell themselves *I'm* the outsider.'

'Is that why you went for the Nazir lad in Nottingham? You decided to make a stand?'

He shrugged. 'I've got a temper drunk. It was bred into men like us. You can change your voice and dance round in a wig, but you can't change who you are underneath, Rook. We're the sons of drinkers built for darkness. You take an animal's purpose away and what's it got left? We're like foxhounds after the hunting ban, and the breeders are sitting around wondering why the dogs got fed up and bit them in the end.'

We were losing track. *I* was losing track, listening too hard to the client. I had to steer the tone.

'The trial,' I said firmly. 'We need to discuss the prospect of you standing up to provide evidence. It's a chance to defend yourself, to give your side of the story, but the prosecution is going to push your buttons. They're going to do whatever it takes to get a rise out of you, and any sort of rise, like the one we just had, could be fatal.'

'I'm not standing. Just do your job.'

'You know how this is going to go, don't you?'

'I have an idea.'

'First thing Monday morning, security personnel from the prison service are going to transport you to the Central Criminal Court, where you'll be held in a cell until they're ready for you in the dock. The judge will enter and the jury will be sworn, ready for the trial to commence at ten o'clock sharp. The prosecution will give all of their evidence first, and then –'

'You're talking like I've never been on trial before,' he snorted through chemically eroded nostrils.

'This is murder at the Bailey, Billy, and your prosecutor, Harlan Garrick, isn't going to fuck around. He'll bring witness after witness until that jury is convinced of your guilt. Whatever happens –' I leaned closer across the table, banging a finger down with each word – '*do not lose your shit*! No matter what the witnesses say. No matter how far you're pushed. If you throw a tantrum in the dock, if you so much as cast a scowl, it could cost you the rest of your life. If they ask us to be upstanding, I want to see you on your feet with your tie done up to the chin before anybody else in the courtroom. You need to cover as many of those tattoos as you can, and you'd better show my junior the respect she deserves.'

His brow firmed into the usual glare. 'I think you're forgetting who's pulling the strings here, *Counsel*.'

'From here on out it'll be the jury making all the big decisions, and unless you're going to fill me in on what really happened that night, your future is entirely in the hands of those twelve strangers.'

'And your future's in mine,' he snarled.

'That's where you're wrong,' I said calmly. 'I'm not playing this game any more. Do you really think people are going to be bothered about a few empty fruit machines in 1983? You think they're going to lock me up for chinning a couple of guys at the footy?'

'They might be interested to know why one of the two lads that battered you ended up in a fucking wheelchair.'

I held on to my poker face, as if I was keeping it level with both hands, and refused to glance up at the camera. '*You* did that, Billy, all on your own. We just wanted you to scare them.'

'Looked pretty fucking scared to me,' he sneered, 'and you're afraid of me too, otherwise why the fuck would you be doing this?'

'I'm doing this for Aidan,' I snapped, and hearing it out loud like that, I knew it to be true. I felt a glow of pain, surely psychological, flash across the scar on my chest, and rubbed it with one palm.

For the first time he seemed genuinely taken aback.

'He could've run,' I said, standing to collect my untouched papers. 'He could've left me behind when he saw the knife, but he didn't. He never would.'

'W-where you going now?' His voice sounded strangely deflated, eyes following me to the door.

'It's Friday. I'm going to get myself a drink.'

'Yeah?' he nodded. 'Keep a can in the fridge for me. Should be nice and cold a couple of weeks from now.'

'See you in three days, Billy,' I said simply, banging on the door for it to be opened from the other side. 'Three days.'

PART THREE

THE TRIAL

24

For a long time, the Central Criminal Court, more commonly known as the Old Bailey, had seemed as distant to me as the Royal Albert Hall must to an overlooked busker on the street. I'd thought the only way I might end up there would be through a guest appearance inside the dock.

I'd first fallen for the tradition of the place, especially the old courts, during my years at Bar school, when I used to climb through the historic entrance on Newgate Street into the public galleries to watch trials with all the enthusiasm of a film buff in the Hollywood Chinese Theatre. The wigs, the gowns, the powerful orations; it soon became all I had to have.

The newer building's modern courts might've been comfier, more suited to my size, but cramped legs had always seemed a reasonable sacrifice for the timeless allure of the wood-panelled walls and hard oak benches of the original rooms, even though the inkwells and ledgers had long been replaced by microphones and laptops.

Such enduring charisma did little to alleviate my mood on the morning of the trial, however, and as I looked up at the bronze statue of Themis, Lady Justice, atop the Bailey's iconic dome, I wondered which instrument she held out for me. The scales or the sword?

'I thought she wore a blindfold,' Zara said as we passed the fountains beneath her shadow.

'No, no blindfold. It's supposed to be her maidenly form that shows blind impartiality.'

'Huh …' I heard her swallow a rattling bagful of nerves. 'Guess whoever made it hadn't gone out with many real women.'

To our right, a crowd of maybe thirty people had already begun to gather, almost all carrying home-made signs with Asian Lives Matter written in bold red and black. They were only the first of many to come, and Zara kept her face turned pointedly away as we passed.

We left the pale October sunrise there at the main entrance, where it bathed Pomeroy's statue of the Recording Angel, Fortitude and Truth in tones of amber and gold, its famous inscription – *Defend the Children of the Poor and Punish the Wrongdoer* – high above the doors and entered the building.

Inside the Great Hall there was the usual Monday-morning hustle of barristers, solicitors and clerks sidestepping one another in suits and shiny black shoes, arms full of papers, box files and briefs.

Though time and familiarity had got me quite used to the grandeur, I still recognised the buzz radiating from Zara as she cooed over the coloured marble and ornate decor, reading aloud the axioms emblazoned around the frieze.

'"The law of the wise is a fountain of life"; "The welfare of the people is supreme"; "Right lives by law and law subsists by power"; "Poise the cause in justice's equal scales"; "Moses gave unto the people the laws of God"; "London shall have all its ancient rights".'

I pointed out which murals had been added after the Blitz, and the shard of glass left by an IRA car bomb in '73, both preserved as symbols of the resolute laws of our land.

I even thought about taking her to see the underground cells that remained of the Dickensian Newgate Prison, the route known as Dead Man's Walk, but couldn't face that cold, narrow passageway to the gallows this morning. The unsettling sense of doom was already close enough.

New barristers carry their wigs and gowns in bags of blue damask with tasselled draw cords, monogrammed with their initials; a senior junior who has done especially well when being led by a silk may be gifted a red bag monogrammed in gold fabric, with a personal message from the silk written inside. Zara, I noticed, was clutching her blue bag tightly to her chest as if it contained the planet's final source of oxygen and might be snatched away from her at any second.

There are three robing rooms at the Bailey: one for men, one for women and a third for silks. While the new resident Judge Taylor of Southwark Crown Court had recently abolished the distinction between genders, allowing women into the much larger men's robing room, no man had been inside the women's room at the Bailey, where I left Zara, but I understood it to be poky. The silks' room is accessed through a door at the rear of the men's. As a junior, I'd conjured up images of marble fountains, valets and an exclusive champagne bar, so, after finally earning the right to go inside, I was severely disappointed to find only another cramped cupboard strewn with clutter and broken lockers.

I didn't rush in robing.

It mightn't be superhero spandex, but the court dress brings a great responsibility, and I allowed myself the time to neaten the starched white linen bands that hung from my winged collar, to straighten the horsehair wig, now a mottled ivory, that had seen such liberty and loss over the years, and to train the heavy, flowing folds of silk, as black and smooth as crude oil, that draped over my waistcoat and trousers like a cape, swallowing my physique whole. Then I gave myself an extra few minutes to stand in utter silence, to breathe in the mantra I've carried since my early, anxious days.

I was to meet Zara in the canteen, but almost failed to recognise her when I first turned from my place at the counter ten minutes later, cups of tea in hand.

'What do you think?' She approached tentatively, turning slightly on the spot, case papers bundled in the crook of one arm.

'Wow. You look so ... grown up!'

I didn't mean for it to sound patronising, but I wasn't lying. Dressed in an immaculate new suit and wig, she looked both competent and in control, and I felt the strangest flush of paternal pride. She was even wearing actual shoes for once, not boots, though I knew by the soles that they were still lace-up Doc Martens.

'Ugh!' she groaned. 'I emptied my whole bloody overdraft for this and look at me! I look like such a *white wig*!'

'You do not.'

Senior juniors are proud of their yellowing wigs and tattered gowns, which signify experience, while a newly called barrister is often dismissed as a white wig.

'Honestly,' I reassured her, 'you look the part completely. A wig that's half fallen to pieces and ragged gowns might rank well in the quirks of the Bar, but to a jury they only signify an impoverished tramp, and you don't want that for your first day, do you?'

She shrugged, eyes on the floor, and hugged herself with both arms. 'Maybe you should've chosen someone with more experience. I bet I'm going to be the youngest person in the court. I feel like a fraud.'

'Most cases are won and lost on their *facts*. We can only make any sort of difference in the small minority. Results are important, of course, but in the long run, things will always even themselves out. The better barristers will win more cases than they lose, and the poorer will level the statistic. All that's expected of you is to do your very best. Be honest, fair and fearless, and you won't go far wrong.'

I believed that. I still do to this day.

She sighed, checking her reflection in the nearest window, and adjusted her glasses.

'It's like a new pair of Converse, I guess. They never look right without a few scuff marks.'

'Then I'd say that leaves us with only one option ...' I handed her one of the teas and took half of the papers, gave her my best smile, and gestured to the corridor. 'Let's go and earn you some scuff marks, shall we?'

She smiled back, sheepishly, and then we walked side by side through the wooden doors into Court One, the most famous courtroom on the planet.

We were early enough to find a caretaker still polishing the face of the dock, cheerily whistling no particular tune to himself as he brightened the same glass box that had once caged the Kray Twins, the Yorkshire Ripper, Ruth Ellis, Lord Haw-Haw and Ian Huntley to name only a handful.

I was wondering how many convicts had gone on to loathe the smell of that floral polish, forever associating it with the moment they were sentenced, when I bumped straight into Fraser Hayes, our freckled fledgling of an instructing solicitor, who had been crouched low, reading the imprint on the court's oak seats.

'Good morning, Mr Hayes,' I grumbled, managing to catch my sliding papers before they hit the floor.

'"Domine, dirige nos",' he read, jabbing his thumb at the inscription, and gave Zara an anxious smile. 'Who knows what that means, eh?'

'Lord, direct us,' I told him simply, leaving him to take his position behind us.

The Bar was originally the section of the court that divided legal professionals from lay people, and so *passing the Bar* earns the right to step down into the well in front of the dock, where advocates line up to face the judge's bench, the focal point of power, which sits before the royal coat of arms under the court's pediment and grand Corinthian columns. The jury box shares the well, always at a right angle to the dock, along with the witness stand.

The usual players filtered into place beneath the light that poured through the room's glass roof – the stenographer, clerk, judicial assistant and usher – and then in marched Harlan Garrick QC, followed closely by Ted Bowen, both bewigged and lugging the weight of the substantial evidence between them in cardboard boxes.

'Is that Garrick?' Zara whispered as they made their way down into the well.

'Yes,' I sighed. 'That's him.'

He hadn't changed much since our last bout, except, I noticed as he neared, fine grey hairs now circled his entire neckline below the wig, which, incidentally, had gone well beyond frayed yellow, into the territory of deep Dijon mustard. He was still as hatchet-faced as I remembered, with a thin line of a mouth above a sharp chin, and deep-set brown eyes that barely glanced at us on approach. A purist Etonian to the core, rumour had it that he planned on entering politics before his upcoming fiftieth birthday.

Any potential for awkwardness with him was effortlessly overshadowed by Bowen. It was the first time I'd cast eyes on him since our encounter on Chancery Lane, and he wore the scrunched expression of a man confronted with a particularly foul stench.

It took great willpower to curb my urge to floor him for all his underhanded perfidy.

'Morning,' I said coolly as they started to scatter loose papers over their half of our shared counsel's row, marking their territory.

'Your client is almost sixty,' Garrick replied without looking up. 'I don't know why he's bothering to contest this case when he's certain to be convicted and to spend the rest of his miserable life behind bars. At least if he pleads guilty, shows some remorse, he might be out in time to receive his telegram from the Queen, assuming a *miner* has ever lived that long.'

'On the contrary.' I tugged my gown straighter across the curve of my stomach, comforted by the smooth silk between my fingertips, and gritted my teeth. 'He'll be out in time to collect his free bus pass, Garrick, and that's in less than a month.'

'Ha!' Bowen had reddened, voice rising like a missile about to go off in my face. 'Not with your hundred per cent losing record against Harlan! If you truly think that –'

'Silence please!' came the voice of the clerk, quelling the retort and smothering the fuse, and silence fell like a stone. 'All persons who have business before the Queen's justices draw near and give your attendance. God save the Queen.'

We all straightened, Zara with military stiffness, as doors creaked open ahead.

High Court judges – known as Red Judges after their distinctive scarlet robes – are always referred to as Mr or Mrs Justice, and addressed as My Lord or My Lady. It was therefore Mr Justice Judge Merton Pike who took his place in the high-backed perch overlooking the court. A short man, even from that angle, he must've been well into his seventies, with lank white hair peeking from the back of his wig and flushed, ruddy skin around the neck, so it was hard to tell where the uniform ended and the man began.

He gazed languidly over the room, seemingly almost stifling a yawn, and then scratched his stubby nose. 'All right, let's have the defendant in, please.'

I rummaged deep for my game face. The moment had finally come.

In unison, we turned to see Billy rising up into the box, inch by inch, one weighty step at a time, as if he might keep coming and coming until he filled the glass completely, like a shark in a goldfish bowl. Even the dock officers, heavy-set as they were, looked like they might have a struggle on their hands if things were to turn ugly, and Garrick's and Bowen's expressions were those of lifelong sceptics gazing upon the most farcical circus attraction one could imagine. I even heard Garrick mutter something about being done in time for lunch, and Bowen sniggered in response.

Billy didn't look much better in a suit. In fact, the outfit only seemed to draw more focus to the incongruity of the tattoos on his face, neck and fists; the Celtic cross under his eye socket looked brasher than ever, the red of the Templar cross clear as blood against the white of his collar. He eyed each of us in turn through the glass, ending on me, on my wig and robes, with the slightest hint of a smug smile. Arrogant to the end.

'Are you William Barber?' the clerk asked.

'That's me,' Billy nodded, and then sat down with the grace of an anvil.

We followed suit, while Garrick remained on his feet for the usual introductions.

'My Lord,' he said with a slight bow, greasing his nose up early for easy insertion, 'this matter is listed for trial in the case of the Crown against William Barber. I appear for the Crown along with Mr Theodore Bowen. Acting for the defendant is my learned friend Mr Elliot Rook QC, who shall be leading Miss –' a pause, an obvious, pointed glance down at his papers before returning to his seat – 'Miss Zara Barnes.'

It was an intentional, wholly disrespectful move.

Mr Justice Pike nodded and glanced over the sheets of the case file. 'Any preliminary legal issues to deal with, Counsel?'

Already incensed, I only shrugged and shook my head.

'Very well,' he said, 'may we have the jury in please?'

Sixteen people shuffled into the room. Twelve names were called to take their place in the jury box, while the remaining four were dismissed.

I've always found jury selection exciting.

It might be the all-powerful state that brings a charge, but the dispensing of justice lies in the hands of twelve complete strangers, twelve ordinary members of the public, as it has done for nearly a thousand years.

Almost anybody can appear on the panel and cannot be challenged without good cause; a juror working in a relevant sector to the crime, in a fraud case for example, may be challenged by the defence, as might a serving police officer with a liable risk of bias, typically in cases where the defence is alleging a copper is lying. Cases are usually tried near to where they happen, unless there is likely to be an adverse local reaction to it, and before the jury is sworn, there's a questionnaire regarding names, addresses and companies, although chances of conflict of interest are generally less common at the Bailey, where cases tend to be geographically distant.

It's a raffle, a lottery, and yet, for the defendant, those strangers are akin to Peter at the Pearly Gates.

I watched their affirmations closely, trying to gauge what we were up against by noting sex, class and ethnicity, imagining the personal experiences each might have had that would affect every decision they ever made. It made me think, as it always did, of what Shakespeare says in *Measure for Measure*: the jury passing on the prisoner's life may in the sworn twelve have a thief or two guiltier than him they try. I've always believed that.

There were five men and seven women dressed in shirts, sweaters and blouses. Eight of the twelve were white, and more than half were already casting thinly veiled grimaces up into the dock. The Bailey had come a long way since shreds of Dr Crippen's dead wife's skin were passed around the same room on a plate for inspection, but the jurors looked every bit as anxious over what may soon await them.

When they were finally sworn and seated, Judge Pike leaned across the bench to address them.

'The evidence upon which you will decide the outcome of this case is that which will be presented in this court,' he told them. 'You should discuss the case among yourselves, but reject the influence of any media reporting or information obtained from outside of court, including social media. As jurors, you have a collective responsibility to ensure that you all act according to your oath, and if you do any Internet research into this case you will be committing a criminal offence for which you might be jailed.' He nodded to the prosecution. 'Please begin, Mr Garrick.'

I heard Zara exhale, slow and steady as a punctured tyre close to my shoulder, and caught Juror Number 6 lean eagerly forward in her seat, holding her breath, while Number 9 looked sick with nerves already.

The pieces were in place, the chessboard was primed, and Garrick rose with a face of iron resolve to make his opening move.

25

'When you all received your summons to do jury service,' Garrick began, after introducing counsel, 'I'm sure you wondered what case you would end up trying. Would it be burglary? An armed robbery? A major drugs conspiracy, perhaps?

'The single count on the indictment today is one of *murder*. The victim, an unidentified teenage girl of Middle Eastern ethnicity, was strangled and beaten so savagely that her nails were torn from her fingertips, her teeth were broken from her mouth, her legs were fractured, and veins burst under the skin all over her body. She was dumped, completely naked, on a disused railway on the evening of the fourteenth of April, the night paradoxically known as *Good Friday*.'

He gesticulated like a composer before an orchestra, enunciating all the finer, horrible details with both hands.

His words seemed to be having the desired effect; shudders of disgust, dismay and morbid curiosity were rippling across the members of the jury like the waves of an aurora.

'It is the Crown's case that the murderer was William Barber, the defendant you see before you today. Mr Barber has been given the choice as to whether he pleads guilty or not guilty to the crime, and he has pleaded *not guilty*. You must therefore enter this trial assuming that he is an innocent man. We, the prosecution, bring the case, and the burden of proving his guilt rests squarely upon our shoulders. It is my duty to present the evidence, and the facts are entirely a matter for you.

'You'll be guided on the law by Mr Justice Pike, who will instruct you on the technical elements of what defines the crime of *murder*, but as a matter of common sense you may conclude that whoever did the terrible things that led to this poor girl's brutal and frightening death clearly intended to end her life, and indeed did so.

'The prosecution say it was the defendant, William Barber, and that his motives for committing such a horrifying crime stem from an unstable, perverse character that is wholly driven by hatred. He is violent to the point of being unhinged. He *enjoys* violence against women, and he is a fundamental racist who *hates anyone* he regards as non-British.

'Now, we don't know where the victim of this murder was from. We don't even know her name. But we *do* know that her ethnicity – the simple fact that she was not *white* – was sufficient enough for William Barber to hate her.'

He folded his arms and turned his mouth down at the corners.

'But what of it? You may well ask. Barber might have hated the victim, even if only for the colour of her skin, but where's the evidence that he killed her?'

These things Garrick counted out on long, curling fingers:

'She was murdered in a cold and remote place outside the village of Cotgrave in Nottinghamshire. It is a place without amenities or purpose, and yet you will hear evidence, *unchallenged by the defence*, that Barber's mobile phone was in use shortly before the murder, accessing the same

213

cell-site mast that serviced the area in which she was killed. The mast had a range of three miles, and the body was discovered just a mile and a half away from it.

'For reasons we don't know, the victim had gone on the evening of her death to the Welfare Scheme Social Club in the heart of the village. She spent roughly fifteen minutes there, using the facilities on the premises, before leaving and walking towards the scene of her death. A woman called Donna Turner was outside when the victim left the club, but she wasn't alone. William Barber, already heavily inebriated, was also there, smoking.

'When the victim came out and walked into the darkness, Barber turned to Mrs Turner and said –' he held up the sheet of paper as if it were physically soiled, and read – '"What the fuck is that Paki doing in Cotgrave? She'll be lucky to make it through the night!" He then extinguished the cigarette he'd only just lit, abandoned his pint, undrunk, and followed her into the darkness. *Broken, bloodied* fingernails would soon stud the trail from that spot to the scene of the murder.

'Mr Barber wasn't seen again until the following morning, when he was not only witnessed, but actually *photographed*, burning the clothes he'd been wearing in a brazier in his back garden. The clothes were charred beyond being of any evidential value, but the defendant's bathroom was also checked, and showed that in the hours between the death and his arrest, he'd taken a shower!'

Garrick shook his head in disbelief, dropping the paper back onto our row.

'Of course, there may well be perfectly innocent explanations for Mr Barber's actions on that night and in the following morning, and he was given the opportunity to elucidate those in his police interview. Perfectly reasonable questions were asked of him. Where was he on the night of the murder? Why did he have a shower and burn his clothes in the early hours? Why did he walk after the victim, away from his home, into the night?

'And what were his answers to these questions? What reasonable explanations did he offer? Simple, really. He answered "no comment" to every question asked. More than eighty questions, and not one single answer.

'No answers were given, the prosecution say, because Barber had no answers to give, except for the one he kept to himself. He *murdered* that poor girl, and he isn't going to stand up and admit to it. One might say that he has every right to provide no answers. The prosecution bring the case, so let the prosecution prove it. Well, we intend to. It is our duty to prove the case to a standard, and you must be *sure* of guilt before you can convict the defendant.

'We will make you sure of the defendant's guilt. We will leave you with absolutely not a single shred of doubt that William Barber is guilty of murder.'

And then he shuffled his papers, bristling with indignation, and left a heavy silence.

An opening speech by the defence is rare, especially in a murder trial, so I was neither asked nor did I request to make one. Instead, I poured water from a carafe out into glasses for Zara and myself and slid one towards her, but she barely seemed to notice for staring upwards.

I followed her wide, brown eyes up to the public gallery and saw Sarah Barber's face there, white and thin as bone, like a flower dying at the front of the moderate crowd.

What remained of the Barber clan had turned up in force. Declan and Caine, the younger brothers, now both in their late forties, watched with deadpan expressions, dressed in what were undoubtedly their usual courtroom suits and quite possibly the same ones I'd seen at Aidan's funeral in '88. Around them, the same bald, hard, craggy faces were repeated again and again through all the cousins and uncles and extended members of the family.

There was nobody there for the victim.

'With My Lord's leave,' Garrick said, 'I'll now call the Crown's first witness ...'

It was a petite police officer who entered the court in full uniform and walked up to the witness box, bowing her neat blonde bob towards the bench before taking the Bible up in one hand, and speaking with the accent of my home.

'I swear by Almighty God that the evidence I shall give shall be the truth, the whole truth, and nothing but the truth.'

'Thank you,' Garrick smiled, a reptile with toothache, old charmer that he was. 'Could you start by introducing yourself to the court?'

She nodded, rubbing her slight hands across her thighs. 'I'm Police Constable Louise Shepherd of Rushcliffe South Police, stationed at Cotgrave Station, Nottinghamshire.'

'Thank you,' Garrick said once more. 'PC Shepherd, were you on duty on the morning of Saturday 15 April this year?'

'I was.'

'And did you receive the call to go to the disused railway that runs from Cotgrave and beyond Radcliffe-on-Trent?'

'I did.'

'Were you in the company of another officer?'

'Yes. Police Constable Lucas Sharp.'

Garrick nodded. 'And, in your own time, can you tell the court what you encountered upon arriving at the scene?'

'Certainly.' She cleared her throat with a slight cough. 'Do I have the court's permission to refer to my own statement?'

From the bench, Pike turned his weary eyes on me, spreading his hands. 'Does the defence have any objections?'

'No,' I said into the microphone, 'none whatsoever, My Lord. The officer's evidence is all agreed upon. My learned friend can lead her through every word of it if he so chooses.'

'Very well. You may continue, Miss Shepherd.'

Another polite nod, another clearing of the throat, and she did.

'PC Sharp and myself responded to a call made by Mr Harold Kennard, a gentleman who had been walking his dog along the old railway tracks from Radcliffe-on-Trent up towards Polser Brook, a small stream north-west of the village, early on Saturday morning. We arrived at the location at seven thirty-seven, but, because the majority of the track cuts through fields that are inaccessible by vehicle, we had no choice but to park our transport at the nearside of Radcliffe Road and proceed northwards on foot.'

'You were assisted by paramedics?' Garrick asked.

'That's right. The first responder ambulance arrived almost instantaneously, and its crew of two paramedics – Miss Lisa Langley and Mr Mark Merchant – joined Constable Sharp and myself. It took us a further five or six minutes to reach Mr Kennard, at which point the victim was confirmed as deceased on our arrival.'

Garrick was intermittently shifting his gaze between the witness, and any impact she might be having on the jury.

217

'Have you visited the scenes of many murders in your time with the force, Miss Shepherd?'

She crossed her hands over her midriff, expression hardening. 'I've seen three in my nine years. I'm thankful to say that these sorts of crimes are few and far between in our community.'

'But this was a particularly gruesome one, wasn't it?'

'My Lord ...' I climbed wearily to my feet, halting the proceedings. 'I've no objection in principle to evidence being given by my learned friend rather than the actual witness, but if he insists on doing so, shouldn't he be sworn, too?'

The judge waggled his bushy white eyebrows disapprovingly at Garrick, whose face coloured slightly, and the witness went on as I returned to my seat.

'It was a very upsetting scene. The victim was only young. Naked, and sprawled out on the tracks like that ... The pedestrian, Mr Kennard, he's in his seventies and was enormously distressed. We cordoned off the area, and the investigation was handed over to DCS DeWitt and crime scene analysis, while Constable Sharp and myself escorted Mr Kennard back to the station.'

'Thank you, Constable Shepherd,' Garrick said. 'We appreciate you taking the time to come down here today. If you wait there, the defence may have some questions for you.'

'No questions, My Lord,' I muttered. 'No questions.'

26

'How come we had no questions? Shouldn't we have cross-examined her? Challenged the evidence?'

We were in the Bar mess, having hung up our wigs and adjourned for lunch. I'd asked for a strong black coffee, but it was so weak I could see the bottom of the cup staring straight back through it. Zara didn't fancy any of the food on offer. I simply didn't fancy eating.

'The nature of cross-examination is to test the evidence of a witness where, on your client's instructions, you disagree with it,' I told her. 'It's not about passing comment on the evidence nor the effect of it unless it's relevant. We don't have any dispute with her findings, so there's no need to cross-examine.'

'I guess,' she sighed, polishing the coffee's condensation from her glasses with one shirtsleeve. 'Still, seems a long way for her to have come just to read her own statement. They must've known we weren't going to argue with whatever she'd found at the scene, so why bother getting her down here at all?'

'Because Garrick's going to lay it on thick with a trowel. He knows it's agreed evidence, but he's aiming for maximum impact. He wants that jury to put faces to names and expressions to faces. He wants a horror show. For now, we just have to bide our time and let the prosecution present their case.'

'Speak of the knob ...' she muttered into her cup, and then, realising I'd heard her, rolled her eyes. 'Sorry.'

Garrick and Bowen had entered the mess, still dressed in full wigs and gowns, and blanked us all the way to the counter. They didn't even sit together, choosing separate tables on opposite sides of the room.

'He's loads older than me, isn't he?' Zara grumbled. She was watching Bowen, who was guiding an egg sandwich into his open mouth with one hand, sullenly flicking through the mess's complimentary copy of *The Times* with the other. 'Must be, what, twice my age?'

I nodded. 'You say that as if it reflects poorly on you.'

'Well, doesn't it?'

'If anything, I'd say it's entirely the opposite. You're half his age and working on the same trial, aren't you?'

'Hmm ...' She sipped her drink, hardly encouraged, watching him still. 'He's from our chambers, isn't he?'

'He is.'

'Doesn't it feel strange, going up against somebody from your set?'

I shrugged. 'It happens quite often. We're self-employed, after all. So, you'd already met him in chambers?'

'No. I recognise the name, but I've never seen him about. You don't get on, do you?'

I could've laughed. 'What gives you that idea?'

Harold Kennard was next to give evidence.

God only knows how they'd got him down there for the day.

He was just a few years older than our own head of chambers but looked as brittle as a bundle of matchsticks by comparison. It took a long, and at times excruciating, three hours for him to describe the morning he'd come across the body, intercut by loosely connected anecdotes covering most of his formative decades.

Whenever Garrick actually managed to steer the distrait ramblings back into focus, it was a miserable, thoroughly depressing picture he painted for the jury.

While I had no doubt that it had indeed been a terrible, traumatising encounter, Kennard's being there was a cheap move by the prosecution and provided no more evidence than the preceding officer had already offered. He had been invited there for sheer emotional impact and little else; a stand-in, to fill the void that might ordinarily belong to a tearful victim impact statement by a member of the family.

For all its skulduggery, it worked wonders.

Juror Number 4 – a white woman with creased hands, the obvious eldest of the dozen in one of the more expensive, neater blouses – mopped her eyes with a tissue.

Billy, on the other hand, looked as if he might've fallen asleep when I glanced back into the dock, and several of his relatives had actually wandered out of the gallery.

For me, there was nothing to do but grimace and bear it until the witness was led out of the courtroom.

'Wow,' Zara whispered while we cleared our row after being adjourned for the evening. 'That was …'

'Painful?' I said.

'I would've gone for agonising.'

I rushed for the robing room, wanting to avoid being cornered with Garrick, and then outside for a smoke. I didn't even bother going down to see Billy before he was returned to his cell for the night, nor did I wait around to speak to his solicitor.

Zara met me out the front, canvas bag of files over one shoulder, blue monogrammed damask against her chest. She hesitated before descending the steps. The throng of thirty or so people there had almost doubled; some were ranting to reporters while others sat cross-legged on the ground, cardboard placards alongside them.

'So, this is it,' she said, 'murder at the Old Bailey.'

'Is it everything you ever dreamed it would be?' I asked drily.

'You mean, did I spend my nights at Bar school dreaming of defending a cruel, bigoted racist?' She shook her head. 'I'd be lying if I said I did.'

'Any regrets?'

'No. Barristers can't be choosers, can they?' She remained close beside me, eyes fixed on the scattered crowd. 'They look like they're waiting for a gig or something.'

'You're apprehensive about going through them?'

'No …' She shrugged. 'A bit, maybe.'

I nodded, smoke billowing out through my nostrils, and began to descend the steps. 'Come on,' I said softly. 'You've been face-to-face with a deranged, suspected killer. What're a few dozen demonstrators compared to that?'

'It's different,' she mumbled, keeping her face turned down from disapproving eyes.

'How so?'

'Because I've come to expect hatred from a man like that,' she said. 'It's everybody else's anger I have a problem with.'

27

The River Fleet still runs beneath the Old Bailey. I haven't seen it myself, but I've been told about it by various people around the court who have.

To get to it, one has to go down through the coal room that heats the courts, an enormous power station with nearly eight-metre-high ceilings hidden entirely below street level. From there, it's just an open hatch and a rusted ladder down to the cold, black Fleet where Elizabeth Fry, the great prison reformer of the early nineteenth century, used to collect water for the inmates of Newgate. By the 1860s, the water had become so fetid that the city was forced to cover it up, to build and live above it, and concede it to the ever-expanding kingdom of the rats that thrive in all those dark, forgotten places.

I was thinking about that the next morning, after having the same dream about Aidan, lost in the mine. Going underground to see Billy didn't help.

'You actually planning on getting up and fucking doing owt today?'

He was suited up in one of the seventy-four subterranean cells, ready for his second day in court.

'I already told you which evidence we'd be challenging,' I said, 'and the witnesses we'd be cross-examining. You didn't seem interested.'

He shrugged, shoulders nearing the low, cracked ceiling, and sniffed. 'Didn't think you'd spend the whole thing just sitting on your fat arse though.'

Both Zara and Fraser Hayes had accompanied me down for the quick morning conference but stood mutely by the cell door. I could scarcely blame them. I hardly had anything more to say to him myself.

'Would you have preferred me to start throwing my weight around? To tear the seventy-something-year-old witness a new one in front of the judge and jury?'

'That'd be worth seeing,' he said with a lopsided grin.

'Look, I don't have time for this,' I snapped. 'So, unless you have some new instructions for us, then we'll be seeing you up there.'

'Can't wait, Rumpole,' he jeered, winking at my wig. 'Which wanker have we got up there this morning, anyway?'

'Ali Abdul Nazir.'

'Ah, the Paki?' He glanced to Zara, his eyes burning. 'No offence, love.'

'None taken,' she replied coolly. 'But tell me, Mr Barber, this Aryan, white, super-race that you're so obsessed with, are you an example of it?'

For once, he had no reply.

Nazir was skinnier than I'd been expecting, though I knew from bitter experience that even the lightest man could throw a blinding jab. Boxing had given him a lean, chiselled look, and at twenty-five years old and well over six feet, he was the tall, dark, handsome antithesis of the stooped elderly witness that had come to the stand before him, his physique pressing against his long-sleeved shirt in all the ways and places mine did not.

'Mr Nazir,' Garrick began, 'could you please tell the court what happened to you on the afternoon of Friday the fourteenth of April this year?'

Nazir shifted lightly on his toes, a professional habit, and stroked his trimmed beard as he cast his mind back six months.

'I was on my way to a mate's, cos we were all off out for bank holiday weekend and that, when I stopped off to use the cashy.'

'That would be the Tesco Express and its cashpoint on Maid Marian Way?' Garrick asked, doing his public-schooled best to translate the quick-fire response.

'Bang on, yeah,' Nazir nodded.

'Do you happen to remember what time this was?'

'I know exactly when it was,' he replied proudly, still bobbing on the spot. 'Four minutes past five.'

Garrick lifted his eyebrows in surprise, as if he hadn't read it in the statement several times already.

'That's incredibly precise, Mr Nazir. How can you be so certain?'

'The machine gave me a receipt, and then later, when I did my statement, I still had the paper in my wallet.'

'Ideal,' Garrick said. 'Now, as you may or may not know, the footage from the cashpoint's camera couldn't be obtained ...' *That's* ideal, I thought, rolling my eyes. 'So, perhaps you could tell the court what occurred at that time?'

Nazir nodded and gazed up into the grey beyond the glass roof.

'I'm standing there, using the hole in the wall, when this bloke comes storming from the corner across the road behind me.'

'Did you recognise this man?'

'Not then, no. Didn't have a clue who he was. I do now, of course.'

'And, since then, you've positively identified him as the defendant,' Garrick said, pointing up to the dock with one limp hand, 'William Barber?'

'Oh yeah,' Nazir said, tilting his head right back so he could glare at Billy. 'He was absolutely leathered, stumbling from one side of the pavement to the other. St James's Street was behind me, so sort of …' He mimed what was presumably the face of a cash machine in the air ahead of him, and then pointed a thumb off behind his right shoulder, '*there*, and that's where he came out of. I turned round as soon as I heard him.'

'And what did you hear?'

'Just noises, really. Aggressive yelling. Sort of singing, I guess, but not …' He frowned, trying to find the right word, and buried the tips of his fingers into his beard, pulling at the hair. 'It was a racket, so I turned round to see what was going on. It's four lanes of traffic on Maid Marian Way, two lanes each way separated by this strip of trees and bushes fenced off in the middle, and he's coming straight across the road towards me. He manages to jump the first fence, stamps through all the bushes and that, and then bins it on the nearest fence.'

'I'm sorry,' Garrick interrupted, raising a palm, 'but what exactly do you mean by "bins it"?'

'Falls over, you know? Into the road. One of the cars has to swerve, pounds its horn, and that's when I realise how drunk he is, and that he's got his eyes fixed on me.'

'Quite the spectacle,' Garrick said coldly. 'What were you doing in the meantime?'

'I was just trying to get my money out fast, but by the time it had given me my card back he was already at the kerb, a couple of metres away.'

'And was he making any more sense, verbally, by then?'

'You could say that,' he sniffed. 'He basically started accusing me of stealing money from the machine. Said I'd come over here to rob him and his family. I mean, technically I was born in Newark, but I don't think that's what he meant ... By that point he was causing a massive scene, and people were slowing down in their cars, watching him through the window of the Bear and Lace, the restaurant next door. He was going ballistic.'

'And how did you react?'

Nazir scratched his left cheek, dampened his lips. 'Well, I told him to get lost, didn't I?'

'In those words?' Judge Pike had leaned forward, eyebrows raised. 'We are looking for the *facts*, Mr Nazir.'

'All right,' he shrugged. 'I told him to fuck right off, if you must know. Told him I work my arse off to earn my own money, and so does everybody in my family. We've never asked for any sort of handout. We're good people. We're British.'

'And how did Mr Barber react to that?' Garrick prodded.

'Not well. He's a big bloke, and the next thing I know is he's coming straight for me. He pulls his fist back, but he's slow, you know? Drunk. I can see it coming a mile off. I give him a quick parry, and drop him with my right –' he imitated the swing in the air, a lightning-quick movement, and then, remembering his audience – 'only to defend myself, of course.'

'You maintain that your actions were in self-defence?'

'One hundred per cent,' he replied firmly. 'I wasn't taking no chances. The way he was carrying on, all them Nazi tattoos and that, I had no idea what he wanted to do, but he wasn't looking to shake my hand, that's for sure!'

'What indeed?' Garrick proposed, raising his eyebrows to the members of the jury, who were hanging on to every word. 'What happened next?'

'Nothing. He was rolling around on the pavement, seeing stars, so I got out of there quick.' He tugged at his shirt, adjusted his belt, and lowered his head to the bench like a pauper doffing his hat. 'I have a licence, M'Lord. British Boxing Board of Control. If they knew about all this, well … It could cause me a lot of grief, and, excuse my language, I wasn't ready to have my licence suspended because of some pissed-up racist who'd come out looking for trouble.'

Pike nodded, scratching beneath his wig with one finger. 'You're certain that he'd come seeking violence?'

'Absolutely. He'd never met me, he didn't know me from Adam, but he wanted to hurt me from the minute he came round that corner and saw the colour of my skin. In a way, I'm glad it was me he found, and not somebody who couldn't have defended himself. Course, whatever might've happened later, that's on my mind a lot, and whether I should've done things differently …'

He trailed off, eyes dropping, and when I glanced to the side I caught Zara thumbing through her notebook.

'Thank you, Mr Nazir,' Garrick said, soft as he could manage, which wasn't too soft at all. 'The defence may have some questions.'

He cast me a flash of a leer as he sat, and I sighed as I got to my feet.

'No, My Lord,' I said once again.

'Then I think that now would be a good time for a break,' Pike said, checking the face of the clock on the wall. 'I'll rise now.'

'Be upstanding!' called the usher, and we were.

'I still can't believe that evidence was admissible,' Zara whispered. 'The witness is providing evidence for a supposed crime our client hasn't even been indicted for, and one that has no relevance to this case! We ought to have his statement dismissed from the record.'

At her side, Garrick shared an especially condescending snort with his own junior and leaned intrusively into our huddle.

'The relevance of Mr Nazir's statement has already been ironed out in our bad character application,' he said. 'This isn't America, my dear. We don't just *strike evidence* from the record willy-nilly. Get at least one trial under your belt, and you might understand the basics.'

Her cheeks flushed, and though he was intentionally being a disdainful arsehole, he was correct, and there was little more I could say.

To further aggravate the moment, Bowen bent slyly across the back of our row, pretending to adjust his shoe, and hissed from the corner of his mouth. 'Bad luck, Rook. I think you ought to tell *the kid* to leave the thinking to the grown-ups in future.'

Zara didn't respond, but her eyes started to shine behind her glasses and she walked out of court with her hands in her pockets, face turned down to the ground. Bowen watched her shrink away, and then snidely clicked his tongue.

'I'd say you've just lost your final hand, Rook. Now you don't even have the race card left to play.'

Another relative trouncing, another lackadaisical lunch, and on to another witness on the stand.

It was the first time I'd seen Denise Dickinson, the Barbers' upstairs neighbour.

The court dress she'd chosen consisted of a low-cut black cotton shirt, black jogging trousers, and black trainers. Her hair was a combination of peroxide kinks and woven extensions hanging down around a heart-shaped face, and her lips were painted a deep plum-purple.

She took the oath with her hands behind her back, pushing her chest outwards, and kept her face turned away from the public gallery at all times.

'Mrs Dickinson,' Garrick began.

'That's Ms Dickinson,' she corrected, 'thank God.'

'Ms Dickinson,' he managed through his tight, hatchet smile. 'Please explain to the court what you witnessed on the morning of the fifteenth of April.'

'All right. I woke up to smoke coming into the bedroom at just before six o'clock in the morning.'

'You're sure of the time? That is, after all, crucial to this case.'

'First thing I did was reach out for my phone. I thought the downstairs flat had gone up in flames, to be honest.'

'What made you think that?'

'The smell. The thickness of the smoke. I couldn't see it yet, but I could taste it, like burning nylon or something, and I thought it was coming up through the floor. My kids were asleep in the next room, so I was straight out of bed, phone in hand, and that's when I realised it was coming in through the window.'

'Your bedroom faces onto the back of the building?'

'That's right. I opened the curtains, and that's when I saw him out there.'

'The defendant?'

'Yeah, Billy, down in the garden.'

'And how did he appear to you?'

'How'd he appear?' She moved her hands forward, gripping the curves of her hips, and scrunched her nose. 'Smashed, for want of a better word! Swaying back and forth, starkers, all except for a sock. He almost looked as if he'd been crying, tell you the truth, all red-eyed and just stuffing his clothes into the patio chimney they keep out there. I was so surprised, it was a couple more minutes before I took the photo.'

'That's this photograph?' Garrick held up a copy, pivoting Billy's naked form for all to see. Up in the gallery, I saw Sarah Barber bury her face into the crooks of her arms, and her brother-in-law – Caine or Declan, it was hard to differentiate these days – lumbered an awkward trunk of an arm around her narrow shoulders.

'That's it,' the neighbour said. 'I couldn't believe what I was seeing.'

'Nor would most, I'm sure.' Garrick laid it back onto the piles before him. 'Why did you post it online?'

She paused, clearly stumped, as if it was an action she hadn't ever thought to question. 'Because I was sick of it, that's why! I wanted everyone to see what I have to put up with every weekend! If it isn't him bringing his mates back to the flat in the early hours, all chanting and mouthing off through the floorboards, then it's him treating his missus like muck! I've got kids trying to sleep, and all they get to hear is effing and blinding and God knows what else. That was the final straw. I'd had enough.'

Garrick mulled over the photograph, nodding to himself, and drummed his fingertips along the edge of the oak. 'What did you think had happened?'

'Well, he's always out scrapping,' she began. 'Wouldn't be the first time he's come home covered in someone else's blood. That's what I thought it would've been. Everyone round our end knows what he's like. Always been the case. Always kicking blokes' heads in for something or other. Hangs out with all these young, fit lads half his age –'

'My Lord,' I groaned, but Pike swiftly swatted away my objection.

'I'll allow it, Mr Rook. The prosecution's bad character application still stands.'

Garrick nodded, grateful. 'What happened after you took the photograph?'

'He went inside. Couldn't have been more than five minutes after that. Just left the fire dying. Must've woken his wife up when he did, because that's around the time they started arguing.'

'About anything specific?'

'Couldn't tell you. He was going wild, even by their standards. I could hear things breaking, thudding, and she was sobbing ... Next thing I know, I've got my kids bursting into my room in tears, and that's when I rang the police. It had all quietened down by the time the blue lights of the panda car got there, of course. It's not right, how he behaves.'

'Thank you, Ms Dickinson.'

As Garrick returned to his seat, Mr Justice leaned forward.

'I don't suppose the defence have any questions for this witness, do they?'

I got up wearily, a broken record in robes, and shook my head. 'The defence have no questions, My Lord.'

'Yeah they fucking do!'

Like a punch to the spine, it knocked the wind right out of me; every head in the room spun at once, and there was Billy, upright in the dock, pressing forward against the glass.

I pivoted completely, a full turn to the dock and then back to the bench, by which time the judge's scarlet shoulders had bunched up around his wig.

'Another outburst like that, Mr Barber, and I'll hold you in contempt of court!' he snarled. 'Mr Rook, is there something you would like to discuss with your client before we continue?'

I held fast and swallowed a mouthful of air.

Dickinson might've been or done any number of things, but I knew she wasn't lying.

'No, My Lord. No questions.'

A terrific crunch was my reward, followed by an instant chorus of gasps, and I didn't have to turn round to know that Billy had just slammed either his forehead or his fist into the glass.

'Ask that lying slut about the fucking gang bang and her rape allegations, why don't you?'

'Get him out of my sight!' Pike roared, and the prosecution positively bounced with delight; up in the gallery, the Barbers went off like dynamite, yelling, jeering and cursing, all except for Sarah, who had shrunk to the size of a small child.

Aghast, I looked back in time to catch the officers wrestling Billy by the shoulders, struggling to pin down King Kong, and then down he went, leaving an empty dock and absolute uproar in his wake.

28

The Viaduct Tavern was one of the original gin palaces of nineteenth-century London.

Directly across from Newgate Prison, it famously gathered lawyers, criminals, judges and government officials together through the years of citywide dipsomania, the reign of Mother's Ruin.

Since the Old Bailey was built in Newgate's place, the pub still tended to gather a similarly mixed bag of clientele under its round, blood-red ceiling, though now it was one of a nationwide chain, serving aubergine and red-pepper toasties along with its drams.

Less than half an hour after Billy had been dragged to the cells we were at a table behind a wooden screen to the left of the bar, fittingly close, I felt, to the lavatories. From the window, I could see the crowds of protesters dispersing once more for the evening; a rival group, mostly made up of white males, had recently begun to multiply across the road, occasionally throwing insults into the throng, while uniformed officers watched every move from nearby. All we needed now was a race riot, I thought. That'd finish the day off perfectly.

'Well,' I said, 'that couldn't have gone much fucking worse.'

I was gazing off into nothing, feeling thoroughly chewed up and spat out, following the light from the etched Victorian mirrors on the opposite wall as it splintered through hundreds of bottles behind the bar. People moved in those mirrors, smiling among friends, and I hoped they'd stay there, lest they be sucked up by the thundercloud in our corner.

Zara was swirling her fruit cider close to the rim of her glass, kicking a smell of sickly sweet berries up over the table. 'He's going to be convicted, isn't he? Did you see the faces in the jury? Number 4's jaw was practically in her lap.'

'I saw.'

'Is it wrong that I don't want that to happen?'

Half my pint disappeared so fast that I missed the floral, hoppy notes advertised on the pump. 'No, it isn't wrong. It's quite normal to build a relationship with the defendant, whatever they're accused of. It should never be about whether you like them or not, and it doesn't mean that you care any less about the indictment, but you are putting yourself in their position. Fighting for their freedom. Even the Devil's advocate wouldn't want to let Lucifer burn.'

She sighed, removed her glasses and folded them on the table. 'It isn't that. Whether he did it or not, I think that William Barber is an abysmal person, and if he's sent down then his children might actually get a half-decent chance in life. He doesn't seem to be a very positive presence ...'

'But?'

'But if he does go down, and he really *didn't* kill The Girl, then the murderer will still be out there. The case will be buried, apparently solved, the victim's name might never be known, and the killer gets to go on with his life. It might even happen again one day, and that's so, so much worse.'

'Which is why it's imperative that we never get bogged down on whether our client is *good or bad* by conventional standards,' I told her. 'We deal in evidence and have to ensure that the law is just, and the truth is found.'

This wasn't entirely honest. Most barristers, in my experience, aren't interested in the truth. We tell lies for money, but I couldn't bring myself to say that to her. I finished the rest of my pint, and found my mind wandering back to one of Rupert's favourite, most heavily recited quotes. '"Beauty is truth, truth beauty. That is all ye know on earth, and all ye need to know."'

'Keats,' she nodded. 'You know the client, don't you, Mr Rook?'

'Who, Barber?' I must've hesitated then, long enough to give her the answer, and she pinched at the tiny indentations left by the glasses on the bridge of her nose.

'Makes sense,' she said. 'It's a small village, I doubt you would've missed him.'

'Does that bother you?'

She shrugged, almost casual, as if she'd barely given it a thought. The way she avoided my eyes told me otherwise. 'You told me to be friendly to defendants, but never to be their friend. You told me not to stick my neck out for them.'

'That's right.' I put my empty glass firmly on the table. 'And before you go on, I would like to make one thing perfectly crystal clear here. I am not, nor have I ever been, friends with William Barber. I knew his family, a lifetime ago, but I barely knew *him*.'

'Then why you? Why this case? Why now?'

I leaned back, weighing the young woman with my gaze, and then rummaged in my coat pocket and slapped my wallet on the table.

'If we're going into this,' I told her, 'we're going to need another couple of drinks over here.'

'I'm all right for another,' she said, finishing her cider and slipping her glasses back onto her nose, 'but thanks.'

'I meant for me.'

Four minutes later she was scratching her head, bewildered, looking as if she seriously regretted turning down the drink.

'Aidan Barber?' she repeated slowly. 'That's the one who died?'

'Correct.'

'You were mates?'

'Best friends through school and beyond,' I said, hearing genuine sadness in the words.

'And you're doing this because, what, you feel like you're *watching out* for his family or something?'

I shook my head and looked down at my bare hands on the table; the heavy, fidgeting thumbs, the yellow stain of nicotine along my middle fingers, and the permanent crack in the knuckle on the right. 'We'd been out drinking in the city centre. We were only seventeen, but things were different then. Fewer ID checks. No mobile phones. We missed the last bus back to the village and had to take the half-hour service to Keyworth, get off in Plumtree, and walk the three miles east to Cotgrave. We'd done it before, so it shouldn't have been a problem, except that there was this group of younger lads on the back seats of the bus, pressed up against the windows and making gestures down to the car behind us.

'The car pulled up as soon as we got off at Plumtree, and the two blokes mistook us for the kids on the bus, I suppose.

We knew how to handle ourselves, until one of them pulled a knife, and I ended up getting slashed from here –' with one finger, I traced the permanent line across the breadth of my chest – 'to here. Aidan had always been fitter than me. He was already halfway down the road when it happened, and he could've left me there, but he didn't. He came at them like a wrecking ball.'

I felt the shiver of a faint, wretched smile at the memory of my friend, my hero, swinging his arms like windmills in the night, and then the smile withered away.

'They cut the tendons in his leg so badly that he never walked right again. Six years after that, when he couldn't manage the walk through the tunnels, he took a ride on the coal belt and went straight into the cutting machine. If he hadn't come back for me ...'

I shrugged, dragging myself out of a deep and treacherous reverie, and reached for my drink.

'That's really sad,' she said, 'but it doesn't –'

'You should be getting off,' I heard myself say, choking the heat from my face. 'We'll see how Judge Pike reacts after he's had the night to cool off.'

'Oh ...' Half a moment passed, and then she nodded the hint of a frown away, throwing both her blue and canvas bags over her shoulders. 'I'm jumping on the Central Line at St Paul's. You going that way?'

'Soon.' I rapped the side of my beer. 'Going to stay here a while. I need to make a phone call.'

'All right,' she said, untangling a knot of headphone wires from her pocket, and glancing towards the activists still milling around outside. 'What happened to them? The guys who put you in hospital? Did they get them?'

'Oh, yeah,' I mumbled. 'They got them.'

As soon as she'd left, hurrying away from the area with her face to the ground, I took my phone out of my pocket.

Nothing from Sean. Nothing whatsoever.

29

'Do you know what happens now?'

All he gave me was a petulant shrug. 'They gonna tell me off? Take me out there and smack my arse in front of the jury?'

I opened my mouth to answer, but, to my surprise, the young solicitor Fraser Hayes answered for me. 'No, Mr Barber,' he began, 'but if there's any more of that behaviour, anything at all, then the trial will proceed in your absence, and you'll be left here, in this cell, to await the verdict.'

Billy slouched, chewing on his lower lip, and glared over at the white paint peeling from the walls, the claw marks in the door. One of the dock officers peered in through the wicket gate, and Billy's mouth curled at the edges.

'They were never coppers,' he leered. 'Warders. They're retired civil servants. Hospital porters. One of the senior officers in Belmarsh, he used to drive buses around the East End.'

Hayes glanced to Zara for support, maybe for guidance, but she only rolled her eyes, well used to the man by now.

'I don't think you're taking this seriously,' I told him. 'It isn't a joke. Do you really want to miss the rest of your own trial, just because you couldn't keep your mouth shut? Didn't you see Sarah up there in the gallery? Your family? They've come a long way, and you're spitting it back in their faces.'

'Don't talk to me about my family,' he grumbled, and turned his face to the blank wall behind him. 'Fucking Belmarsh. It's boring. All that High Security bollocks, as if I can't handle myself in the main building. I practically *ran* Nottingham Prison from '97. Saw the millennium in with a bottle of Jack in the warder's office.'

He grinned to himself, eyes clouding over, actually pining for days in prison.

'Really?' I asked, feigning interest. 'Well, I saw it in at home with my wife. It was nice.'

He turned back towards me, and his face had dropped an inch.

'One more chance,' I said. 'That's all you've got.'

And we went upstairs, leaving him underground.

On the receiving end of Garrick's questions this morning was a large Indian man with small button eyes in a soft, round face, his skin mottled by dry patches after a close morning shave. He breathed deeply through his nose, sending a faint whistling down the microphone, and repeatedly straightened his grandad jumper and peppered hair with what seemed to be surprisingly delicate hands.

'Dr Munjal,' Garrick said, thumbs buried in the folds of his silk, 'you are a senior forensic scientist, correct?'

'Yes. I was a pathologist with the Forensic Science Service for fifteen years until its dissolution, and now I work for Forensic Facts, a private, Home Office-sanctioned company.'

'And, as an expert witness, can you provide the court with your professional analysis of the fatal injuries sustained by the victim?'

'I can.'

'Then, before you do –' Garrick fed the jury a grave expression, the trace of a glint in his eye – 'I must ask the members of the jury to steel themselves for the horrific details that are to come ...' Number 4 fished a handkerchief out ready, while Number 6 took a long, apprehensive drink of water. 'Go ahead, Doctor ...'

Munjal nodded, and utter silence fell from the gallery down.

'The subject was approximately sixteen years old at the time of her death. Toxicological reports came back negative for drugs and alcohol, and examination of the vagina and vaginal material revealed no signs of intercourse; her hymen membrane was still largely intact. Tissue damage to the throat and left side of the body indicated that the attack was committed by a right-handed person, the sheer force suggesting a male with large, powerful hands. There was no evidence to show that any other weapon had been used.

'The first, most forceful impact came from behind, possibly at speed, connecting with the back of the skull and knocking the victim to the ground. Microscopic traces of rust and iron inside her face and gums suggested that she'd fallen with considerable weight onto the railway, dislodging her upper incisors. At least fifty-seven subsequent blows were recorded, and damage to both sides of the neck revealed strangulation from both in front and behind, suggesting that she rolled several times.

'Blood pattern analysis revealed primary blood transfer more than twenty metres away from where the body was found, and flecks expelled from the airways were consistent with the damage to her left lung, which was collapsed. Inside that lung was where we discovered one of the broken teeth. The only clothing recovered from the scene was the yellow polyester jacket, torn at the seams after being forcibly removed, and though it was eventually laid over the body, impact splatter and cast-off placed it approximately two metres away at the time of the assault.

'Seven fingernails were missing from the hands, three on the left and four on the right, and her legs had been broken posthumously. There was a displaced fracture in the femur of the right, and a compound fracture in the left, which had forced both the tibia and fibula out through the flesh. This was most likely the result of either a sustained attack shortly after the point of death, or attempted movement of the body.

'The post-mortem examination indicated the time of death to have been between two and four o'clock in the morning.'

Clack-clack-clack went the stenographer, still catching up.

I moved to pour myself some water, and realised Zara had drained the whole carafe while he'd been talking.

'So much blood,' Garrick sighed, 'would it be fair to assume that the assailant's skin, hair and clothes would've been covered?'

'I'd certainly say so.'

A low murmuring rumbled through the court; I distinctly heard the word 'burned' whispered by somebody on the jury, and Garrick smiled involuntarily.

'Thank you, Doctor.'

I stretched as I got to my feet, and several members of the jury seemed visibly surprised.

'Dr Munjal,' I said, still racking my brain for a reasonable line of inquiry, 'perhaps you could shed some light on the realities of the post-mortem process? For starters, did you visit the crime scene yourself?'

'No. That role goes to the scene-of-crime officers, while my work is largely confined to the laboratory.'

'But you *did* conduct the post-mortem examination?'

'I was one of the pathologists, yes, though such an examination involves a whole team of experts and weeks of analysis, from DNA, bloodstain patterning and toxicology, to studying insects and pollen to determine time since death. That's without ballistics and fire investigation, where such variables are necessary.'

'And without identification, how were you able to establish the victim's age?'

'Bone and dental X-rays are first used to indicate maturity, followed by analysis of a DNA process called methylation to determine lifespan.'

'But you couldn't conclude with absolute certainty on her home country?'

He shook his head. 'Genetics do not abide by concepts of *race*. Biologically speaking, all humans are more than ninety-nine per cent identical. Genetics can't provide a precise birthplace, but they *can* indicate more relatives in one place than any another. The victim's ancestry, we discovered, was primarily a mix of Syrian, Jordanian and Iraqi.'

'Fascinating,' I said. 'You mentioned a whole team of experts, but are you personally skilled in DNA profiling?'

'I am, as well as identifying bodily fluids, textile fibres, and plant, animal and human hairs.'

'So, it'd be fair to say you spend a lot of your working life with one eye on the business end of a microscope?'

'Ahem.' Pike cleared his throat from the bench. 'Is there a relevant question coming from the defence any time soon?'

'Yes, My Lord, there is …' I was stalling, and it obviously showed. 'I'm just trying to ascertain the expert witness's opinion on the likelihood of an assailant leaving no trace of DNA in such a frenzied attack, without prior preparation.'

'The witness hasn't been brought here for his opinion, Mr Rook, just as *you* haven't been brought to pass comment on the evidence.'

I swallowed my retort, nodding, just as the doctor leaned towards the microphone with a frown. 'But, of course, there *was* DNA found on the victim.'

I almost fell flat on my arse. 'I beg your pardon?'

'A microscopic trace of DNA was recovered from underneath what fingernails remained on the right hand …'

I couldn't say how long I'd been standing there, but all eyes were on me when I came back to the room.

'You'll have to forgive me,' I said, regaining my balance, 'but the defence weren't aware of these findings.'

Zara was rummaging through our case papers, scouring every page, while the pathologist looked suddenly panicked. 'These findings *were* included in my report.'

'And the DNA recovered …' I took a steady breath. 'Did it match that of the defendant, William Barber?'

You could've heard a pin hit the oak. All ears turned towards the man.

It felt like a long time before he shook his head.

'No. The trace gave only a partial profile, not enough to positively identify anybody.'

'But was the profile sufficient enough to *exclude* anybody?'

He nodded stiffly, batting his eyes up to the bench. 'It was.'

My heart began to beat a vicious tattoo against my throat. 'Like the defendant, William Barber?'

The first lesson learned in advocacy training is a simple one: never ask a question to which you don't already know the answer.

The room strained for its response; the kick-drum rhythm in my chest increased.

'We couldn't say who it was,' the doctor replied, 'but the DNA profile did not come from William Barber.'

'Thank you, Dr Munjal.' I said, flopping back into my seat as steadily as I could manage. 'No more questions. You've been very, very helpful.'

I caught up with Garrick and Bowen before they'd scurried back into the robing room.

'Shabby doesn't even come close,' I said, halting their escape along the corridor. 'Why wasn't that evidence disclosed to the defence?'

Garrick appeared to be in physical pain, so damaged was his pride, and it took a long time for him to respond through a clenched jaw. 'I can only offer my apologies, Rook,' he managed, flashing a disdainful look to Bowen. 'I left the task of deciding what was disclosable to my *junior*.'

'Is that so?' I said, and turned to Zara. 'Miss Barnes, do you happen to know the rules on disclosure?'

She nodded. 'The prosecution should serve all material that potentially undermines the prosecution case or assists the defence.'

'In which case,' I continued, shifting my gaze onto Bowen, who had mostly disappeared behind his leader's shoulders by now, 'this was either dishonesty or gross incompetence, and only you know which it was.'

'It's all right,' Zara added, turning to lead us off down the corridor in the opposite direction, 'any time you *grown-ups* need a refresher, let me know. Otherwise, maybe leave the thinking to the kid in future?'

30

DCS John DeWitt might as well have ridden a Harley into the courtroom.

He came in loud and hard, shiny black shoes stomping, cock and shoulders swinging, determined to let everybody know he meant business, and that business was to see Barber locked up for the rest of his natural life.

It was the first time I'd seen him by the light of day, and his greying, ice-blond moustache made him look like a Victorian prizefighter; I'd almost forgotten how tall he was. Instead of the rugged barn coat and jeans, he'd come dressed in full uniform: an immaculate tunic with insignia on the epaulettes, black tie and a peaked cap with black-and-white-chequered dicing.

He pivoted into the witness box, spat the oath without prompting, and never lowered his glower from the dock. Black eyes met black, separated only by glass, as if the rest of the room, and the world beyond, had suddenly ceased to be there.

'Detective Chief Superintendent DeWitt,' Garrick said, after the officer had introduced himself to the room, 'you led the investigation for this case, yes?'

'That's right,' he boomed, placing his hat by the microphone. It really was a peculiar accent he had, and I struggled to pin it between varying shades of Nottingham, the Netherlands and New Zealand.

'You've been a police officer for ...?'

'Thirty years.'

'Could you walk us through the morning of the fifteenth?'

'It'd be my pleasure,' he said, and I truly believed that. 'I initially responded to a domestic disturbance at Mr Barber's residence at around half past six that morning. When I arrived, I found the house to be in disarray. The child was distraught, and Mrs Barber seemed to have suffered a swelling to the left side of her face as a result of the fracas.'

'And *Mr* Barber?'

'He was unconscious in the shower, door wide open, water still running.'

'Did he stir upon your arrival?'

'He did not. It was only after maybe two more minutes that I noticed a thin trail of smoke rising from the patio chimney in the garden, and upon going outside to investigate, I noticed what appeared to be the remnants of bloodied clothes smouldering in the flames. Based on this, and the obvious risk still posed to his family, I decided to take Mr Barber into custody, and transported him to Central Station.'

'And did he, for lack of a better expression, *come quietly*?'

'Not exactly, though the effort of dressing seemed to take most of the fight out of him. He was unconscious for the majority of the journey, or else babbling to himself in the back seat.'

'Babbling?' Garrick repeated. 'Did you happen to hear anything of note among these ramblings?'

DeWitt nodded. 'From what I was able to gather, he spent most of the journey mumbling about some sort of "holy war".'

An undertone of murmurs swept the court. My stomach stiffened, mind flashing to our last conversation at Belmarsh. Billy and his big mouth.

'The body of the victim was discovered shortly after we arrived at the station, at which point I had to leave the pleasure of Barber's company while I went out to the scene. It became almost immediately apparent that there were unquestionable parallels emerging between the two situations.'

'How long until you were able to make the charge?'

'It took a little more than nine hours.'

'An unusually long amount of time?' Garrick asked, knowing it wasn't.

'On the contrary, it was quite fast, a testament to how soon the pieces began to fall into place. The majority of arrest proceedings take between four and eight hours, once you take into account the interviewing, administration and liaising with the CPS for a charging decision. Murder is usually considerably longer.'

'Were you present for Mr Barber's interview?'

'I was, for all it was worth. Two hours we questioned him, once he was sober enough to talk, and he didn't answer a single question. Not one.'

'*Not one,*' Garrick repeated, adding a theatrical sigh for good measure. 'And did you warn him that, while he had the right to give no answers, the jury might be invited to draw an adverse inference if he sought to rely upon a defence that he hadn't mentioned in the interview?'

'I did, and still he gave us no explanation whatsoever.'

'Is that common among suspects?'

'Common among *guilty men,*' DeWitt jabbed.

'My Lord,' I groaned, but the judge was ahead of me this time.

'We want your evidence, Superintendent DeWitt, not your opinion.'

He bristled and shrugged.

'With neither answer nor explanation,' Garrick went on, 'how were you able to narrow down Mr Barber's whereabouts at the time of the killing?'

'Once it became clear that we were dealing with a suspected murder case, we were forced to act quickly. Fortunately, Billy – Mr Barber – is well known to us by now. We know where he tends to socialise and who with. We know his drinking patterns, and it took no time at all to pinpoint his whereabouts up until he left the social club. That's when we learned of his brief interaction with the victim, and how he'd followed her from the club. Intelligence officers were able to use cell-site analysis to show that his phone had been in use in the same rural area that the body was discovered, before it was turned off at half past one in the morning.'

Garrick nodded slowly, leaning forward to set his palms flat on the polished surface of our row. 'You say that Mr Barber is "well known" to your officers ... Would it be fair to say that you have something of a *history* with the defendant?'

DeWitt smirked, moustache scratching his nose.

'I have personally arrested Mr Barber more times than I could count. Fifteen of those arrests have led to convictions. He is a blight on the local community.'

'*Opinions,*' the judge interjected once more, 'please keep them to yourself.' He nodded to Garrick to continue.

'Would any of the previous offences for which you arrested Mr Barber fall into the category of hate crimes?'

'Yes. Most of them, actually.'

'Could you tell the jury the definition of a racist or religious hate crime?'

DeWitt nodded; of course he could. 'The Crown Prosecution Service defines a *racist or religious hate crime* as one that demonstrates hostility based on the victim's presumed race or religion, typically identified by excessive violence, cruelty, humiliation and degradation, *especially* when undertaken at a time coinciding with a specific religious festival.'

'And what about the crime the defendant is currently being tried for?' Garrick went on. 'What was it, exactly, that made it a racist or religious hate crime?'

'The victim was, as we know, Middle Eastern, and killed, violently, on the evening of *Good Friday*. It would be fair to argue that the crime therefore fits into this category. The definition also states that the alleged perpetrator will most likely have previous incidents involving systematic, regular, targeted antisocial behaviour, which have escalated in severity and frequency.'

'Could you tell the jury about those of Barber's previous convictions that demonstrate a propensity to violence, including against women, and racism?'

Judge Pike nodded to the superintendent and DeWitt clasped his heavy hands together like a man before a buffet.

'Where would you like me to start?'

'With anything you deem at all relevant,' Garrick said.

'Let's see,' he sniffed. 'William Barber is a member of what we call the *extreme right wing*. This term indicates an activist who is motivated by politics, racism, extreme nationalism and fascism. In 2012, he was convicted of distributing a terrorist publication for a proscribed far-right organisation, contrary to the Terrorism Act, and sentenced to thirteen months in HMP Nottingham.'

'Were you involved in that arrest?'

'I was. The defendant had attended an underground convention for white supremacists on the twenty-third of April that year.'

'That is St George's Day?' Garrick interrupted, with a pointed glance around the room.

'Correct. The publication was, as I recall, entitled "A European Declaration of Independence", written by Norwegian mass murderer Anders Breivik. It endorsed a violent, militant opposition to Islam, immigration and feminism. Barber also has at least eight convictions that I can think of for actual bodily harm, a dozen or so more for common assault, and has served another three years in Nottingham for the unlawful wounding of a former girlfriend.'

'Thank you,' Garrick replied gravely. 'On that note, I believe you have some video footage to play for the court?'

'I do,' DeWitt confirmed.

I hadn't watched it, but Zara had warned me about it. I'd been putting it off because we had no argument to raise. It was a mouthful of bitter medicine we'd both known was coming sooner or later. I tried to look nonchalant, but suspected I was failing.

They used to wheel videocassette players into the courtroom on stands; now there are flat screens fixed to the walls, with speakers hidden among the oak veneer.

'This video,' DeWitt said, 'was uploaded to Mr Barber's Twitter page in March of this year.'

A fast, fretful glance shared with Zara. I must've been cringing by then, but it was nothing compared to what I did when the video started, and I was forced into a ball, like an animal cowed.

It wasn't merely a twenty-second video. It was a twenty-second suicide note captured by Billy's own hand in that unflattering selfie-pose, with dozens more angry, white, middle-aged men cheering and waving St George's crosses behind him. In the near distance, behind the rabble, I recognised the emerald dome of Nottingham's Central Mosque, separated from the crowd by a line of uniformed officers.

And led by Billy, to the tune of Sanders and Kelley's 'I'm a Little Teapot', the mob began to sing:

'We are the English, fierce and loud,
This is our home, and we are proud!
When we think of ISIS, hear us shout!
KICK – THE FUCKIN' – PAKIS – OUT!'

When I dared to look round, through the bottomless quiet that followed, I could see heads visibly shaking across the jury. Many eyes had turned to Zara for a reaction, who happened to be the sole Asian in the room, who was pinching her eyes shut tight.

'That was posted *twenty-one days* before the killing,' DeWitt said, 'at a rally outside the city's Central Mosque. Worshipping families had to be sequestered inside for their own safety.'

'Thank you, Superintendent DeWitt,' Garrick said, brushing his palms together. 'I believe the defence might have some questions …'

'Such as might the indictment be put again to my client?' Bowen muttered as I stood slowly, wearily, trying to rouse the razor-sharp vigilance that had served me so well through my younger years of competitive debating. The reserves were hard to find.

Cross-examination is a rapid contest of individual moments that can change the course of a trial. It's a lightning-fast back-and-forth of reactions and responses that might uncover a truth or lie to change everything. The human brain is, by design, a contemplative machine, preferring to reflect on confrontations over hours, forever imagining better retorts long after the encounter; cross-examination has little use for hindsight. A barrister might well have one chance to find the truth.

And if a witness bares their teeth in the crossfire, then all the better for it.

'Detective Chief Superintendent DeWitt,' I started, bringing his glower onto me, 'why *did* you go to William Barber's home on the morning of the fifteenth?'

'As I explained not twenty minutes ago, I was responding to a report of a domestic disturbance.'

The pseudo-amicable demeanour on which we'd parted in Nottingham was nowhere to be seen.

'No, I heard you,' I told him. 'It's just that the report came from Ms Dickinson, the upstairs neighbour, and yet upon arriving, Mrs Barber didn't corroborate the neighbour's side of the story, did she?'

'Little surprise there,' he scoffed. 'Mrs Barber has always remained dutiful to her husband, no matter the risk to her own personal safety, or the safety of her son.'

'So, she denied the dispute?'

His moustache bobbed from side to side. 'She did, though it was immediately obvious from the state of her face that there had been a physical altercation'

'Therefore, you took it upon yourself to arrest Mr Barber, despite his wife denying any incident?'

'It's my job to protect people, even when they won't admit that they require protection.'

I nodded, tugged at the silk around my wrists, straightening the flow of material. 'You also said that the defendant was unconscious in the shower with the water running when you arrived. Tell me, DCS DeWitt, do you consider an unconscious man particularly threatening?'

'An unconscious violent man is perfectly capable of waking up at any moment.'

'So, one more time, if you wouldn't mind,' I pressed. 'You, personally, went into the defendant's home after the neighbour had heard some sort of unidentifiable ruckus, and found Mr Barber sleeping in his own bathroom. His wife denied any wrongdoing, but you decided to haul him into custody all the same?'

'You seem to be forgetting that there were clothes, saturated in blood, burning in the garden. That gave me enough *reasonable grounds* to take him in.'

A knowing waggle of the eyebrows, a reference to the past, to the night neither of us was going to mention.

'For what? Murder? Are you a full-time police officer, Superintendent DeWitt, or do you occasionally moonlight as a clairvoyant?'

'I beg your pardon?'

'I simply don't understand how you could've arrested him for murder *before* the body had been discovered.'

'Not murder then,' DeWitt snapped, the cool slipping in his grasp, 'but it was obvious that he'd been up to something.'

'Six thirty on a Saturday morning,' I said. 'Do you personally respond to many domestic disturbances at the crack of dawn, in your role as Detective Chief Superintendent?'

He wasn't quite showing his teeth yet, but I could hear that they were gritted.

I could've mentioned his peculiar drive in the centre of the city, but I'd only be throwing myself under the bus for my own suspicious actions, and part of me suspected that he knew that.

'Mr Barber happens to be an intimidating, violent man, which he has proven time and time again.'

'His previous convictions have been admitted, those sentences served. He has never, however, been accused of killing anybody before now.'

'Neither have most murderers,' he bristled, 'until they are. There's history between us, and I know how to handle him better than some of the younger officers might. Otherwise, it would've most likely been Constable Louise Shepherd and, capable as she is, I took it upon myself to go instead; a precautionary measure for the safety of your client, his family and my officers.'

I folded my arms above my gut. 'Interesting that you use that word, "history", once more. You have, as you boasted, personally arrested Mr Barber more times than you can count?'

He shrugged. 'If he stopped committing crimes, then I might stop arresting him for them.'

'Alternatively,' I countered, 'one might argue that you have something of a *vendetta* against him. Do you, DCS DeWitt?'

I was clutching at straws, filling dead air, looking for cracks in the lines of his poker face, but they were nigh on impossible to find.

A cold, straight smile was all he revealed. 'I'd happily see Barber spend the rest of his life behind bars, if that's what you mean, but why would I waste my energy on a vendetta against a man like *that*?'

'Fine words, Superintendent DeWitt, and yet you *have* wasted so much energy on it.'

He straightened his tunic. 'Do you enjoy cross-examining police officers, Mr Rook?'

'Not half as much as you enjoy arresting the defendant, it would seem.'

We stared, locked in stalemate. A minute must've passed.

'If I may interject,' the judge swept in slowly, 'it is almost quarter past four. Perhaps now would be a good time to adjourn for the evening, and continue this examination at ten thirty tomorrow?'

'Perhaps it would,' I said, eyes fixed on DeWitt until long after the rest of the room had risen around us.

'Ten thirty tomorrow morning,' I said to Zara as we swept out of the courtroom. 'That gives us eighteen hours.'

'To do what?'

'To find an answer that'll turn this trial around.'

'What are you thinking?'

'Something isn't adding up here. DeWitt turns up at Barber's home, alone, an hour before the body is discovered?

He's full of shit, and I can smell it on him from the other side of the well.'

She nodded, clutching our case papers in a bundle. 'So, what do we need?'

'Proof. Suspicions and opinions are nothing without evidence. I need you to trawl the Net for anything you can find on him. There were allegations of misconduct a few years ago, I'd say that's as good a place as any to start, but I'll take anything, from which supermarket he uses to where he gets his bloody car washed.'

'All right,' she said tentatively. 'I'll do my best. What are you going to do?'

'I'm going back to Nottingham to talk to McCarthy.'

'Tonight?' she sputtered. 'We're halfway through the cross-examination!'

'Exactly,' I said, taking off down the corridor towards the robing room. 'Eighteen hours, that's all we've got! The clock is ticking, Miss Barnes. It's time we got some answers.'

31

Despite all my haste I still found myself swallowed by the gridlock of rush-hour traffic, eyes on the unrelenting march of the clock above the steering wheel, as the sun set over England. It was already coming up to seven when Sean finally returned my frantic calls.

Crawling along the lower half of the M1, I pulled in to the nearest service station to talk.

'Now then, Rook,' he said, as I came to a stop in the car park. 'If you were ringing about that website, well, I hit a bit of a brick wall with the boys over in tech.'

'That's not it,' I said, 'but thanks for trying.'

'No? So, what's up?'

'DeWitt. I need to know everything about him.'

'DeWitt?' He was quiet for a few seconds, and then I heard a slap, as if he'd just smacked his forehead with one palm. 'You mean DCS DeWitt? As in, my fucking *boss*?'

'There were accusations of misconduct before he came to Nottingham. What do you know? Your colleagues must like to gossip as much as anybody else.'

'For Christ's sake, Rook. I might not *love* the guy, but I can't just roll him over and let the lawyers have at him! My life wouldn't be worth living around the station! You really want me to kiss ta-ta to my uniform for *this*? I'd be lynched before the week is out.'

I lit a smoke and checked the mirrors; a carful of teenagers with long hair and leather jackets had pulled in to the space behind me. They came clambering out of the doors in a clatter of empty cans before rushing for a piss-stop on what looked to be a boozy, cross-country drive. I was feeling edgy, and could see it in the reflection of my own eyes.

'I'm on my way to Notts now,' I said. 'We should meet up somewhere and talk about it. Somewhere safe.'

'I'm working all evening.'

'Didn't stop you before,' I tossed back. 'How about the country park? It won't take long. Half an hour, tops.'

He clicked his tongue down the line.

'Look, I know you're stressed, mate, but you can't come storming up here out of the blue, hoping to get me to flip on another copper. It's not happening. Not ever. Not for Billy.'

'Fine,' I said moodily, 'cheers,' and then hung up on him. I had no time to waste.

I finished the smoke and went into the services. The stress tightening my head craved alcohol, but I had to stay sharp, and settled instead for a can of Red Bull. I went back to the car and smoked another two cigarettes so fast I felt sick from nicotine.

Words were rattling around my head, banging off the inner surface of my skull; at first, I thought they were Rupert's, and then I realised they were my own:

When you defend, do so fearlessly, but honestly. Try and win your cases, but don't ever cheat. Be friendly to defendants, but never forget one crucial point – they are not your friends. Don't ever stick your neck out for them, no matter what you do.

And what was I doing now? I wondered.

What was I turning into?

Unless I did something drastic, DeWitt was going to bury us tomorrow. That much was clear. It was also obvious that Billy was lying about his whereabouts on that night, his opportune amnesia, and I couldn't shake the inkling I'd carried all along; I knew what it was to forge a life on lies and misdirection. Billy was hiding, doing so in plain sight, but from what I had no idea. There had to be a reason he wasn't with his right-wing cronies that night, and, to my mind, the reaction of the prostitute in that bathroom had said it all. She'd known his face and known it well enough to set the whole house upon me.

I glanced around the car park, wary of the open Wi-Fi network as I opened my laptop, wondering if my fellow travellers would be able to see my actions online. There were a few lorry drivers scattered around, noses buried in their phones and laptops, and I had to reason that I would be neither the first nor the last man to visit an escort directory halfway up the motorway.

With that in mind, I went onto Red Sheets.

My ill-conceived scraping of a plan was to message any of the working girls in the Cotgrave or Nottingham area and ask to meet up. After that, well, I'd just have to improvise.

When it came to drafting my message, however, or choosing the right girl for the job, I didn't know where to start. Had it really come to this?

'Come on, you old bastard,' I muttered to myself, slamming my face into my palms. 'Think!'

Minutes passed with few sparks in my head. I chucked the laptop onto the passenger seat, necked half the energy drink, and stared vacantly at the logo on the can. Two eponymous bulls were charging towards one another there, horns down and ready to maim. On the left, I could almost see DeWitt; the right was surely Billy, and where would I, the advocate, be in that situation?

Standing in the middle, I supposed, waving a big red flag, ready to be skewered from either side.

That's when I felt my face crease into a frown.

An image had come to mind, of standing with that red flag, baiting destruction from both sides. Only instead of standing in some torero's ring, I was tattooed across the skin of a young man's back.

My hands had begun to shake when I went back to the laptop and changed the search filter from female escorts to the much shorter list of males. That's where I found him.

His face had been cropped, but he was shirtless in the photograph, bent over before a mirror, and on his naked back was the tattoo of a bullfighter, fluttering a great crimson flag.

Underneath that was a banner in green: *online and available for escort now!*

Sending an anonymous request to talk was, alarmingly, as simple as ordering from Amazon. I just had to sit and wait for a reply.

I must've refreshed the page almost a hundred times in about six minutes. Then there was a knock on the glass beside me.

'Rook?'

The laptop closed so fast I thought I might've shattered the screen.

Fraser Hayes, Billy's solicitor, was standing beside the car with a cup of coffee and a doughnut from one of those gourmet cabinets.

'Not running out on us now, are you?' he joked as I lowered the window, apparently too anxious to back it up with a smile.

'No,' I swallowed, palms clamped tight over the laptop. 'Following leads. Yourself?'

'Going home,' he sighed. 'I can't take one more night in a hotel when my missus is only a couple of hours away, even if it means setting off from Notts at daft o'clock in the morning.'

I nodded, thinking of Jenny and how I probably should've done the same every once in a while, but the thought was stricken by the sound of a woman moaning with pleasure, a lewd message alert blaring out from the speaker of the laptop.

My hands clenched across the surface, cheeks aflame.

'Well,' Hayes said, raising his eyebrows, 'I'll leave you to your *leads* and see you in the morning.'

'Bright and early,' I managed through a dry mouth, and didn't loosen my grip until he was across the car park and in his own car.

When I opened the laptop, I discovered two things. The screen was, thankfully, still intact, and there was a message blinking at the bottom of my browser.

When and where? X

When was nine o'clock.

Where was at the south-west entrance of Nottingham's Arboretum Park on Waverley Street, appropriately close to Forest Road, the city's old red-light district.

First, I watched him from a distance.

A dark, slender figure, he was there fifteen minutes early, hood up and leaning quite casually against one of the four stone gateposts, the black iron gates locked shut already.

I kept the brim of my hat down low, smoking and loitering some forty metres away at the junction with Cromwell Street against the wall of the cemetery that mirrored the park for a hefty stretch of the road. I was trying to make sure that his hulking guardian was nowhere to be seen, along with any companions who might be waiting to jump me on arrival, but the road was clear, the darkness empty. I'd left my own car parked at the Gooseberry Bush, the Wetherspoon's round the corner to the south.

At two minutes to nine he started checking his phone, thin face glowing in the damp-blue light of the screen, and I knew I had to move.

Now or never. My palms were slick, heart hammering as I crossed the road towards the entrance of the park.

On his profile, it said his name was Luke, and so that's what I started with when I'd made it within earshot.

'Luke?'

He lowered his hood with a cool, friendly smile, revealing the face I could just about remember, the pronounced cheekbones of a model juxtaposed against the web of faded scarring around the right eye.

He was silent for a moment. Then the smile drained. 'You!'

'Wait!' I tried, but he'd already bolted, scrambling nimbly over the park gate like a cat from a bag and landing softly on the other side. 'Shit!'

I jumped onto the bars, heaved my bulk up and over the spikes, and slammed down without grace on the other side. My only lead was already a fair way off to the left, sprinting round the smooth black expanse of the pond. He was fast, and I was painfully slow; I cursed every damn cigarette I'd ever lit.

He glanced back over his shoulder – a momentary twist in the shadow rapidly shrinking into the surrounding black of the distance – and if he hadn't done that, he would've made it. As it happened, there was a great crack as he pelted straight into an overhanging branch, and down he went, skidding like a jet without landing gear. Desperation, anger and exhaustion launched me on top of him with my entire weight, pinning him to the spot. His eyes were as wide and white as two autumn mushrooms on the lawn in the dark. The sound of panting filled the air.

I stood up, dusting the dirt from my knees, and then slumped against the trunk of the tree he'd hit.

'Pig!' he spat, rubbing his head and wavering from side to side as he stood. 'What you want?'

'I'm not a copper,' I wheezed, 'and all I want after that is a goddamn pint, that's all.' I rummaged for my smokes and held one out towards him. 'What would you say to a drink?'

He seemed to be weighing his options, bright eyes shining in the dark, and then, just when I was afraid he wouldn't take it, slowly, begrudgingly, he did.

Up close, in the light of the pub round the corner, he looked younger than the twenty-five years his online profile had claimed.

Perhaps it was the way he ate, as if he hadn't seen a real meal in weeks, making short work of a large mixed grill and chips, half a rack of barbecue ribs, grilled halloumi and a dozen onion rings on the side. With the five pints he washed that away with, all on my wallet, it came to almost double the hour for which I'd had to pay.

'Luke. Is that your real name?'

He shook his head, licking the blunt edge of his steak knife clean. 'Louis, if you really want to know.'

'How long have you been in the UK, Louis?'

He thought about it as if he hadn't considered it for a while. 'Three years.'

Those three years and their habits had yellowed his natural skin tone, though his accent remained. The scarring around his right eye was raised and webbed, a gruesome imitation of Paul Stanley's star in scalding shades of pink and pure white. 'You're Spanish?'

'Catalan,' he replied sharply. 'Just outside of Barcelona.'

'Lovely city,' I nodded, slicing a length from my own cut of beef. 'I saw that Catalonia declared independence last week. That must be exciting?'

He didn't answer. I'd just opened my mouth to try a different angle when a member of the floor staff – not quite a waiter here – was suddenly standing by our booth.

'Everything all right with your meals? Can I get you any more sauces?'

'Fine, thanks,' I said brusquely, shooing him away, though when I looked up he was still hovering, treating us to a brief, disapproving stare before leaving again.

'I come here to teach,' Louis said, tearing his field mushroom to pieces. 'Spanish at the university, I thought, but it doesn't happen that way.'

'I can see that. You still up in St Ann's?'

'No,' he replied bitterly, glaring at me from beneath the scarred tissue. 'Thanks to this *capullo* starting a fire, the landlord kicks us out.'

'That was all just a misunderstanding,' I said. 'What happened to your pimp?'

'My *pimp?*'

'Big bloke, chased me out of there.'

He cocked his head and laughed, a surprisingly boyish titter. 'Marcel? He's no *pimp*. He's protection.'

'Protection from what?' I asked, fleetingly hopeful, but he pointed the steak knife level across the table.

'From people like you, friend.'

I turned to my own pint.

'There was a girl when we work on the streets,' he went on, finishing his drink and holding the empty glass high above his plate. 'Group of men pay, but she doesn't want all of them at once. She was pretty, so they boil a kettle, hold it over her face, and …' He tipped the glass upside down, sending the last drops cascading, and caught them on his tongue. 'Safer in houses. Safer together.'

I looked over his face, the searing glow of the scars, and nodded.

'I need to talk to the girls,' I said. 'Anybody who was working down in Cotgrave about six months ago. I need to find out about their clientele. Could we meet them?'

He rolled his eyes. 'I don't know where they are. Girls come, girls go.'

I took the folded paper from my pocket – it looked as if I'd found it in a bin – and opened it out onto the tabletop.

'This man. I need to know if you've ever seen him with the girls. It's important. It could save his life. It could help to save even more.'

He leaned forward, looked at the mugshot, and, to my surprise, smiled.

Then he cut the rump of his lamb in half and stuffed it into his mouth.

'Why?' he asked through a mouthful of food. 'What do you want to know about Billy?'

It was coming up to midnight when my phone rang, buzzing in my coat pocket, causing me to jump.

Zara.

'Mr Rook!' she panted from the other end. 'I've found something! Holy shit, have I found something!'

'What've you got?'

'What *haven't* I got?' She sounded like she might explode at any moment. 'I hope you're sitting down, because you're not going to believe this!'

I glanced back from the open doorway to the young Catalan sitting in the office behind me, Fraser Hayes, exhausted at his side, taking his statement down word for word.

'I don't know about that,' I said, rubbing my eyes, grinning in spite of myself. 'I'm just about ready to believe anything at this point.'

32

I hadn't slept.

Not for the first time, I felt the weight of the briefcase hanging from my fist, the presence of the danger inside, like a bomb I was carrying into the courthouse.

I'd got back to London at dawn, followed along the dark, empty motorway by the lights of Fraser Hayes's chugging Peugeot, and went straight to the Bailey, unwashed, unshaven, and dressed in yesterday's clothes.

If Zara had managed to get a minute's sleep, it didn't show, and what a shattered, ragged trio we must've looked when we gathered under the marble of the Great Hall.

'You ready for this?' she asked, robed and waiting with armfuls of freshly bound paper, the smell of warm printer ink still drying on crisp, white pages.

'Ready as I'll ever be. You?'

She managed a half-nod, ruffling the wig above her glasses, and blinked against the dark circles around her eyes. 'Reckon so.'

Hayes yawned, checked his watch, and tousled his increasingly ratty hair to stop himself falling asleep on the spot. 'I'm off to neck a few espressos before we start. Think I'm going to need them. Can I get you anything?'

'Same for me, espresso,' I said, 'triple,' and off he went to fetch them.

We hovered in the hall a moment longer, and Zara handed me copies of a document she'd drafted at some ridiculous hour of the morning.

'Fantastic work,' I said, checking the pages. 'Well beyond your call of duty. You really are a fine junior.'

'I know,' she smiled. 'Just tell me everything's cool.'

'I'm in my fifties. The day I tell you that *everything is cool* will be the day I need some serious assistance.'

'I'll remember that, Grandad.' She gestured to the staircase. 'Shall we?'

Bowen and Garrick were in the well, relaxed and refreshed, apparently ready to make their final putt.

Bowen looked me up and down. 'I don't know about DeWitt moonlighting as a clairvoyant, Rook, but you look like you've been moonlighting selling the *Big Issue*.'

'Glad to hear that homelessness is amusing to you,' I said. 'I'm fresh out of *Big Issues* but let me give you a copy of this document to make up for that.'

'What is it?' Garrick asked suspiciously, snatching the papers from my hand.

'A bad character application. It's time the jury met the *real* Detective Chief Superintendent.'

Garrick flicked through the pages, face scrunching further with every new sheet, and shook his head. 'You're wasting your time and everybody else's, Rook. Judge Pike will never allow this.'

I couldn't help but smile. 'I wouldn't be so sure.'

Criticisms might be made of our criminal justice system, but the independence and fair-mindedness of the judiciary remains a shining beacon. The judge allowed it, and when we reconvened with the jury after our successful application,

DeWitt having returned to the stand, I knew it was time to take the gloves off once and for all.

I took a drink of water, readying my throat. There was a long way left to go.

'Superintendent DeWitt,' I smiled, turning upon him, 'you emigrated here from South Africa, is that correct?'

He shrugged, blasé, but with a twitch around the eyes. 'That's right.'

'Whereabouts?' I asked, though Zara had already answered that for me.

'Pretoria.'

'Ah, Pretoria!' I clasped my palms together. 'One of the country's three capitals, an academic city of cutting-edge research, as I understand. When did you decide to relocate to the UK?'

His eyes were narrowing with each passing moment. 'I came to England in '96.'

'In '96?' I repeated, raising my brow. 'You said yesterday that you've been in law enforcement for thirty years. Now, the Bureau of State Security would have been replaced for some years by '87, but it would still have been your duty to uphold apartheid, would it not?'

A shallow nod. 'That was the law.'

'Absolutely,' I said, 'and far it be it from me, of all people, to criticise the laws of any land.'

'My Lord …' Garrick sighed, shaking his head so hard it almost spun his wig. 'Judging by those bags around their eyes, perhaps the defence have forgotten the point of this trial, but I can only wonder whether there'll be any *relevant* questions any time soon?'

'Indeed,' Pike said, though he dipped his chin and eyed me with some modicum of unmistakable curiosity.

'My learned friend is absolutely right,' I said, 'it was indeed a long and interesting night, and perhaps I'm getting ahead of myself. Let's put a pin in that for now, shall we?' I rubbed the sting from my eyes, shuffled the papers in front of me, and stroked my palm along the coarseness of my jaw. I couldn't remember the last time I'd shaved. 'So, where were we? How about cell-site analysis? That was, after all, a hefty part of your evidence against the defendant, and placed him squarely in the vicinity of the killing at the recorded time of death, did it not?'

'It did,' DeWitt replied.

'And yet, we can see in the report by the cell-site expert that only *one* phone mast was servicing the entire area at that time, from the social club to the scene of the death and beyond! Wouldn't that, therefore, make every resident of Cotgrave a potential suspect, as their phones were, technically, all in use in that same vicinity?'

An icy smirk. 'Our investigation was based on a lot more than that. Besides, there's nobody quite like William Barber in that village. He has the most prolific criminal record in the area, and his fellow residents don't post the same sort of racist, inflammatory garbage across the Internet.'

'You're right,' I sighed, straightening my robes, as another sheet was handed to me – 'Thank you, Miss Barnes' – and I held it close to my face. 'Here, for example, is a post from just *last month*. "Another attack in London by a loser terrorist. These are sick and demented people who were in the sights of Scotland Yard. Must be proactive!" Is that one of Mr Barber's?'

He nodded. 'Sounds like the sort of racist drivel he'd come up with.'

'Yes?' I paused, frowning at the sheet. 'Oh, my mistake, that post actually came from the personal Twitter account of the President of the United States. Should Donald Trump, consequently, be a suspect, too?'

'Mr Rook!' Judge Pike barked, reddening faster than a crustacean on the boil. 'I will *not* have my court's time wasted with pseudo-political statements!'

'Hear, hear!' Garrick declared, and Bowen banged his feet beneath our bench in agreement.

DeWitt was shaking his head. 'I've heard some defences in my time, but *this* ...'

We were losing the room already. I glanced to Zara, and she nodded. It was time.

'Perhaps you're right,' I said, 'but what options did we have? It's not, after all, as if the defendant had an alibi to rely on, is it?'

'Precisely my point,' DeWitt said, flattening his tunic with both hands. 'Now, if that's all ...' He lifted one foot out of the box, ready to be dismissed.

'No.' I held up a hand to halt him. 'That was actually a question, DCS DeWitt. Mr Barber didn't have an alibi on the night in question, did he?'

Slowly, he moved back into the box, towards the microphone, and frowned. 'You really must've had a late night. Have you paid attention to any of this case, Mr Rook?'

'Oh, I've paid attention. We all have. We all heard, for example, the failure to disclose the evidence of the DNA found under the victim's fingernails.'

'It was a partial profile, and the results were inconclusive.'

'And yet they were conclusive enough to rule out the defendant as the source of the DNA?'

He blinked hard. 'There's plenty more evidence against the defendant.'

'As the jury have heard. But could there, similarly, have been anything *else* that you forgot to disclose to the CPS?'

He leaned forward, wrapping his fingers around the balustrade of the stand, and for the first time I noticed how large his hands were. 'If you have a point, Mr Rook, why don't you get to it?' he snarled.

Fair enough, I thought, and lit the fuse.

'DCS DeWitt, are you familiar with a young man by the name of Louis Galos?'

His lower lip shifted, a hairline fracture in the concrete facade he'd maintained so well, and his fingers tightened around wood. 'No.'

'Really?' I cocked my head. 'You do not know Mr Galos?'

He shrugged. 'Never heard of him.'

'Huh …' I turned to survey the bemused expressions of the faces across the jury, up in the gallery, before coming to rest on Billy.

The rage, the absolute, earth-shattering terror in his face; as soon as I saw that, I knew it to be true.

'Well,' I said, turning back to the witness, 'the two of you *have* met. You've personally arrested the young man on four separate occasions, in fact.'

Another shrug. 'I've arrested a lot of people. You expect me to remember them all?'

'What I expect, DCS DeWitt, and all I ask for, is honesty. What do you know about Mr Louis Galos?'

'*Rook!*'

The voice was Billy's, but I, like everybody else in the room, kept my eyes squarely upon the witness. I would not, could not, be stopped.

'Well,' I said, 'would you like to tell the court, Superintendent DeWitt, or should I?'

His eyes had turned to stones in his skull, jaw tight as a vice. He didn't say a word.

I sighed and glanced back to Billy. The look of devastation that had gripped his squashed-up features meant little to me now. I was thinking instead about the humiliation and the cruelty, the arrogance, violence and manipulation.

You wanted me to win at any cost, did you? How about the truth?

'Mr Galos is a sex worker,' I said, turning back to the sweating brow of DeWitt. 'A Spanish immigrant currently based in the centre of Nottingham. Six months ago, however, Mr Galos was sharing a small house on East Acres, a residential road in Cotgrave, which happens to fall precisely along the route between the Welfare Scheme Social Club and the country park, beyond which is the site of the killing.'

Zara handed me the next sheet in the pile, and I smoothed it across the oak, rapping upon it with one knuckle.

'Allow me to ask a basic question,' I went on. 'Does evidence of an alibi either undermine the prosecution case or assist the defence case?'

Stunned silence from DeWitt.

It was a few more seconds before the judge interceded. 'Could you answer the question please, Superintendent DeWitt?'

'Yes,' he conceded grudgingly. 'Evidence of an alibi assists the defence.'

'It does,' I nodded firmly, 'and yet you didn't think it necessary to disclose the fact that our client, Mr Barber, had an alibi between the hours of one and five o'clock on the morning of the murder?'

A few gasps, but mostly perplexed frowns stretched from the jury to the prosecution and beyond. I had to go for broke.

'In simple terms,' I sighed, 'Mr Galos and William Barber were engaged in sexual intercourse with one another, *during* and *beyond* the time of The Girl's killing. And you knew about this all along, didn't you, Detective Chief Superintendent?'

33

It was well over a minute before the silence in the court-room was broken by a long howl echoing from the public gallery.

Glancing up, I saw the last of Sarah Barber as she was shepherded, retching, from the balcony by several ashen members of the family, while Billy buried his head in the massive crooks of his arms.

There was nothing to do but carry on.

'Mr Barber was a regular client of Mr Galos, a relationship he'd begun almost a year before the killing. Furthermore, you *knew* of this! It had been revealed to you after one of Mr Galos's aforementioned arrests. You were entirely aware about this alibi from day one of the investigation! So, I ask, why did you decide not to disclose that fact?'

DeWitt's eyes were burning now, but he did a surprising job of holding in his temper.

'Fact?' he scoffed. 'You have absolutely no evidence of this, beyond the word of some drug-abusing *rent boy*! If this were true, why wouldn't Barber have admitted it from the start? You seriously expect the jury to believe that a man would risk being sent down for a murder he didn't commit, simply to hide his *homosexuality*?'

'Most men, no, of course not. But *this* man? Absolutely! Just as *you* were banking on him doing!'

'My Lord!' Garrick was on his feet alongside me. 'This is an *outrageous, totally inappropriate* attack on a commended chief of police! Where is this so-called witness, I ask?'

Mr Justice Pike frowned, scratching his nose. Then, to my surprise, gave me the slightest of nods. 'Go on, Mr Rook.'

By now, DeWitt was spinning wildly between judge, jury and myself. 'I suppose Galos gave you an explanation for the burned clothes while he was at it, did he?' he growled.

'Evidence of an affair that Mr Barber would, understandably, have wanted to destroy. Would it be fair to say that in this courtroom, your job as an investigating officer is to present the evidence, all of the evidence, to the jury?'

'Only the credible evidence,' he snapped.

'Whether evidence is credible is not a matter for you to decide, Officer, but for the jury.'

There came no reply, so I altered my approach. 'Let's go back to the arrest of Mr Barber, shall we? You bundled him into the back seat of ... what car was it, again?'

He was paling now, blond as the hair upon his head. 'What *car*?'

'Yes. I'm sure that you, commended Chief Super, rarely have to squabble for the keys from the board in the parade room. Having your own, unmarked car is one of the perks of your position, isn't it? No logbook to fill. No officers to share it with. In fact, you drive an unmarked BMW 5 Series, don't you?'

Of course you do, I thought. You tried to haul me into it, and I wasn't the first.

He nodded.

'Nodding doesn't help, DCS DeWitt,' Pike said. 'You need to say yes or no so it can be recorded.'

'Yes.'

'So,' I went on, 'it goes without saying that you were driving your unmarked BMW that morning?'

'I don't remember what car I was driving.'

'But wait,' I said, 'Ms Dickinson, the upstairs neighbour, clearly told this courtroom yesterday of her relief when the *panda car* arrived on the scene! It certainly stuck in my mind, as people rarely use that expression these days, but I'm sure we can have the court reporter go back to that evidence if memories need refreshing?'

'I told you, I don't remember *what* I was driving. Maybe she was speaking metaphorically?'

'Maybe so. But tell me, if you took the defendant straight out of the shower, dressed in what must have been clean clothes, then how did he make such a mess in the back seat?'

DeWitt held my gaze, blinking rapidly. More papers came up to me from the pile; God bless Zara and her night of work.

'Are you familiar,' I asked, 'with Nottinghamshire Constabulary's Use and Maintenance of Police Vehicles Guidance?'

'Yes,' he managed through tight teeth.

'Including the passage that states: "Where professional cleaning of a police vehicle is required to remove bodily fluids or other contamination, Business Services can arrange for completion of any witness statements, and all cleaning should be done through approved contract arrangements"?'

'Yes.'

'So, all police cars have to be taken to the same approved car wash – is that right?'

'Yes.'

'Then tell me, Superintendent DeWitt, was there any particularly pressing reason for one of your cars to be taken for a full valet, by you personally, only minutes after the car wash opened on the morning of the fifteenth. This is while Mr Barber was in your custody, sobering up, and you were supposedly on your way to the scene of a young girl's murder?'

He looked like he was getting short of breath, leaning against the balustrade. 'What are you insinuating?'

Cross-examination. A chance to find the truth.

'Answer the question, please,' came the steely voice of the judge.

'I don't remember! The car was probably dirty – what of it?'

'Well, let's recap, shall we?' I said. 'You *knew* that the defendant had an alibi, but it was one he'd never use. You decided not to disclose details of that alibi to anybody. You picked him up in a standard patrol car, while your unmarked vehicle was waiting to be cleaned of bodily fluids, only hours after a killing. There was another failure to disclose evidence of DNA found under the victim's fingernails, which did not come from the defendant, and you were *so eager* to arrest Mr Barber for this murder that you did so before the body had even been discovered! As if by psychic ability you arrested him for a crime which, at that moment, nobody else knew had been committed! Nobody, but the killer, of course. How was this possible?'

He didn't answer. Along the panel, faces were turning to and fro like spectators of a Grand Slam tournament. I had him on the ropes.

'Why *did* you move to Nottingham, DCS DeWitt? You were previously working in Sheffield, up until you were subject to police disciplinary proceedings, weren't you?'

'I was cleared,' he managed.

'Of all allegations?' I raised an eyebrow. 'Cleared or not, the charges of misconduct were severe enough to be reported in the national news at the time. Without detail, of course.'

'Cleared of all, yes, except one, and all I got for that was a rap on the knuckles.'

'A rap on the knuckles?' I ran my finger along the printed article. 'Is that how you describe a warning over future conduct?'

'It was nothing.' Sweat was gathering now, rolling from his temples to his jaw.

'Again, that's a matter for the jury to decide, not you,' I said coolly. 'Why don't you tell us what you were accused of? It might be in the court's interest, after all.'

'There were some issues …' he mumbled, and then swallowed. It took him a while to finish. 'With disclosure.'

I tried not to smile. 'In other words, you were accused of withholding evidence?'

'The allegations were a load of rubbish! Everything I did, I did to –'

'But those allegations were enough to make you move to a new city, weren't they?' I pressed. 'I wonder, if that was enough to make you leave Sheffield, then what must have driven you to leave Pretoria in '96?'

'What the hell has me leaving South Africa got to do with this case?' he blustered.

'Well, you were a police officer in South Africa, were you not? You willingly upheld apartheid, in a city only ten miles east of Vlakplaas, the farm infamously used by death squads, and only *after* the collapse of apartheid did you come to England. I suppose it had nothing to do with the Truth and Reconciliation Commission coming down hard on members of the South African Police?'

He was falling apart at the seams, and then he uttered two simple words that changed everything.

'No comment.'

On hearing these words, my legs seemed to vacate the floor. Checkmate. 'No comment? Did you not tell this jury, only yesterday, that such an expression is common among *guilty men?*'

Ten seconds of silence. Twenty. Thirty.

Mr Justice Pike leaned forward. 'Well?'

Across the balustrade, the detective's hands were shaking.

'DCS DeWitt,' I said, 'do you consider yourself a guilty man?'

'Guilty of what?' He looked broken, confused, lost.

'Before this continues,' I said, 'I am obligated to warn you of the rule against self-incrimination. This essentially means that, should the answer to the question I'm about to ask you be incriminating, you have the right to refuse to answer.'

He only blinked, so I took a huge breath.

'Did you have something to do with the victim's murder on the night of Good Friday?'

His answer came without words.

Time distorts in moments like this, and what happened next somehow occurred both quickly and incredibly slowly. DeWitt was out of the witness box. He was charging across the well. He threw his bulk onto our row, sending a storm of papers into the air, and reached for me with both hands.

All I could think to do was shunt my head forwards, butting my wig down over my face and into his nose, knocking him back before Harlan Garrick, Zara and two court officers managed to prise him away.

34

'Ladies and gentlemen of the jury,' Garrick said, relocating a cracked version of his earlier voice twenty minutes after DeWitt had been escorted from the room. 'In my opening statement, I undertook the task of convincing you that this man, this pathological liar, this *proven reoffender*, is nothing better than a cold-blooded murderer.

'We, the prosecution, have called witness after witness to testify to his unstable, violent character, while the defence have provided no physical witness of their own. Instead, they are relying on a sudden, supposed and, you may think, *unbelievable* alibi, which they have conjured out of little more than thin air.

'The defence would have you believe that the defendant – this *extremist* of far-right principles – was engaged in a homosexual affair on the night of the victim's death. In making your decision, I implore you to consider the credibility of this statement, and the witness who made it. A sex worker with no registered address, and with his own history of prior arrests. The defence might have caused a stir with their cross-examination, but I will remind you that it is their job to do so, and simply because Detective Chief Superintendent DeWitt allowed my learned friend Mr Rook of Queen's Counsel to get under his skin, that doesn't undermine the evidence called by the prosecution one jot.

'I ask you, then, to look at the defendant, who still hasn't stepped forward to confirm or deny this alleged alibi. Focus on his behaviour in the dock during this very trial! Focus on the *fact* that he was in the area at the time, he was discovered burning evidence, and he did, most certainly, murder that poor young girl, with the sheer strength of his own brutal hands.

'We, the prosecution, ask that you find the defendant guilty as charged.'

As I stood to make my closing speech, I could feel the bump already growing on my forehead, my hands still trembling from all that had just happened.

I looked back into the dock, and saw him there.

Billy – the outlaw, the mountain, the monster of my youth – now utterly broken.

All the glib, sarcastic comments, the cruelty and the arrogance that had brought us to this moment had vanished, and what remained was a man so much smaller than before.

'Ladies and gentlemen of the jury,' I said. 'As a barrister, I see a lot of pride. People live by it, and people die by it. We all have private lives, and things we will hide at any cost.

'Is it really *so* unbelievable, considering the defendant's public image, that he would go to any lengths, including the sacrifice of his own liberty, to hide the truth of his sexuality from family and peers?

'From the moment of his arrest, Mr Barber has been the victim of a case laden with lies, subterfuge and repeated failings to disclose evidence and answer crucial questions. The entire investigation, in fact, was spearheaded by a man so desperate for a hasty solution that he himself may have skirted the boundaries of the laws he is sworn to protect.

A man who has responded to the simplest of questions with absolute aggression, the likes of which I have never witnessed in the courtroom.

'In this case, the prosecution bear the burden and standard of proof, which is to prove the defendant's guilt *beyond reasonable doubt.* In closing the case for the Crown, Mr Garrick invited you to find Mr Barber guilty. I'm not going to tell you to find him not guilty, but simply ask you to consider the evidence in this case, and bear in mind that burden and standard of proof. If you *are* sure, beyond reasonable doubt, that William Barber murdered that poor girl, well, then you go ahead and find him guilty, and he will deserve it.

'If, on the other hand, as a result of the things that have come to light during this trial, there is any *doubt* in your mind as to what happened, doubt as to who did it, then William Barber – ghastly, racist, violent thug though he may well be – is entitled to a verdict of not guilty.

'Thank you.'

We sat on the stone steps outside, watching the protesters nearby, the news cameras around them, the banners sailing above.

The members of the jury were off doing their *Twelve Angry Men* routine around a large table, hashing it out over sandwiches and coffee; soon, one would be elected as foreman or forewoman, and asked to deliver their unanimous verdict.

I was chain-smoking, working my way through a whole pack until my throat would surely burn.

Beside me, Zara was tugging at loose hair that had slipped out from underneath her wig, staring past the crowd.

I followed her eye, and saw Caine and Declan Barber, surrounded by a handful of family members, walking away. They weren't even waiting around for the verdict.

I hadn't gone down to see Billy, even though the nervousness that had plagued my earlier visits had withered altogether. In some deep, hidden place I almost felt sorry for him, though I'd never speak of it out loud. It certainly wasn't sympathy, but it might've had roots in some sort of empathy.

'It's funny, isn't it?' Zara said. 'What really frightens people. You look at a man like that, harbinger of hostility, and yet he's more frightened than anybody I've ever met. He's so utterly petrified of himself, of his own sexuality, that he'd risk spending the rest of his life in a cell. He'd sacrifice the entire world just to save face, and for what?'

'For the life he wanted,' I muttered, more to myself than to her. 'For the man he so desperately wanted to be.'

'He's a coward,' she said, 'that's all. He unloads his self-pity onto others by being vile. He could've been true to himself from the beginning and spared those around him so much anger. So much misery.'

'He could have,' I nodded, 'but would anybody in his shoes, I wonder? In that culture? In his world?'

She turned to face me, removed her glasses, and studied me hard. 'All people face judgement in some shape or form, Mr Rook. That's life. Shit, half of my extended family are strict practising Muslims, and *I* still managed to come out. The people around you get over it, eventually, or you just have to get over them. Nobody ought to live a lie.'

It took me another moment to catch on. 'You're ...'

'Gay?' She laughed lightly. 'I thought silks were meant to be pros at reading people?'

'Hmm,' I flushed. 'I suppose I didn't think about it one way or the other.'

'Which is all I've ever wanted,' she smiled. 'I've had labels enough before now. I just want to be taken for, well … *me*.'

'Some people don't have your courage, Miss Barnes. Who knows? Perhaps Billy always wanted to be sent down in the end. Maybe he thinks he deserves it.'

'And he probably does, for plenty of other reasons,' she said, 'but if a man truly wants to be punished, then isn't the very concept of punishment made redundant? Wouldn't that undermine the legal process altogether, in giving him what he wants?'

'Punishment takes many forms,' I told her. 'Whether he's found guilty or not, his life will never be the same again. All we did in there was present facts.'

'And beauty is truth, truth beauty, right?'

'Right,' I said, though I knew that wasn't always true. 'Those are very eloquent thoughts. What happened to the ruffian that stepped into my room not so many weeks ago?'

'Well, I guess we all pick things up along the way, don't we?'

'We do,' I said. 'We certainly do.'

'What about DeWitt?' she asked. 'What happens now? I thought he'd be in cuffs. I thought we had this solved.'

Honestly, I thought to myself, so did I. 'As far as the law is concerned, we have no proof. Discrepancies alone never won the day. All we had was a theory, enough to blow the prosecution's case open, and little more than that. All we ever had was doubt to cast, and that's what we needed. We were never going to discover what really happened that night ourselves, and neither should we. That's not our job.'

'But there'll be an investigation, won't there? There *has* to be …'

I couldn't say. She picked at her nails, fiddled with her collar and sighed.

'The Girl,' she said, eyes locking onto mine. 'Where will she end up?'

I tapped the end of my cigarette onto the steps. 'Do you really want to know?'

She thought about it for a moment. Looked to her shoes and nodded. 'Yes.'

'I'd imagine she would've been kept on ice until now. She is evidence until conviction.'

'So if Barber is convicted and the case is closed?'

'That'll be up to the coroner,' I said. 'There are more than a hundred unidentified bodies found in the UK every year. They're often used for teaching.'

'You mean they'll butcher her up some more for trainees to study?' She shook her head sadly. 'Then what?'

'She'll be burned.'

'Or buried in an unmarked grave,' she added.

We didn't say another word until the door behind us opened several minutes later.

'Mr Rook? Miss Barnes?'

Fraser Hayes was standing there, fiddling with his tie.

'It's time.'

35

'Will the defendant please stand?'

Billy raised himself on weary legs, and looked up to the public gallery. His wife hadn't returned, nor had most of his family.

In the end, I thought, perhaps you really do get what you deserve.

'Would the foreman please stand?'

The elected forewoman stood. It was, to my surprise, Number 4, the oldest woman with the nicest blouse. She adjusted her glasses and looked up to the bench, wetting her lips.

'Have you, the jury, reached a verdict upon which you are all agreed?'

She took a deep breath. 'We have.'

'And on this indictment, that William Barber did, on the morning of the fifteenth of April this year, commit murder, do you find the defendant guilty or not guilty?'

The quiet that followed seemed to stretch on for a thousand years.

Something warm gripped around my forearm, and I looked down to see Zara's white-knuckled fist welded to my robe.

The forewoman cleared her throat, and nodded to the bench.

'Not guilty.'

PART FOUR

THE TRUTH, AND
NOTHING BUT

36

It was December when I decided to make a start on organising my life.

There was no single leaf to turn. Clearing out meant chipping away, hour by hour, one old case file at a time, and that was just the physical work. My wedding ring, like so much more bric-a-brac, I'd got used to carrying around in my coat pocket, still unwilling to renounce it entirely.

Baby steps, I kept on saying to myself. Let's start with the litter and the paperwork and take it from there. There'll be plenty of time to face the trivialities of divorce, obesity, alcoholism and cigarettes.

We were finally on top of the prep for the fraud case, and I hadn't heard anything of Billy in almost six weeks. I suspected – and hoped in no small measure – that I never would again. That's the way it is, being a barrister. Lives hang in the balance, and we give it our all, but once the verdict comes, they're just another case file in the stack.

I did think about the Barber household from time to time though, and on more than one occasion I found myself wondering if we'd done the right thing, outing him in the way we did.

At those times, usually in the darkest, loneliest hours of the night, I had to remind myself that justice is a concept that reaches far beyond the pages of English law, and all we'd done was present the facts to the best of our ability. Nothing more, and nothing less. The holes are often the ones we dig entirely for ourselves.

As for DeWitt, there'd been only the briefest mention of repercussions in the news at the conclusion of the trial, some whispers of an internal investigation, but nothing had ever surfaced. I wasn't sure if anything would, but Zara seemed to hold on to the belief of some greater justice, and I could still see the thought of the *killer at large* come back to her in quiet moments.

If there was anything for the pupil to have learned from her first trial, it was that the whole truth is rarely uncovered, in the courtroom, prison cell or beyond.

Sometimes the client walks, and sometimes the client doesn't, but our lives go on all the same. The jury verdict always includes the word *guilty*; it's the *not*, three letters, that changes so much.

It was a Friday when the door to my chambers opened without a knock shortly before lunch, and I didn't even turn; I was well used to her comings and goings by now.

'How'd it go?' I asked, shaking the dust of old paperwork from my hands.

She collapsed into the chair by the bureau I'd emptied out for her and buried her face in her hands. 'Shit,' she grunted.

I sighed. 'Don't beat yourself up about it. The magistrates can be harder than you'd think. What was the sentence?'

She managed less than two seconds before I spotted the grin breaking out between the strands of falling hair. 'Acquitted!'

'You're a terrible liar,' I laughed as she leapt up out of the chair.

'Honestly, Mr Rook, you should've seen me! I totally smashed it!'

'Never had a doubt about it. What did Stein have to say about it?'

'Haven't seen him yet, I came straight here. *And*, as if that wasn't enough, look outside! It's snowing!'

'Really?' I'd spent the morning so buried in files that I hadn't noticed the weather. I looked out past the stacks of semi-organised boxes ready for storage to see spots of white clinging to the glass. 'So it is.'

'We should celebrate!' She reached over to the nearest shelf, three rows beneath the first-edition copy of *To Kill a Mockingbird*, and picked up the bottle of whiskey that Rupert had sent down after Billy's trial. It was still sealed, and his simple, elegant note – *Well done, Pupil* – remained around the neck. Strangely, I hadn't felt up to opening it yet. I couldn't ignore the feeling that, though the trial was most certainly finished, the case hadn't ended as it should have.

She plonked the bottle on the desk, and I indicated the clutter around us. 'I don't know, I've really got a lot to be getting on with here ...'

'Ah, come on!' she beamed, bouncing around in her boots. 'That's what New Year's Resolutions are for! Live now, tidy later, that's what I always say, don't I?'

'I have not once heard you say that. Besides, I've already got my resolutions sorted. No more pupils under my feet, and that's just for starters.'

'Yeah, yeah,' she said, 'I didn't hear you complaining when I was traipsing through all of these!' She tapped the nearest box with the toe of her boot. 'Come on, this is my last week before I go home for Christmas!'

'Don't remind me,' I groaned. 'I can't bloody wait for my brother-in-law to regale me with all the countless benefits of being a self-employed plumber, as he has done every other time I've seen him. He's his own boss, don't you know? Humbug!'

It was to be my first Christmas with the family for more years than I could remember, and I told myself that it was pure coincidence I'd organised it only a day after Billy walked out of the Old Bailey, alone. I was already anxious, but it was too late to rescind the invitation now.

I kept thinking about my mother. I kept thinking about family, and the importance of a name. Mostly, I kept thinking of The Girl, and how she'd left the world with neither, and how sad that really was.

'I'm not buying that Scrooge crap,' Zara snapped, rummaging through what little progress I'd made in sorting the boxes. 'I think one of the reasons my mum gave up on religion after meeting Dad was for Christmas. It's the best.'

'Isn't there some irony in that?' I asked. 'What are you looking for anyway?'

'Didn't you used to have some old speakers in here somewhere?'

'They're not that old,' I grumbled, and pointed to the wires emerging from the middle of one of the stacks, still sitting precisely where I'd dumped them after clearing the bureau out for Zara.

'Yeah, right, they could've come from Noah's Ark.' She heaved the topmost box off, kicking up a cloud of dust and loose paper, and weighed it in her hands. 'These were the first boxes I ever went through here. Took me the whole of that first week to get through about a billion bank statements and receipts, remember?'

'I know,' I said, 'just be careful, before –'

She dropped the box before I finished, upturning it, and hundreds of loose papers went spilling out across the floor like a good dealer's cards over a table.

'Great,' I said. 'Just when I was actually getting somewhere …'

'Sorry!' She started scooping handfuls of the sheets back up into her arms. 'I'd actually forgotten how much there was in –'

And she stopped. Froze entirely, in fact.

'What's up? Seen something that'll save this bloody fraudster before the trial begins?'

But she didn't laugh. Didn't smile. She was staring at the paper in her hands.

'Parinda Malik …'

'Beg your pardon?' The name did ring a bell, but the bell was far away, almost forgotten altogether. 'Parinda *what*?'

'Look!' She thrust the page over my desk, complexion draining. 'Right here! I *knew* I recognised the name!'

It was a copy of a billing record. A list of maybe two hundred names and consultations submitted for reimbursement from the legal aid fund. Every so often, a name had been circled in red ink, representing those clients whose identity we hadn't been able to confirm. It was only as I met Zara's eyes once more that it clicked.

'Oh shit.'

We cleared the narrow staircase down through the building, leapt out into the flurry of snowfall and ran, Zara a few paces ahead, coats unfastened and billowing, to my car, which was parked at the top of Chancery Lane.

Ice cracked as I threw open the door, leaned over the gear-stick, and scrambled through the clutter inside the glovebox.

And there she was, all but forgotten, paper cold to the touch.

My phone was at my ear before I'd even made it out of the car.

'Kessler speaking,' the voice said after a couple of rings.

'This is Rook,' I panted. 'We need you to come into chambers.'

'All right,' our client said, and I heard the rustle of pages. 'Hmm, what day are you thinking? Have you found something in the case?'

I handed Zara the clutch of posters, where the face of Parinda Malik was staring out from the top, missing now for more than three years.

'Now,' I told him. 'You need to come here now.'

Kessler hadn't been especially thrilled about rushing through the city snow to sit in my ransacked office, that much was immediately obvious, but when I handed him the make-shift poster, complete with Arabic annotations, he quickly progressed to a state somewhere between livid and mystified.

'What am I looking at here?' he asked, glancing between us both.

'Parinda Malik,' I said, giving him the billing receipt. 'You billed for giving her an hour of legal advice, *here*.' I pointed to the date circled in red Sharpie.

'So? You're telling me you've tracked her down? That's good, right?'

Zara was sitting by the bureau; she shook her head. 'We need to know what she came to you about. It's important.'

'To the case?' He leaned closer to the small print and shook his head. 'This was a consultation in Nottinghamshire, more than three years ago. It would have been somebody else in the firm.'

'Who?' we both asked at once. Snow was building up the lower half of the window by now, and the lamp on the desk was fighting a losing battle against the gloom.

'I have no idea,' he said, scratching his jaw. 'I'd have to check the online records.'

I slid my laptop across the desk towards him, knocking a couple of sheets of paper onto the floor. 'By all means, Mr Kessler.'

He rolled his eyes and went into his coat pocket. 'My phone is fine.'

A long, slow minute passed. I found myself looking at his fine Italian shoes, his manicured hands, and decided that, guilty or not, he clearly had no compunction dressing ostentatiously.

'All right,' he said. 'She attended one of the free consultations with Jack Aaronson, one of our junior solicitors.'

'You have this Aaronson's number?'

He frowned, wary, and looked back to the poster, the pinholes still visible in the corners. 'What's this all about, Mr Rook?'

'Parinda Malik spoke to one of your representatives on the nineteenth of June 2014. According to this poster, that was only a day before she went missing from the Nottingham area. We have to know what she spoke to your man about.'

'Why? I mean, even if Jack *could* remember, and I can all but guarantee you that he *won't*, you know full well that we can't disclose that sort of information. Why do you think we had more than thirty tonnes of paperwork inde-pendently vetted down to the seventeen tonnes you were given? I'm lucky I haven't been suspended pending inves-tigation; I can't breach legal professional privilege – these regulators would tear me a new arsehole if anybody found out, you know that.' He shook his head. 'I'm sorry, but I'm going to have to put my foot down here. There's no require-ment for me to break legal professional privilege on this.'

'Oh, come on, Kessler! I'm not asking for much here. I've spent months working through all this, and –'

'And that's precisely what you've been paid to do – and *nothing* more than that.'

Stalemate. Snow turned grey on the windowpane, muddying the world outside, and wind rattled the wood of the frame.

'If there's nothing else …' he said, standing, pocketing his phone and striding impatiently towards the door, 'I'd appreciate it if we can keep future meetings to *my* trial, thank you very much.'

'Hang on …' Zara's voice came slowly from where her bureau was. 'You said that Miss Malik attended a free consultation, and yet you've billed the legal aid fund for the session … How does that work?'

He paused in the doorway, turned back into the room, checking the hallway behind him.

'You've always done great work for me, Rook,' he said quietly. 'Always done right by our clients, and for that reason, I'll give you a name, but you *did not* get it from me …' He leaned further into the room. 'Flora McNally – find her, and maybe you'll find whatever it is you're looking for.'

Zara had the name up on the screen of her iPad before the door had even closed behind him.

'Well, Rookie?' I was pacing back and forth, plunging my hands into my hair.

'This can't be right,' she muttered, scrolling. 'That guy's full of shit – I bet he pulled the name out of thin air to keep us busy.'

'Why? What have you found?'

'Well, there's an eighty-one-year-old Flora McNally up in Glasgow, another currently living out in Spain, and a *Professor* Flora McNally lecturing at Birmingham Uni.'

'A professor? What's her subject?'

'Um ... English Language and Applied Linguistics, apparently.'

I stopped pacing. She caught my eye over the glow of the screen and read my mind in an instant.

'That's what they were claiming the legal aid for ...' she gasped.

'Yes.' I was already reaching for my keys. 'An interpreter!'

37

Birmingham's College of Arts and Law is situated on a leafy campus of grand old red-brick buildings, and each was a hive of studious young people sheltering from the snowfall, cramming in last-minute essays before the holidays, when we turned up more than three hours after leaving chambers.

Zara had wanted to phone ahead, and fretted over it several times after we'd found ourselves trapped behind a procession of salt spreaders on the treacherous journey up the sleet-battered M40, but I'd told her it was a bad idea; asking a stranger to surrender her professional ethics seemed especially difficult to do over the phone. Fortunately, we managed to find the Department of English Language and Applied Linguistics before our woman had disappeared for the evening, and were promptly invited into her cramped little office at the rear of a winding corridor.

'Professor McNally,' I started, ducking into the room and pulling the door to as she powered on a halogen heater in the corner, 'what's your role here at the university?'

'Please, call me Flora.' She spoke with the lingering trace of a Scottish accent; mid-forties, nothing stern or immediately intimidating about her for such an educated woman. 'I run both the Applied Linguistics MA, and the night school for teaching English to speakers of other languages.'

'We understand that you've done some work with solicitors.'

'Sure. I'm often engaged as an interpreter for the courts. Assisting with trial proceedings for asylum seekers, mostly. People who can't afford an interpreter and have no family or friends to do it for them. Defence solicitors hire me to translate for defendants and, likewise, the CPS has me translate for prosecution witnesses.'

'What languages do you work with?' I asked, genuinely impressed. I'd seen only a handful of the courts' interpreters at work over the years, and always been a little envious of the skill.

'Oh boy ...' She blew a mouthful of air. 'Arabic, Kurdish, Turkish, Farsi, Azerbaijani ... It's mainly hearings, appeal forms, property disputes in civil courts, domestic violence and forced marriage in family courts.'

I nodded to Zara. We were in the right place.

'You once did some work with a solicitor named Jack Aaronson in Nottinghamshire?'

'That's right. Must've been, wow, three, three and a half years ago now? They were running a legal advice service, so they had a lot of queries about rights of tenants and the like.'

'You didn't happen to make any notes or transcripts during these meetings, did you?' Zara interjected.

'No ...' She frowned slightly. 'That wouldn't have been appropriate. Why do you ask?'

I took the poster out of my pocket, unfolded Parinda Malik's blurred features, and handed it over. 'It's a long shot, we understand, but do you happen to remember this client coming in for a consultation?'

The sensible portion of my heart wasn't expecting much, so I was surprised to see, from the way her eyes hollowed, that she did.

Her hands tightened their grip on the printout. 'What's this about, exactly?'

'We're not sure,' I admitted, 'but this woman went missing a matter of hours after she came to that consultation. You were present, weren't you? You translated for her?'

'Yes.' She got to her feet, crossed the room, and checked the door. Sat back down and stared at the paper. 'Parinda Malik was the last person to come in that day. I remember well, because she put me in a strange mood, one that stuck with me for the entire weekend. She seemed so ... afraid.'

I hoped she wouldn't notice my hands shaking with excitement. 'Do you remember what she was there for? It'd be a big help. It might even help us find her.'

'I remember,' she said quietly, glancing back and forth between us. 'She said that she was being harassed. She wanted advice on what to do about it. If I'd have thought, even for a *second*, that ...' She fell silent and remained that way for a while.

'Anything else?' I asked, barely able to draw the breath needed to do so.

'Yes ...' She licked her lips, looked back down at the poster, and then stared me dead in the eyes. 'She was being harassed by a senior police officer.'

Back through the snow, slipping on ice, we dived into the refuge of my car, causing the golf clubs to clatter off the back seat and into the well. I shook the snow from my hat and tossed it onto the seat behind me.

'Oh, we've got him!' Zara yelled, slamming the passenger door, sending a lump of snow dropping from the roof. 'We've got that fucker *nailed*! This is the link, isn't it? If we can get her to submit a statement, then we can tie it all together. Girls going missing across Nottinghamshire, and a report of harassment only hours before one suddenly disappeared!'

'Maybe ...' I nodded, turning the key and blasting the heater. 'Though it's only another word against DeWitt's, and McNally would have to breach code of conduct to submit it. That's risky, and we have to avoid more risks. We need something solid. I've *got* to convince McCarthy to roll on his boss.'

'So, let's do it!' She drummed the dashboard with her gloves. 'To Notts!'

'Slow down a moment.' I took a deep breath. 'Think about it. You really want to start your career by taking this further and officially accusing a senior commanding officer of ... well, *what* exactly? Perverting the course of justice? Murder? Conspiracy?' I shook my head. 'No. First, I should get you back to London, and then I'll give McCarthy a call when I've had time to –'

'No way, Mr Rook! You think I don't know what's at stake here? We started this together, and we're finishing this together.'

I opened my palms against the heater, and Zara placed a hand on my shoulder.

'I once told you that I want to defend those who are powerless to defend themselves,' she said. 'Well, that goes for outside the courtroom, too. What if we could save a life? What if we could find out what really happened? Isn't that worth trying for?'

I looked at the ferocious light coming from her eyes; I wanted to be the responsible mentor, but I couldn't quell my own excitement. She was right, after all. Wasn't this why we'd got our wigs in the first place?

'All right,' I relented. 'I'll try ringing him now, see if we can arrange a meeting.'

'Yes!'

The only problem, which Zara didn't know, was that I hadn't spoken to Sean since hanging up on him the night before the verdict. It therefore came as little surprise to me when the phone rang and rang until it went to voicemail, every time I tried.

'Shit!' I slammed the phone down onto my lap and returned my palms to the vents of the blower. The snow was getting heavier, landing with soft thumps across the windscreen of the car.

'So, what, that's it?' she cried. 'Come on! Nottingham is only a couple of hours from here, we could be there by eight o'clock if we got a move on! Let's just turn up to the station, then we'll see if he ignores us!'

'Don't forget that DeWitt runs that station,' I chided. 'No. We need to be clever about this.'

'Well, I don't know ...' She folded her arms and pushed back into her seat. 'Don't suppose you know McCarthy's home address, do you?'

'No, I ...' I paused and frowned; funnily enough, I did.

I looked up at the blanket of white through the dark, checked the petrol in the tank, and pulled my seat belt across my chest.

'You'd better put your belt on, too,' I said. 'This could be dangerous.'

I was absolutely right.

38

Ralph Dickinson didn't gel with our Cotgrave gang, but it wasn't down to a lack of trying on his part. He was too soft for our liking; he wasn't handy in a fight, and so he wasn't especially handy to have around at the weekends.

He was, however, an avid Forest supporter, and relatively wealthy compared to the rest of us, so we'd always make the effort to troop up to his legendary summer parties at his family's house in Radcliffe-on-Trent, the village north of Cotgrave.

Back then, in the early eighties, the house had stood alone on farmland, but now it was surrounded by new builds and it took me almost half an hour of circling through the snowstorm to gather my bearings.

'It's *got* to be around here somewhere …' I muttered, peering through the blinding white.

None of the houses on the adjoining roads matched; there were small bungalows with motorhomes in the driveways, windscreens covered up and retired for winter, alongside larger two-storey houses with boxy UPVC porches. I had my phone on my lap, still trying Sean's number, while Zara used her own to track our movements via satellite on Google Maps.

'You're sure it's around here?' she asked once we'd come to another dead end.

'It *has* to be,' I reasoned. 'There's woodland ahead that used to be part of the grounds, I'm sure of –'

I'd spun the wheel towards what I thought was the edge of the road, but the snow had fallen so heavily that it masked the kerb completely, and my car slid into it with a dull, ominous thud.

'For Christ's sake,' I groaned. 'I can't see a thing through this. I'm going to get out and have a look.'

She unclipped her belt, one hand on the door, and I shook my head.

'You stay here with the engine running. It's a blizzard out there, last thing we need now is for the car to seize up.'

'The start of a horror film if ever I've heard one,' she said, looking out onto nothing. 'What am I supposed to do in the meantime?'

'I don't know. Check the map again, maybe? Make sure it's really out here? I'll be back in a minute or two.'

'All right.' She turned to her phone. 'Well, if you're not back in an hour I'm leaving you for dead.'

I nodded, put my hat on, turned my collar up, and shoved the door hard against the force of the blizzard.

It took me another few minutes to make it to the towering wall of bushes at the rear of the turning circle, which were gathering white on every branch; emerging from those, topped by nearly ten centimetres of snow, was a small mailbox, and behind that was a long, narrow driveway cutting through the middle of the hedgerow.

'Blind as a bat,' I mumbled, holding my hat in place, and crunched through the virgin snow up to the property.

At the top of the driveway a garage faced me, with the house off to the left, hidden by those bushes at the front and dense woodland separated by a low wall to the rear.

The house wasn't quite as grand as I remembered – I suppose I hadn't seen much real grandeur to compare it with back then – and the ensuing years of enhancements and adjustments had left it almost unrecognisable to me. Almost, but not entirely.

I didn't head for the front door, instinctively cutting into the large garden at the side instead, guessing where the walkway might now be under crisp, untouched white. Perhaps it was only a small-town phenomenon, but we all used to call for one another through the back door, never the front, and so that's where my feet led me. A small wooden shed stood out there, a swing set hanging static; the woodland beyond was already blanketed, and the silence it created was dense.

None of the lights were on inside the house, but I gave the door a hard knock in the hope that one of the children might be squirrelled away on the top floor.

Nothing. No answer. No sound. No sign of life whatsoever.

It was only when I pushed my bare hands up against the ice forming across the window of the door, making a warm spot large enough to peer inside, that I realised I'd made a mistake. This obviously wasn't the McCarthys' home.

I was looking into a kitchen, and it was a familiar sight.

Filthy pots were stacked high upon the worktop, and there were empty lager cans scattered all over every surface. Beside the washing machine, clothes were piled up haphazardly, large white shirts and black trousers all bundled together. This was a bachelor pad. I knew it as surely as if I'd been able to smell my own kind through the door.

I still had my hands up against the glass, watching my breath cloud the pane, when my phone rang, vibrating in my coat pocket. Wary of leaving more footprints, I moved for the only patch of garden where the weather hadn't settled – a cracked, concrete area beneath the shelter of the overhanging trees by the back wall – and fumbled for the phone. *Now* you decide to reply, Sean?

I pulled it out of my pocket and something came along with it, landing with a light, clinking, metallic sound on the wet concrete.

'Shit!'

It rolled, following a trickle of freezing water down towards sunken cracks by the wall, and when I turned the screen of my phone – still vibrating in my palm – for light, I saw only the briefest glimpse of gold before it was swallowed by a fracture in the ground.

'No, no, no!' I flung myself onto the cold and reached into the crack, fingertips wiggling blindly, numbing in the wet. Eventually, to my great relief, I managed to prise the wedding ring out of the earth, but a small pebble – little more than a piece of grit – snagged at the back of my index finger, causing me to gasp in surprise. I poked it once more, found it astonishingly sharp, and lifted it out with the ring.

My phone vibrated again, a message this time, and I finally looked at the screen. It hadn't been Sean after all. It was Zara, and now she'd sent a message.

!!! was all it said, accompanied by an image.

I waited for the picture to download, signal struggling to hold so far from what we'd learned was the only cell-site mast in the area. While it loaded, I pocketed the ring, turned the light back to the odd-shaped pebble that had scratched my hand, and held it closer to my face.

The small, gritty substance had turned so black and rotten at the edges that it took me a moment to figure out what it was in the low light. Then I realised.

There are moments when the body appears to enter into absolute free fall; it's a form of shock that seems to send the brain hurtling out through the back of the skull, the nervous system plunging into unfathomable cold.

That's how it felt when Jenny told me she'd fallen in love with somebody else.

And that's precisely how it felt there, in that instant, when I realised it wasn't a stone in my hand at all. It was a broken human tooth.

I didn't run. I didn't move. I didn't breathe.

I didn't even hear the crunch of footsteps approaching, until they were right behind me.

'Rook? Is that you?'

Sean McCarthy was home.

39

In one hand he was holding three or four shopping bags. In the other, a crate of lager.

The coat he was dressed in was long and black, and when he knocked the hood back with a sharp jerk of his head, the falling snow was promptly lost in his grey hair. A memory came back to me then, of a photograph I'd seen framed in the Barber household, Sean marching around in a similar black coat at some sort of fancy-dress party. Always keen to shock.

Say something, I thought. Say *anything*.

'Tried ringing you ...' It came out higher than I'd been expecting. Despite the cold, I was blinking the salt of sweat out of my eyes.

'Really?' He shrugged. 'Been out for most of the afternoon. Thought this snow might've cleared off if I waited it out at the pub before walking back. No such luck. Left my phone here.'

I tried to nod, couldn't tell if I'd managed, and slowly turned my own phone over in my right hand. The image had loaded. It was a screenshot from Zara's iPhone, a satellite view from Google Maps. There was the house, but that wasn't the point of her message: *!!!*

The building had been circled in bright red – I could picture her doing it with one index finger on the screen – and from that circle was an arrow pointing westward, through the trees beside me. On the western side of those trees, a couple of hundred metres away from the place I was standing, was a red X, also drawn by her hand; a thin, bird's-eye view of a curve I knew well enough by now – the tracks of the abandoned railway.

'What've you got there, mate?' Sean asked.

I hadn't realised I was still holding the tooth in the palm of my open left hand.

He came close. Peered at it. We stood in silence for a while.

'Ah, the pleasures of kids running wild,' he said cheerily. 'Bet that's the one Annie lost when she came off the swing a few years back. She wears a fake one now, but you wouldn't tell.'

This time I managed the nod, but it was as stiff and brittle as the icicles forming on the nearby branches. The snow cast its pale glow over everything, and in it, I saw Sean break into a grin.

'Since you're here …' He held up the crate. 'I know you aren't going to say no to one, are you? I need a drink after that trek.'

He turned away, placed the bags down by the door, unlocked it with keys from his pocket, and stepped into the shelter of the kitchen, casually gesturing for me to follow.

'Come on,' he said. 'I'll show you what I've done with the old place.'

I hesitated.

I could almost smell the fuel from the Jag's engine still running only a short sprint away to the right, but I was watching my body make all the decisions now, and follow my body did, phone still in my right hand, tooth now clenched in the fist of my left.

Sean clasped his hands together after dumping the shopping among the litter on the kitchen surfaces, rubbed his palms, and then hit the light switch, the strip bulb stuttering into life like a failing engine.

'So, what d'you think?' he asked.

I cleared my throat. 'About what, Sean?'

'Well, it's a bit different to when Dickinson lived here, isn't it?'

I looked around. The small part of my brain that was neither falling nor desperately racing to put the pieces together noticed again that there were no children's clothes buried in that pile by the washing machine. The calendar on the wall hadn't been changed since January, if not this year's, the one before that.

'Shut the door, would you? Costs a fortune heating this place!'

'Where's Tracey?' I asked, closing the door, shaking the handle to ensure it hadn't locked behind us. 'The kids?'

'Gone.' He removed his coat, snow turning to a puddle on the tiled floor, hung it from a hook on the wall alongside his uniform jacket, and took a couple of cans from the crate. Opened them up.

'When?' I was looking at the golden band on his left hand.

'While ago now,' he said. 'I'd appreciate it if you kept that between us. You know how it is, don't you?'

Ordinarily, yes, I did know how it was – very much so – but nothing here was making sense to me. I'd spoken to Sean a matter of weeks ago, heard his wife in the background of that conversation, but it looked as though there hadn't been a steady partner here for months. Years, maybe. I took myself back to that conversation: what *had* I heard, really? Sean, of course, and a shrill, feminine voice rising in the background. Screaming, almost, before …

'Rook?'

Back in the room, Sean, my old friend, was smiling again. He slid one of the open beers along the worktop and it came to a rest alongside me, frothing over the rim.

'You're still holding it,' he said gently.

I was. I uncurled my fist and it was heavy as lead in my palm. I thought I could smell the decay, the warm stench of an open mouth being picked apart by a dentist, but it was most likely my imagination. We both stared down at the blackened lump until my phone shook in my other hand like one of those practical joke buzzers.

Zara's name strobed onscreen. It rang, and rang, and rang.

Sean raised his eyebrows. 'Are you not getting that?'

I couldn't focus. Thoughts were smashing around my skull like rocks in a spin cycle.

It was only when the phone abruptly stopped vibrating, the last of its battery swallowed, that Sean rolled his eyes and reached into my left palm. He took the tooth, studied it for a moment, then slipped it into his jean pocket.

He sighed, and I smelled whiskey. 'Stop that.'

'Stop what?' I asked.

'Stop those wheels turning up there.' Pointing at my head. 'I can see it happening.'

'What can you see, Sean?' It must've been obvious; I could feel the impossible, sickening whiteness spreading across the surface of my skin as clear as the frost on the windows around us.

'For fuck's sake.' He stamped his boot, shaking more slush off onto the floor, and necked half the can. 'Come on,' he said, catching the overspill from his chin with the sleeve of his sweatshirt. 'Come and have a sit-down. Have a drink, for God's sake.'

I pushed my weight against the exit, clenching the dead phone so hard it hurt all the way up my arm. 'What are you going to do if I don't, Sean?'

'I'm not gonna do a damn thing,' he said, turning his back on me.

'No?'

He shrugged, finishing the beer, and swapped it for another two cans. 'What were you expecting? You want me to tell you I'm off to get Dad's old Browning? We're mates, aren't we? We both know you're going to come and have a sit-down anyway.'

'Why's that?' I was trying to push the veiled threat of the gun to the back of my mind.

He took a step away. Paused. 'Because you've got to know, haven't you? I can see the bit between your teeth, driving you up the wall. So, let's just sit down, have a beer, and talk about this like a couple of grown men, shall we?'

I didn't answer.

I should've walked away, but as he'd guessed, I couldn't. Not without knowing.

He reached towards his uniform hanging from the coat hook, unclipped the expandable baton from his jacket, and hooked it neatly onto his hip. 'Just in case you're thinking of doing anything stupid,' he said, before disappearing further into the dark of the house.

I followed.

Like Billy Barber before him, he had me. He had me, and he fucking knew it.

40

We went into the sitting room, and that's all it was: a perfectly ordinary sitting room in a perfectly ordinary house.

It was untidy – dirty plates on the floor, more empty cans and bottles piled around a fifty-five-inch television, Xbox wires in a tangle, and a stack of pornographic DVDs by the open wooden staircase leading upstairs – but it was far from squalid.

I could've been wrong. It wouldn't have been the first time.

He closed the curtains, blocking out the snowfall, turned on the lamps in opposite corners, and invited me to sit. I remained squarely on my feet. It stank of stale smoke and sour beer. There were photographs of children – *his* children, I assumed – at varying ages framed around the room. No sign of a wife.

'She isn't dead,' he said coolly, reading my thoughts as he collapsed wearily onto the sofa and opened his second can. 'She's dead *to me*, but she's still got some life in her body, as well as the cock of a twenty-five-year-old wog, last I heard.'

A long drink, shaking his head. The low lamplight cast shadows from his high, handsome cheekbones.

'*Twenty-five*,' he said. 'That's only five years older than Brett, our eldest.' He gestured to a photograph of a teenager who bore a fierce resemblance to the feisty blond hooligan I'd known – or thought I'd known – many years ago.

'She's a sick cunt,' he added, and then spat on the rug in the middle of the room and left it there.

I was still clutching the phone.

'I'm gonna have to take that from you,' he said. 'Just for now. You understand, don't you, mate?'

Mate. Though I hadn't realised it at the time, the word had made me happy when we'd been able to say it to one another upon meeting again; it had felt like a long time since I'd been able to do that, and mean it, with anybody.

Now the word sounded thin.

'It's dead,' I told him, indicating the lifeless screen.

He nodded apologetically. 'Probably for the best, but still …'

I handed it over, trying to play it cool, painfully aware that I'd just surrendered my last bullet to the firing squad.

As he slipped it into his pocket with the tooth, my thoughts leapt to Zara, sitting within throwing distance in the passenger seat.

It seemed unlikely that he hadn't noticed her in what was unmistakably *my* car with the headlights on, but why hadn't he mentioned it?

Perhaps he couldn't see her through the snow; maybe he'd already come to the conclusion that I'd left the engine running because I hadn't planned on staying, and he was more than happy to leave it unmentioned, knowing that my only escape was, with every passing moment, entering the same terminal death throe as my phone.

But Zara … What if she –

'Would you sit down?' he said, derailing my train of thought. 'And take that stupid hat off. You're making me nervous.'

I chose the most distant seat available, a threadbare foot-stool close to the television, and placed my hat on the floor.

He offered me a cigarette, menthol, and lit them in turn, laying a heavy glass ashtray onto the cluttered coffee table between us.

I wondered, if it was to come down to it, whether he could take me in a fight. Once upon a time, almost certainly, and he wouldn't have needed a skull-cracking truncheon to do it either. I reached for the cigarette.

'You and DeWitt were in this together?' I asked, thinking out loud, filling my lungs.

'DeWitt?' He actually chuckled. 'Christ almighty, I thought *you'd* be more understanding of a man born in the wrong place at the wrong time. He's done well for himself, our Chief Super, but a past is a hard thing to leave behind, especially when it gets dragged up in the courtroom once a year by every half-arsed defence lawyer with access to the Internet. No wonder the fucker finally snapped on you.'

A tiny, delicate part of my pride was wounded by that. I'd thought we were unique in our discovery.

He drained the second can, tossed it alongside the drying streak of spit, and opened the next.

'Let me ask you something, Rook ...' With one long finger he tapped the cigarette's ash onto his boots. 'Why do you care?'

I blinked, smoking as fast as he was drinking. 'Why do I care about what?'

'Any of this. You won, didn't you? Got paid. So, why do you care? Why are you here, skulking around my property on the coldest night in December?'

'Parinda Malik,' I told him, keeping my tone conversational, keeping his mind off the alleged pistol somewhere in the building.

'*Prindo* what?'

I took the poster out from my pocket and held her face up for him to see.

'Who's that then?' he asked nonchalantly.

'A young woman who disappeared from Nottingham three and something years back, but I think you probably know that already. What you probably never knew was that she spoke to a solicitor the day before she vanished. Had a lot to say about being harassed by a local copper.'

His eyes widened a notch, pupils smothering green. 'Sounds like bullshit to me.'

'No bullshit, Sean.' I flattened the paper onto the coffee table. 'We've got the solicitor's receipts to prove it.'

'To prove what? Do you know how many complaints are filed against the force each year? She probably got stopped and searched one too many times and fucked off back to wherever she came from.'

'I don't think so.' I watched him steadily, drenching my tight throat with lager, casting my mind back to our meeting in the country park: *there isn't a girl alive who could resist. Why else do you think I became a copper?*

I stubbed the menthol out in the ashtray. He did the same, splitting his filter in two.

'How many, Sean?' I asked quietly. 'How many girls? Two? Three? More?'

He watched me back, fingers rapping his aluminium can. 'You didn't answer *my* question.' His words were slurring at the edges.

'What question?'

'Why do you care about any of this? You're in no position to determine what's right or wrong. How many criminals have you fought to defend? How many killers have you freed?'

'This is different.'

'Is it?' He raised his eyebrows. 'You'd rather see a man like Billy walk, would you? Billy fucking Barber. Come off it!'

'You told me that Billy had tried to blackmail you ...' I recalled slowly. 'Over what?'

'A load of shit,' he snapped. 'We both spent some time in the BNP a few years back, but so what? Nothing illegal in that ...' He leaned closer. 'What if you were *my* barrister? You'd do everything you could to keep me out of prison, wouldn't you? You're not a copper. You're not a grass. You'd never stand as a witness for the prosecution. So, what's the difference?'

I couldn't find an answer; somehow, I was being lectured on morality by *him*. 'What happened over Easter weekend, Sean? How did she end up out there, alone, with nothing but that jacket? Why break her legs when she was already dead? Why did you do it?'

He rolled his eyes. 'Come on, Rook. You're talking to a copper for Christ's sake.'

'Only on the outside. You might as well wear fancy dress to work.'

'Well, that makes two of us then.' He lit another cigarette; clenched it between his teeth, thinking hard, before exhaling. 'Our uniforms mean something, don't they? That's why we put them on. Why we worked so hard to get them. Our uniforms are power.'

'I don't abuse that power.'

'No?' He clicked his tongue, leaned back into the sofa and eyed me through rings of smoke. 'You don't use it to your advantage? Please. Before our uniforms, we had nothing. No power. No choices. You were born in the Midlands in '65, you went down the pit. Back in Belfast, things were even clearer. I was born Catholic, so I went to Catholic school and knew only Catholic people. Maybe that's how society is *supposed* to be, you know? My old man said there was a reason they called them Peace Walls. Segregation is peace, and when you blur those lines you get war. It's inevitable. It's coming.'

'Fitting words to come out of a war zone,' I said drily, 'especially from a nationalist who left his own country.'

He shrugged. 'Dad was complicated, I'll give you that, but he knew the power of a uniform. That's the whole reason he started a paramilitary with my uncle. They thought the IRA was too soft on outsiders. Got tanked up one night in '75 and shot a couple of black citizens to prove the point.' He smiled at the memory, introspective, almost proud. 'Course, the IRA had to punish them for it. Uncle Pat got his throat cut, and Dad spent the next seven years hiding down the pit in fucking Cotgrave, the arse end of nowhere, before they tracked him down. And what did he do wrong, really? He drew a line in the fucking sand, that's all.'

I was shaking my head. I'd known Sean's dad – we all had – up until he'd walked out on the family. He was certainly a hard man, like the rest, but a killer?

'You are so full of shit,' I said coldly. 'You always were.'

The temperature shifted fast. Sean glowered. He smashed his second cigarette to dust in the ashtray, half smoked. 'You boys were always pulling me to fucking bits. Everything I ever said, just like my wife. Just like all those stupid slags! What the fuck would *you* know about *my* dad?'

I sipped my lager, watching the heat rise in his cheeks. Sean McCarthy, like any cornered defendant, had lashed out. Every criminal has a weakness. I took a steady breath, battling nerves.

'Your father was a lot of things, Sean,' I told him, 'but at the end of the day, he was just another lousy shit who didn't come back from the bookies one morning. Whatever lies he told you, whatever fantasies you've cooked up to help justify what you've done –'

'*Fantasies?*' He slammed his beer onto the coffee table, sending droplets into the air between us, and I flinched. 'You want to fucking bet on that, do you?'

Sean had a weakness all right, and that weakness had always been pride.

I managed a cool, unconvinced shrug, goading him.

He staggered across the room to the wooden staircase, ducked into the cupboard underneath, and began rummaging through a jumble of old shoes and coats inside, cursing beneath his breath. Something hidden at the back of the cupboard beeped five times. The keypad of a safe. I glanced through the kitchen. Snow was still falling beyond the glass door, covering the tracks I'd made in the garden. I was just wagering the probability of outrunning Sean when I found myself thinking of the Copper at the Door, the test I'd played with Zara.

A uniformed police officer comes across an attractive young girl on the morning of Good Friday in the quiet village of Cotgrave. He attempts to lure her into his marked vehicle.

'Has he done this before?' imaginary Zara interjected, bobbing in Sean's former seat on the sofa.

Almost certainly. Perhaps the girl speaks English, maybe not, but she *does* have enough wits to get away. Hours later, she stops to use the toilet at the Welfare Scheme Social Club, still rattled, and then walks northwards in the direction of the country park.

'But she never steps foot inside the park after all, does she, Mr Rook?'

No. She never does.

The same officer finds her a few streets away from the social club, not by accident, but because he's been looking for her. This time he refuses to take no for an answer. He gets her into the car – *his* car by now, after finishing work for a supposed weekend holiday – and drives her north, entirely parallel to the railway, bringing her *here*.

She fights back as he undresses her. Escapes somehow, grabbing only her jacket on the way out. She slips in the rain trying to scale the garden wall and loses the first tooth. He catches up to her a few hundred metres west. He beats her, strangles her under the cover of the storm, and the crime is pinned on a local racist.

The killer is going to get away with it. How?

The Zara of my imagination tossed her hair back over one shoulder.

'You just said it, Mr Rook. The pieces of the puzzle are all there. He gets away with it because he *is* a copper. He gets away with it because he knows how, and he has the patience to spend the night placing broken finger-nails along the railway line, tracing a make-believe path back to the last place she was seen alive. It's a storm, its flooding fast, so he can't move her to a better burial site – he tries, but a body is heavy, the ground is a swamp, and he snaps her legs with the effort – but he *can* easily cover his tracks in the groundwater. Everybody believes he's away with his family because he still wears the ring. Mostly, he gets away with it because he knows we'll do nothing about it.'

No, I thought to myself. No, he doesn't.

'There!' Sean interrupted, slapping a clutch of papers onto the coffee table. 'Who's full of shit now?'

They were photographs – four or five faded seventies Polaroids – of Sean's father as I almost remembered him, only younger, dressed in a mercenary trench coat and beret, holding a shotgun here, a pistol there, some with a scarf over his mouth.

I shrugged again. 'Your father's been out of the picture for a long time now, Sean. Whatever he might have done, one thing doesn't excuse the other.'

'I'm not making *excuses*!' he roared, pacing the room, fists clenching at his sides. 'I'm proving that you don't know shit, Rook! I'm *proud* of my dad! I'm –'

He stopped talking.

The silence that fell was as thick as the snow outside; somewhere upstairs, a lone pipe creaked, but that was all I heard.

Sean was staring back down the length of the kitchen, out through the glass in the door, as if somebody had just pressed pause on the moment. His fingers absently stroked the steel at his hip.

I got to my feet slowly, praying that Zara had called the police, ready to welcome blue lights over the garden.

327

But there were no lights. There were only two brown eyes, magnified by thick Ginsberg glasses, and an inquisitive face pressed close against the window.

I heard my hand tighten around the beer, the crunch of tin, and half registered the cold liquid leaking onto my wrist.

Sean raised an eyebrow.

'Well ...' he said slowly. 'Isn't *this* interesting?'

41

'Your junior?' he asked quietly, walking through the kitchen and holding a single finger up to Zara on the other side of the door: *one moment, please.*

'Sean ...' I croaked.

'Here's what's about to happen, Rook,' he said. 'The three of us are going to sit down, and you're gonna use that brain of yours to put this under the rug. The two of you can go home tonight, and she never has to know a thing. Put this to the back of your mind. Forget about it.' He met my eyes. 'You can save her life. What do you say?'

What I said was nothing whatsoever; I was standing in the doorway to the kitchen now, straining my eyes at Zara in a hopeless signal for her to run back to the car and drive.

All she did was stare right back, pupils darting between the two of us, measuring the baton at his hip.

Sean opened the door with a welcoming grin, the perfect host, and a wave of cold swept through the house. 'Sorry, I thought it was locked! You must be the junior.'

He offered his hand. She might've been a statue for all it was worth, hands clasped behind her back, chewing her lips. 'Everything all right, Mr Rook?'

Sean nodded towards me. 'Course, we were just talking about old times. Come inside, you'll catch your death out there!'

She didn't move an inch, but she rolled her shoulders, hands still hidden.

'Mr Rook?'

'It's fine,' I heard myself say, shuffling towards, and crucially *between*, the two of them. I put my crushed beer onto the worktop. 'My phone died before I had chance to reply, but I got your text. Everything's cool.'

Her head cocked, a glint through the lenses at her eyes, as we came almost nose to nose at the threshold. 'Everything's ... *cool*? You sure?'

'Yes.' The bite of the weather outside caught sweat on the nape of my neck and sent a violent shiver down the length of my back. 'It's all cool.'

'All right.' She blinked at Sean, who was standing at my left shoulder. 'Well, if you say so ...'

She brought her hands out from behind her back, took my own, and placed something there.

I didn't have to break eye contact to recognise what it was; even after so long abandoned to the back seat, it fitted my grip like a tailored glove.

'Tell her to come inside already, mate!' Sean said cheerily. 'You're letting all the damn heat –'

He didn't finish.

I turned back with the perfect swing, feet apart and rolling like thunder, and brought the golf club screaming up into his jaw. My heavy iron. Lucky number 9. Goodnight, Inspector McCarthy.

There was a spray of blood as he clamped through his tongue, a scattering of teeth, and he went down hard, crashing on to the tiles, beer can rolling into the pile of unwashed clothes.

'*Holy fuck!*' Zara screamed, plunging her hands into her hair. 'I thought you were going to, like, *threaten* him or something!'

'Tell me you rang the police.'

'Of course, but isn't *he* the police?' she sputtered. Sean made a long, thin, whining sound.

He turned onto his back, blood and saliva pooling upon his jumper, and reached towards his waist. I held the club high, eyes on the truncheon, but he didn't touch it. Instead, he slipped his fingers into his jean pocket and pulled out the decaying, broken tooth from the garden.

Even with the lower half of his face misshapen as it was, I could've sworn the bastard smiled as he shoved that hunk of tooth into his own blood-soaked mouth; he swallowed hard, and then his eyes rolled back, and he was out cold.

'Fuck!' I yelled, grabbing his mangled, swelling jaw with one hand, cracking it as wide as the bones would still allow, but it was already gone. 'The tooth!'

'The *what?*' Zara cried.

'The Girl's missing tooth! It was here, our only evidence, and he just swallowed it!'

'He *swallowed* it? What the fuck do we do now?'

'We find evidence, fast,' I said, wiping spit and blood from my hand onto a nearby tea towel, 'or else we are fucked.'

Zara was shaking so much I thought she might be having a fit. 'G-GBH on an officer,' she stammered, 'aggravated burglary ... attempted murder ...' She fell against the open door, wheezing.

I tried to gather my thoughts. My eyes traced over Sean, back to the living room, to the staircase and the open cupboard beneath it. 'What else were you hiding, you piece of shit?'

'M-Mr Rook?'

'Go outside,' I told her flatly. 'Keep an eye out for the police.'

'But –'

'Take this,' I stuffed the club back into her trembling hands. 'He's unconscious. He can't do any more harm.'

She managed to compose herself enough to nod, tearing her eyes away from the blood on the tiles and holding the iron like a baseball bat over her right shoulder, and then disappeared into the snow. I waited until the crunch of foot-steps was out of range before moving.

As I stepped over Sean's body, stalking towards the cupboard beneath the staircase, I felt physically sick; not because of the violence behind me, but for whatever I might find ahead. My heart was beating so fast it hurt.

The cupboard was dark, tight, and I had to crawl inside on my hands and knees, fumbling through the smell of dust and worn leather. The safe was around the size of a shoebox, the steel kind often found in hotel rooms, and it looked as if it had been buried under several anoraks and dust sheets for quite some time until Sean had dug it out only minutes before. The door was still open.

I caught my breath, deafened by my own pulse, and reached inside blindly.

My fingertips found two objects.

The first was heavy steel, cold to the touch: the barrel of a semi-automatic handgun. Sean hadn't been lying about that. I snapped my fingers away from it, only now remem-bering to exhale.

The second item was smaller: frayed cardboard, a rectan-gular box, it took me no time to recognise it as a standard pack of playing cards, but when I picked it up in one hand the weight was far too light for a full deck.

I backed out of the cupboard on all fours, box quaking in my grip, and glanced up over my right shoulder as I came out into the light.

I didn't see Sean. Not really, but there was just enough time to distinguish sleek black metal before the truncheon smashed down above my forehead. Agony drove through my skull, snatching the air from my lungs, and my vision went white.

An enormous weight collapsed on top of me – Sean, moments after his vengeful swansong – as blood ran through my hair and onto the nape of my neck like water from a kettle.

My eyes cleared, and I saw the golf club fall to the carpet, Zara standing over us both, screaming at Sean to stay down, but the sound had gone out. I reached for her, playing cards still in my hand, but she faded to a dream, the ghost of a girl I'd never seen alive, with a halo of blue light around her face.

Then the blue light was pulsing, a strobe across the ceiling, and I finally let go, heat pouring over my face, cold spreading through the rest of my body, and allowed the impossible weight of my eyelids to simply sweep the world away.

42

I was on a hospital bed. That much was clear.

The white ceiling, the sound of machines beeping along the corridor, the smell of antiseptic.

My head felt as if I'd been playing chicken on the old railway, like some of the Cotgrave kids used to do, only I'd refused to retreat and my skull had been smeared halfway back to the village.

I turned slowly to the left, peering through fog, and saw a face I just about recognised.

A petite woman in full uniform, blonde hair tied back. Not a nurse, I realised, but Constable Louise Shepherd of Rushcliffe South Police. I must've groaned out loud; seeing that I was awake, she disappeared from view, but I could hear her voice outside.

'Looks like he's awake, sir.'

'Is that so?' someone replied, and into my fading delirium strolled none other than Detective Chief Superintendent John DeWitt.

He was dressed in the same brown barn coat I'd seen him wearing by the roadside, smoothing his moustache out with one hand, peering down at me as if I were something caught beneath his shoe.

'Before you ask,' he boomed, coming to rest in my narrow frame of vision, 'you aren't in heaven.'

I coughed, ruffled my face, and felt the tightness of glue and dressings all pulling from somewhere above.

'How long was I out?' I croaked weakly, as if upon waking from the strangest comatose dream; I imagined a beard all over my face by now.

'How long?' He looked at his watch. Shrugged. 'About forty-five minutes, give or take.'

'Oh ...' I lifted myself and leaned back against the pillows. It felt as if I'd gained a few extra kilos in my skull. 'Zara?'

'Being questioned.'

I looked down. Somebody had stripped me of my shirt and replaced it with a thin white gown that hung over my trousers. 'Am I under arrest?'

'Right now?' He shook his head. 'No charge yet. We'll need a statement in the morning, and you're staying here tonight.'

'No chance, I've got to –' But he silenced me with one swiftly raised hand, and if I'd been any more alert I might've flinched. I crumpled down, relenting, and sighed. 'Sean?'

'McCarthy is receiving urgent medical care. He doesn't have much jaw left to tell us anything right now, thanks to you, but it's only a matter of time.'

I blinked. 'What do you know?'

'We have a good enough idea for now,' he sniffed. 'First thing in the morning, Rook. You have a lot of explaining to do.'

'It'd be my pleasure,' I said, and I truly meant it.

A few moments of silence passed between us, uncomfortable and strained.

'It was my kid,' he said eventually. 'Oscar. He threw up over the back seat of my car on Good Friday, and I had to take it in to get cleaned. We're not insured for domestic use, so I didn't volunteer that information. It wasn't exactly something I'd expected to have to answer.'

I nodded, heard the dressings crinkle on my scalp.

He turned on his heel and made it to the door before stopping.

'I was an officer in BOSS, yes. After that, I had to get out of the country. I came to England. My first real case was a teenager stabbed to death in broad daylight. Took me half a decade to hunt down the bastards who did it. Said they did it for a laugh. Nothing more. Just a laugh. They'd spread like rats from a sinking ship, right out across the country, but I did what I had to do. I got them all, Rook. It wasn't pretty, and I had to bend the rules to do it, but I got them.'

'Yes,' I said. 'I know that now.'

'Did you also know that they're all free men? That kid is still buried, his mother was sectioned after a total nervous breakdown, but they're all out because their *barristers* struck a plea deal before the trial ever made it to court.'

I sighed, looking over to the frost on the window, the white clouds parting beyond. '*Noble cause corruption* is still corruption, Superintendent DeWitt.'

He walked out of the room without another word and I was left alone, to close my eyes again.

The next time I woke, it was to see Zara snoring in the plastic chair by the bed, head tipped back, jaw hanging wide open.

Clenched in her hands, buckled upon her lap, was my hat, retrieved from the scene.

I watched her for a minute or two, warmth filling my chest. I'd never felt so proud of anyone in my whole life.

She must've sensed that I was awake because she opened her eyes and wiped the dribble away from her chin with the back of one hand.

She caught my eye and grinned, all the way from the boots up, and it really did suit her entirely.

'Thought you were worm food,' she said, tossing the hat onto my middle.

I clutched my temples with both hands. 'Wish I was.'

She nodded stiffly. When I looked closer, I could see tears brimming up in her eyes; one escaped, only one, and it rolled down the softness of her cheek. 'You found them. You actually found them.'

'Found what?' I frowned.

She wiped her face with one sleeve. 'Names. IDs. Travel papers. He'd kept them all. He'd kept their names. Five altogether.'

She lunged forward, catching me off guard, and threw her skinny arms around my shoulders. We stayed that way for what felt like a long time, and when the sting of tears crept into my own eyes, I told myself it must've been a symptom of the head injury and nothing more.

'We got him together,' I said. '*We* did it.'

She fell back into the chair and blew her nose into a tissue from a box beside the bed. 'But there's still the trial, you know. What if he gets away with it somehow? What if he walks?'

To this, I only smiled. 'Not without us representing him he won't. The fucker hasn't got a chance.'

A realisation came upon me then. Billy Barber had been right all along: this case would end up with me standing on the opposite side of the courtroom, after all.

'So,' Zara said, 'what do we do now?'

I pulled my hat over the dressings, swung my feet off the edge of the bed, and grimaced at the dizzy barb of pain it sent behind my eyes.

'What time is it?' I groaned.

'Coming up to midnight.'

'Know anywhere we can still get a drink at this ungodly hour?'

'Well, yeah, but DeWitt told me that you're not supposed to ...' Her voice faded away, she cocked her head, and smiled once more. 'You know what? I reckon I know *just* the place.'

I looked down at my gown, weighing it against the bloody shirt in the corner of the room, and pulled my coat on over it. 'Think I'll fit in, looking like this?'

'About as well as I do in chambers, I'd imagine.'

We stepped out of the hospital arm in arm, my thoughts still tangled on Sean: the secrets he'd kept, the lies he'd told, and all the terrible things he'd done. Like the light of so many dead stars above us, only just coming into view. I shuddered, and Zara tightened her grip on my elbow.

'You all right, Mr Rook?'

'Yes,' I said. 'Yes, I think I will be. So, where do we go, Rookie?'

'Rookie?' Zara shook her head and gave my arm another squeeze. 'Didn't I say it was a serial killer all along?'

I laughed. It was entirely inappropriate but warm and natural, right from the belly up, and together we walked into the darkness of the city.

That railway – the final fragment of Cotgrave colliery – was torn up the following February.

The route was resurfaced only a month after Sean McCarthy was convicted and, after his sentencing, news of The Girl's death finally made it back to her family in Lebanon.

Her name was placed upon her remains, wherever they'd been interred, only to be forgotten in good time, like all, destined to become nothing more than coal under this green earth.

Her name was Sonia, for whatever it was worth.

And worth a great deal it was.

Acknowledgements

My name is the only one on the cover of this book, but the words inside it are a true collaboration between my co-writer, the brilliant wordsmith Scott Kershaw, and me. I would like to thank our inspirational agent Rory Scarfe, who had the vision to put Scott and me together. Scott's industry, and the sheer brilliance of his prose, had me feeling at times that my role in our collaboration was akin to Andrew Ridgeley's in Wham. As soon as the first draft of the book was finished Rory sent it to Bloomsbury where, within days, it was snapped up by the Raven Books Editorial Director Alison Hennessey. After further polishing of our work by the extraordinarily talented Alison, it was ready for publication. Here's to a glittering future for me, Scott, Rory, Alison and, of course, Elliot Rook QC.

Note on the Authors

Born into a coal mining family, Gary Bell was an apprentice mechanic, production line worker and door-to-door salesman before being arrested for fraud in his mid-twenties. After taking his exams at night school, he went on to study law as a mature student at Bristol University and has now spent over thirty years at the Bar, before becoming a QC specialising in criminal defence in 2012.

Scott Kershaw is the author of two novels. Prior to becoming an author, Scott worked as a professional chef for several years, and travelled the continent as a music journalist.

Note on the Type

The text of this book is set in Linotype Sabon, a typeface named after the type founder, Jacques Sabon. It was designed by Jan Tschichold and jointly developed by Linotype, Monotype and Stempel in response to a need for a typeface to be available in identical form for mechanical hot metal composition and hand composition using foundry type.

Tschichold based his design for Sabon roman on a font engraved by Garamond, and Sabon italic on a font by Granjon. It was first used in 1966 and has proved an enduring modern classic.